Valentine's Day is Killing Me

Valentine's Day is Killing Me

MaryJanice Davidson

Leslie Esdaile

Susanna Carr

KENSINGTON PUBLISHING CORP.

http://www.kensingtonbooks.com

BRAVA BOOKS are published by

Kensington Publishing Corp.
850 Third Avenue
New York, NY 10022

All Kensington titles, imprints and distributed lines are available at special quantity discounts for bulk purchases for sales promotion, premiums, fund-raising, educational or institutional use.

Special book excerpts or customized printings can also be created to fit specific needs. For details, write or phone the office of the Kensington Special Sales Manager: Kensington Publishing Corp., 850 Third Avenue, New York, NY, 10022. Attn. Special Sales Department. Phone: 1-800-221-2647.

ISBN 0-7582-1284-4

First Kensington Trade Paperback Printing: January 2006
10 9 8 7 6 5 4 3 2 1

Printed in the United States of America

CONTENTS

Cuffs and Coffee Breaks

MaryJanice Davidson

For everyone who ever dreaded
the approach of Valentine's Day,
this one's for you.

Acknowledgments

Thanks to my editor, Kate, for asking me. Who could resist such a premise?

Thanks also to the women who shared their "date from hell" stories, especially Sara, Kirsten, Cathie, and Donna. I'm praying you were exaggerating for humorous effect. You've all got medals now, right?

"It is good to love the unknown."

—Charles Lamb on Valentine's Day

"Watch this, Lisa. You can actually pinpoint the second when his heart rips in half."

—Bart Simpson, *The Simpsons*

Chapter One

EconoHart
Corporate Headquarters
Minneapolis, Minnesota
February 13, 2006

——Original Message——
From: Scott Wythe
To: Julie Kay About
Sent: Tuesday, February 13, 2006 12:02 PM
Subject: latest draft

hey girl so here it is i made some changes but it's looking really good, maybe tweak the dog a little more and then it'll be perfect. way cool girl!
scotty

——Original Message——
From: Julie Kay About
To: Scott Wythe
Sent: Tuesday, February 13, 2006 12:12 PM
Subject: Re: latest draft

Stop doing that. You're a grown man (I'm assuming, as we've never met face-to-face) and you write e-mails like you just escaped the second grade.

Say it with me: punctuation. Capital letters. "I" is always capitalized, even when it's in the middle of the sentence. We might write for a bad greeting card company, but we're still writers, for Christ's sake.

Now: I will not tweak the dog, I will do nothing to the dog. The damned dog is fine the way it is. Let's let this thing GO already.

J.K.

—— Original Message ——
From: Fred Hammer, I.T. Department
To: Julie Kay About
Cc: Scott Wythe
Sent: Tuesday, February 13, 2006 1:02 PM
Subject: Re: re: latest draft

Ms. About, during a random check of company e-mails, the I.T. department noted unacceptable language use in your account. Please consider this your fifth warning. Further warnings may result in disciplinary action. Remember, wherever you go, you are representing EconoHart Corporate.

Have a nice day! ☺

—— Original Message ——
From: Julie Kay About
To: Fred Hammer, I.T. Department
Cc: Scott Wythe
Cc: Mr. Donald Erickson, CEO
Sent: Tuesday, February 13, 2006 1:06 PM
Subject: Re: re: re: latest draft

Stay out of my e-mails, you jackbooted Nazis! If you prying motherfuckers don't pull your thumbs out of MY business, I'm going to dump a coffee milkshake into the main server! Don't you have anything better to do than spy on me like a bunch of virgin idiot losers? We've got viruses up the ass and our firewall is constantly going down, so you can't tell me you've got nothing better to do than read e-mails.

Don, if you want to fire me, then fucking fire me. If you want me to get my work done, call off the goddamned dogs. And if I see another smiley face emoticon in any corporate communication, I WILL NOT BE RESPONSIBLE FOR WHAT HAPPENS.

—— Original Message ——
From: Don Erickson
To: Julie Kay About
Cc: Scott Wythe
Cc: I.T. Department
Sent: Tuesday, February 13, 2006 1:22 PM
Subject: Everyone get back to work

Julie, sorry to bother you. Keep up the good work. I can assure you, the I.T. department will not be bothering you again.

Right, fellas?

Scott, I hope recent events aren't putting you off the work environment here at EconoHart. We're one big, happy family and we're glad you've joined us!

Chapter Two

Julie Kay leaned back in her office chair and smirked at the screen. Good old Don-o, swinging to the rescue. He didn't spend eight months wooing her away from Hallmark only to have I.T. weenies drive her out the door over some silly bullshit.

Although, cc'ing the big boss was kind of a dirty trick. But then, who played nice these days? It slowed you down, if nothing else.

Her computer beeped at her and she frowned—hadn't there been enough of this stuff today?—then called up the e-mail.

—— Original Message ——
From: Scott Wythe
To: Julie Kay About
Sent: Tuesday, February 13, 2006 2:30 PM
Subject: still waiting

hey so glad we got that cleared up you were totally awesome grrrl but i'm still waiting for the last draft of the card. do u want me to come over there and pick it up cuz it's no prob.

good job with the weenies. maybe we can have a drink sometime

scotty

"*Arrrrggggghhh!*" she yowled, and slammed her fists on the keyboard. Instantly, "sdlkjfa;slektjwpeoituwpoeitu-wopetuiw" streamed across the screen and she hastily took her fingers away and cleared the mess.

Would the boy never learn? Why wouldn't he let the stupid card go to Production? She was the one with the degrees in Creative Writing and Graphic Arts. He was—what? Was he even her age? He sure didn't write like it.

But then, who did these days? It was like most people assumed having e-mail meant never having to spell or capitalize. She was shocked at the number of high-level executives who would never dream of sending out a business letter without punctuation, but thought nothing of e-mailing "how u doon grrrl?" to a colleague.

Although . . . she was at Corporate, and Scott was forty miles away in the Marketing building at Brooklyn Park. Not exactly a hop, skip, and a jump; plus, they had couriers to pick up the hard stuff.

That was kind of nice of him, offering to come over . . . must be because he was the new guy. New guys were always anxious to make a good impression.

She took another look at the final sketch. Stupid dog on the cover, stupid, insipid saying on the inside, Happy Birthday, buh-bye. She had planned to write the Great American Short Story, and instead she drew dogs and thought up words that rhymed with "birthday."

And no matter how hard she worked, how hard they all worked, business was steadily dropping off. The homemade card craze—Julie Kay mused, rubbing her lips, then scowling at the bright red stain on her fingers—is killing us.

So, it made sense to put forth her best effort, always. And Scott was a pair of fresh eyes. Maybe the puppy could use a little more definition in the face and paws . . . wouldn't hurt to try and it would only be another five minutes or so . . .

—— Original Message ——
From: Julie Kay About
To: Scott Wythe
Sent: Tuesday, February 13, 2006 3:21 PM
Subject: Absolute final draft

Scott,

(I'm assuming you're a grown man, thus I refuse to refer to you as Scotty. Puppies and pet rabbits are named Scotty.)

I gave it one more tweak, as you suggested, and though I can't tell the difference, you might. I'm sending the final version over by courier right now; you should have it within the hour. So off my back, hosehead.

Sorry about the mess you got in earlier. The I.T. department (and I know you're reading this, you Gestapo bastards, and why don't you go fuck yourselves?) and I have a history. They think the Third Reich is alive and well, and I think that as long as I'm working here sixty hours a week and getting more work done than anyone else in the department, it's none of their damn business what I put in an e-mail.

Don't forget what I said about capitalizing and punctuation. Even if you are only a sixteen-year-old intern, you can do better than that.

J.K.

Chapter Three

"I'm holding up fine."

"I didn't say anything."

"So don't start."

"Who's starting?"

"I love my life."

"I love your life, too."

"Okay, then."

"Okay."

Julie Kay sipped coffee and studied her sister with narrowed eyes. Four years younger, Kara Jay was her psychic and physical opposite: short, plump, blond, radiant with sunshine and fulfillment. She had two under two at home, and another baby due in April. She had the open, friendly face of a foundation model, light blue eyes, and a small nose—a classic Swedish face, coupled with a classic Midwestern temperament. Her husband made a great living in construction, and looked like he modeled for Speedo calendars in his spare time. They went to Disney World for a week every year, and cut down their own Christmas trees. They had been happily married for five years, and made their own baby food.

It's like she's an alien come to observe me, Julie Kay marveled, counting the freckles on her sister's nose, *right in my own family*!

"So what are you doing tomorrow?" Kara Jay asked. "And stop counting my freckles."

"Basking in the joy of my single lifestyle."

"No, really."

"No. Really."

"If you just—"

"No."

"—he's a very nice guy—"

"No."

"—has his own roofing company—"

"No."

"—showed him your picture—"

"No-no-no-no-no-no-no."

"He thought you were cute," her sister peeped, then took a hurried gulp of her double-tall, caffeine-free skinny latte.

"No blind dates. And that . . ." she added, pointing, ". . . is not a coffee."

"Now who's starting?"

"Kara Jay, I'm just saying. I know you don't believe me, but let's go through it one more time. I like being single. I like being able to stay up as late as I want—like a real grownup!—and never once have to read, or think about reading, *Everybody Poops*."

"It was just that one month," her sister grumbled. "To get Willie over the hump."

"I like being able to eat cold pizza from any room in my house at any time. I like having the bed to myself. I like having the place to myself. I like having my *life* to myself."

"Except tomorrow," Kara Jay pointed out triumphantly. Literally pointed out, and Julie Kay noticed her sister was in sore need of a manicure.

"Well. Tomorrow."

"Valentine's Day. *The* holiday. You can't be alone that

day, you just can't. It breaks my heart to think about it. It's practically a law."

"Would that be federal or state?"

"And look where you work! You'll be surrounded by plush things all day. You'll be deluged in pink and red! Everywhere you look: hearts and chocolate. If you don't have a date to look forward to after work, how will you get through it?"

"I had planned," she admitted, "to bring my friend Captain Morgan to work."

"No, don't get drunk again—Don will only overlook so much."

"I have to spread my creative wings," Julie Kay declared. "And since I'm the best graphic designer he's got, Don will overlook a lot."

"Well, your wings aren't helped by getting sloppo at work and then picking fights with the I.T. guys. Ugh, remember the Christmas party? It was so mean—you were bigger than all of them."

"Weenies."

"Considerably bigger," her sister added, which was a good one, given that she wasn't exactly a lightweight herself. "And before you say it, *I'm* creating life. What's your excuse?"

"You're also creating my ulcer. And there's nothing wrong with an extra ten pounds here and there."

"And everywhere!" Kara Jay added brightly. "It's a good thing you're tall."

"Kara Jay . . ."

"That's all I'm saying. You can hide almost anything on that long frame of yours, you lucky cow."

"Kara Jay."

"It's just, you're so pretty without half trying! That's what makes me nuts!" Her sister ruffled her own streaked hair in frustration. "Think how great you'd look if you'd actually—you know—make an effort." She nearly spilled her latte in her excitement. "You know, get a haircut, some bangs, stop wearing it in that tacky long braid all the time. You look like Xena—"

"I think Lucy Lawless has bangs," she said mildly.

"—started wearing some color instead of black all the time, start wearing pretty shoes instead of those clunky—er—whatever they are . . ."

"Clogs. And they're comfortable."

"You sit down all day! What do you need comfortable shoes for? You could stand to wear a pair of nice pumps every other day."

"You forgot to tell me that colored contacts will rid me of my boring brown eyes," she prompted, "and the glasses."

"Your eyes are beautiful—don't you dare touch them! But you should get contacts, definitely get rid of the glasses, so everyone can see how pretty they are."

"And . . . ?"

"Well, the usual."

"Get married and have babies."

"Yes."

"Death first," she said grimly, and finished her coffee in a scalding gulp.

Chapter Four

She didn't even have to look at the Caller I.D. on her phone to see who it was. She debated letting her sister yammer into voice mail, but there would be no forgiveness if there wasn't an immediate call back.

"Johnny's Mortuary," she said, cradling the receiver between her neck and ear. "You stab 'em, we slab 'em."

"That is so old," her sister said. "That was old when we were in training bras."

"I still am. What is it now? I'm busy." Julie Kay stared at the galley—a galley! for a get-well card!—before her.

Thought this might cheer you up
And make you feel frisky as a pup.

Ugh! "Is it dog week around here and nobody told me?" she asked. *The last thing I want to feel like is a frisky pup.*

"Not that I know of," Kara Jay replied impatiently. "Listen, we didn't really get a chance to finish talking about your date at lunch."

"No blind dates!" She picked up a pen and angrily slashed through the insipid text.

"Julie Kay . . . be reasonable. Just once, to see what it feels like."

"Just *once*? How can your memory be so shitty?"

"No, I meant try a blind date for once, not be reasonable for once. Besides, Sean really thinks you two will hit it off."

Thoughts of your imminent demise
Make me wish we had come to a compromise

"No, no, no."

"What? Julie Kay?"

"Never mind. I mean, do mind! No blind dates—jeez, do I have to tattoo it on my shoulder?"

"That reminds me, do you have any tattoos? Sean asked me to find out so he can tell this guy. I remember you were threatening to get one of a run-over Road Runner on your ass, but you never showed it to me, so I honestly don't—"

"Kara Jay! Why aren't you listening to me? You can hear a toddler drop a Cheerio from half a block away, but 'no blind dates' doesn't hit your radar?"

"It's a totally different thing," her sister insisted.

"The next time your kids come over," she warned, slashing through the new, equally awful text, "I'm stuffing them with ice cream and chocolate."

"You do that every time."

"Need I remind you?"

"What? I already know; I'm the one who has to talk them down from the ceiling at 10:30 P.M."

"No, I mean, need I remind you of my track record with blind dates?"

"A few bad experiences shouldn't—"

"What? Are you on drugs?"

"That's none of your business," her sister said primly.

"Remember that guy, the Iowan who took us out with your then-boyfriend? We went to the state gymnastics trials? On the way there, he talked and talked about 'the Republican way of life,' got *out of the car* to try to shoot the deer that had crossed the road—who brings a shotgun on a date, by the way?—then sulked through the sets because he missed the poor thing."

"He was just trying too hard."

"*Trying* too hard? I'd hate to see him slacking off. Then—remember? I make the casual comment that I think gymnasts are really gifted, and he gets all huffy, like, 'You saying I can't do that?' and stomps down to the floor and tries, actually *tries* one of the routines, and breaks an ankle! Then got pissed when I wouldn't ride in the ambulance with him!"

"That just put you off Republicans," her sister said reasonably. "Not blind dates."

"Okay, fine. You want to play rough? How about the model you set me up with during college?"

"The watch model, or the dress-sock model?"

"The entire date he kept checking himself out in the mirror behind me. I mean, he was good-looking, but nobody's that much of an Adonis. The whole time I had the creepy feeling someone was sneaking up on me. I had to constantly fight the urge to turn around and check. Then I find out his nickname . . . Trojan? It wasn't because he was a Greek major, like he told me. It was from the condom brand! Yerrrgggh!"

"Anything sounds bad," Kara Jay said, "when you put it like that."

"And you! You have no perspective when it comes to this stuff! What was it Sean told you on your first date? 'Make yourself at home—my apartment is your apartment, my penis is your penis'."

"He grew on me."

"Like a foot fungus!"

"What about Bradley? Bradley was okay."

"Ha! He spent the entire date talking about all his super-secret Army exploits, which of course he couldn't tell me about because they were soooo secret (shyeah!). Then he started babbling about his Klingon costume for the convention, and how he was going to dress up as Data for the *Star Trek* convention . . . and then . . . then! Two days later, a Princess Leia costume shows up in the mail for me. After one date! Exit, stage right."

"But you have to admit, he was nice. You—"

"I've had dates tell me I could order anything I want. Thanks, jackass, I *know* that. I've had *first* dates present me with written proof they have a clean bill of health . . . like that was going to be a huge issue. I mean, can I at least finish my risotto before I have to read about a guy's white count?"

"Okay, so you've had some bad experiences. We all have."

"You're blissfully married to your high-school sweetheart, you jerk."

"Well, I meant 'we' in the . . . uh . . . universal sense. Right! I—"

Her computer binked at her again and she swung around in her chair to see the latest horror.

From: Scott Wythe
To: Julie Kay About
Sent: Tuesday, February 13, 2006 4:22 PM
Subject: How about dinner?

The new proof looks terrific. My boss is thrilled. (I.T. guys, you should be thrilled, too.) How about dinner? You've probably got plans for tomorrow, but how about Friday?

If you refuse, i'm gonna keep writing u letters like this and u will be sorry, grrrrl!

"Oh dear God," she breathed, hypnotized by the screen.

"What? What?" Kara Jay squawked in her ear. "Is it the I.T. guys again? Have they mobilized? Did they feed your computer another virus?"

"No, it's . . . a guy I work with, the new guy down in Marketing, asked me out for tomorrow night."

"Well, there you go!"

"He says he's sure I've got plans for tomorrow so maybe we could get together another time."

"It's nice that he's not assuming you're a mean, lonely freak," Kara Jay observed.

"I'm not lonely," she said defensively.

"But you'll let the other two slide? You are a freak. A freak who doesn't have a date for tomorrow. And you work with him! So that's not a blind date at all. It doesn't break your dumb dating rule."

"It is. I've never laid eyes on him. Eight thousand people work here, you know, and most of us aren't here in the main building. He could walk right up to me and slap me in the face and I wouldn't know him."

"Wait," her sister said, and chuckled.

Chapter Five

Julie Kay spotted the crowd outside Tables of Content and hesitated. Typical V-Day mob, all right. All googly-eyed couples and starchy waiters. She definitely should have followed her instincts and stayed home. *There was nothing wrong with being single, dammit!* Why didn't married people get it? Why had she weakened? Why was her bra itching? Why had she swapped her comfortable gray clogs for black flats?

Well, there was nothing for it. Time to bite the bullet, take the bull by the horns, pick your annoying cliché. It was only one night, anyway. How bad could it possibly be? It couldn't be worse than the Republican who brought a shotgun along. Or the model. Right? Because the chances of topping her worst date records were so slim as to be—

The dying wail of a siren cut the air and an ambulance screeched up to the curb. She heard someone yell out, "You're too late—the poor guy's dead!" and someone else yell out, "No, no, hurry! He'll be okay!" and knew. In that moment, Julie Kay About had her first and last psychic flash: her date had a date with the paramedics.

She shoved past the crowd—there were only two officers there so far for crowd control—and burst into the small restaurant. Even in this moment of stress, she couldn't repress a shudder at the *de rigueur* white tablecloths with a single red rosebud in a tall glass vase in the center of each one. Most of the tables were empty; everyone, it seemed, was grouped around her date.

She knelt beside Scott Wythe, the artist formerly known as blind date, now known as dead date . . . because he was dead, all right. You didn't have to be a health-care pro to know *that*. It was the peculiar gray color, the way his eyes looked like poached eggs. Oh, and the way the shrimp fork was sticking out of the middle of his chest. The blood stain was shaped like a fish on a bicycle. Were murder-scene bloodstains some sort of Rorschach test? Would a married couple see a pair of gold wedding bands? And why was she thinking of that now?

She tried not to be selfish, but couldn't quash the thought: worst blind date ever! Poor Scott! Poor her! Why did this have to happen? To either of them?

"Let us through," one of the paramedics ordered, and she obediently moved aside. Should she ride to the hospital in the ambulance with her date? Her dead date? Because that was creepy, even if it was also the right thing to do. Drive along behind in her own car? And then do what? She couldn't even identify him for the doctors. All she could do was give out his e-mail address and tell them he had terrible grammar in life.

"Julie?"

And he was so young! Ridiculously, amazingly young. She knew he would have to be, but if the dead guy had seen his twenty-fifth birthday, she'd . . . well, she didn't know what she'd do. He still had traces of acne on his perfectly unlined face, poor fellow.

"Julie Kay?"

"That's enough," someone else said, and she looked up in time to see an utterly gorgeous man being clapped into cuffs. He looked at her and even from across the restaurant . . .

(their eyes met across a crowded crime scene . . .)
(focus, Julie Kay)

. . . she could see how blue his eyes were—the color of an Easter sky. He was hunched over slightly as the cuffs were put on, and was looking up at her with a friendly expression on his face.

"Yes?" she asked. Wow, they'd caught the killer already! Unless the cuffs were recreational. But no, the fellow in the bad suit had a badge clipped to his belt, and the gal beside him—much better dressed—was reading him his rights.

"I guess I'm going to be a little late," Blue Eyes explained.

". . . the right to have an attorney present now and during any future questioning . . ."

"What?" she asked. She was a little nervous to be talking to the killer.

". . . one will be appointed to you free of charge if you wish . . ."

"You know. For our date," Blue Eyes added helpfully. She noticed he was dressed in excellent first-date fashion: khakis, a dark blue work shirt, loafers, dark socks. His shoulders looked impossibly broad in the shirt—swimmer's shoulders. He was ridiculously tall, too . . . he towered over the detectives. His dark brown hair hung in his eyes, and he jerked his head back so he could look right at her some more.

"What?" she said again, catching on but not wanting to, figuring it out but not wanting a bit of this mess, not one piece—no, thank you.

"I bought you some flowers," he said, jerking his head at a table to her left. "But I can't get them for you right now."

"You didn't," she said faintly.

"Buy flowers?"

"Kill this guy."

"Oh, hell no!"

Well, that was something. Still, Julie Kay had no idea

how to feel about recent events. Was it better that her date was the dead guy, or the murder suspect?

"I thought I had a psychic flash," she said faintly. "My very first one."

"Oh. Well, no offense, but I don't believe in that stuff."

"Me neither."

"That's enough, sir. You're coming with us now," the lady detective said, kindly enough.

"Oh, okay. Well, it was nice to meet you in person."

"Thanks," she said through numb lips.

"Sorry about all this," he added, gesturing with his shoulders to the crime scene.

"Me, too." She sat down before she fell down.

Chapter Six

"At least he didn't stand you up," her sister said comfortingly.

"For Christ's sake, will you try to focus!" Julie Kay hissed into her cell phone. She slammed on her brakes so she wouldn't hit the unmarked car in front of her. Her date had enough problems without being put in traction as well. "I have a big fucking problem here, and I'd like you to *help me*."

"Sweetie, I'm a homemaker, not Matlock. What do you want me to do?"

"Can I go off and leave him?" she asked anxiously. "It's not like we have this deep, meaningful relationship."

"He said he didn't do it, right?"

"Yeah, but *I'm* not Matlock, either. If he's innocent, the cops or the D.A. will figure it out. Right?"

"Riiiight," her sister said doubtfully.

"So what's my date responsibility here?"

"It's a new one on me," her sister admitted. "I'm just glad he turned out to be alive."

"Yeah," she said, taking a left on Hiawatha, "there's that."

"So, that's an improvement, right? Especially if he's

telling the truth about not killing—who'd he supposedly kill?"

"I have no idea."

"Well, I hate to go all Miss Marple on you . . ."

"Let me talk to him first. If they'll let me, I guess. Man, oh man," she muttered. "And I thought Valentine's Day was killing *me* . . ."

"That'll learn you. Silver lining behind every cloud, and all that."

"You've been super-helpful. And by that I mean, of course, you have not been remotely helpful, and I'm hanging up now."

"Call me back!" her sister begged. "Tell me whodunit!"

Like I'm going to have a clue myself, she thought, and slapped the phone closed.

Chapter Seven

"Well," her date said cheerfully. "This is awkward."

"It's not funny, Scott."

"I'm with you, but it's either try to make a joke out of it or burst into unmanly tears, and I'm trying to make a good impression on you."

"It's a little late for that," she pointed out.

"Thanks for coming to the station."

"Mmmm."

It was an evening of firsts: she was standing outside a holding cell, which Scott had all to himself. Getting in to see him had been relatively simple, once she'd signed about six reams of paperwork. It had certainly gone better than her last annual review.

"So, what? What happens next?"

"Well, I called my dad and he's sending a lawyer down to try to get me out of here . . ."

"You haven't seen a lawyer yet? You saw me but not your attorney?"

"What can I say. That black cardigan makes my heart go trippity-trip."

She yanked the cardigan closed. "Scott, this is serious."

"I know. You can tell because, the more serious it is, the more dumb jokes I'll be cracking."

"How old are you?" she asked suspiciously.

"If you'll take a peek at my rap sheet, you'll see I'm a doddering twenty-four."

"Well, even if this murder thing wasn't hanging over our heads, I could tell you this never would have worked. I've got almost ten years on you."

"So? You speak your mind and you've got an ass that won't quit. That's really all I require in a woman."

"Scott, I'm not sure you're getting exactly what's going on here . . ."

"Sure I am. Somebody killed our waiter while I was in the men's. I fell over the body and got blood all over me." He gestured to his dark shirt which, Julie Kay now noticed, had a dark stain on the upper left shoulder.

"You fell on the dead guy?"

"Yeah, and it's as gross as it sounds, believe me. Basically, I did everything you're not supposed to do . . . I mean, have I not seen any episode of the *Law & Order* franchise? I rolled the guy over, tried to see if he was okay, got my prints all over the shrimp fork—it was my shrimp fork, by the way—"

She covered her eyes. "Oh, boy."

"—started yelling for help and, annoyingly, *that's* when people noticed the body: when they looked over and saw me crouching practically on top of him."

"Great."

"Worst date ever," he finished.

"I was just having that same thought."

"Honey," he told her, giving her a penetrating look from those amazing eyes, "you're out there. I'm in here. So I win the Worst Date Prize."

"Agreed. So, now what?"

"I tell my lawyer what happened—when he shows up—and justice prevails."

"It's not like you had a motive, right?"

"Never saw the guy before tonight. Although, I was kind of annoyed he didn't give us a better table."

"Well, for God's sake, keep that to yourself. Maybe somebody at the restaurant saw what happened."

"If someone did, no one said shit to the cops while I was there. Of course, they could have feared my murderous rage and clammed up as a result . . ."

"Sure." Who could fear long legs and blue eyes and a narrow waist? Scott was a little on the skinny side, but she liked tall guys. And he was really tall. Yum. "Well, I guess I'll just wait with you until your lawyer gets around to showing up."

"Aw, you don't have to do that," he protested as she looked around for a place to sit. "You should go grab something to eat. Aren't you hungry? It's after nine o'clock and we never got a chance to . . ."

"I couldn't eat. Not after seeing that poor guy. Did you see his eyes?" She shivered. "I've never seen a real dead guy before. TV doesn't count."

"I have," Scott said glumly. He had a place to sit, she noticed—a small bench in the far corner, not to mention the toilet—but didn't. Instead, he stayed close to the bars. Close enough to reach out and touch her, if he wanted. "I used to work in a funeral home."

"And you left to design greeting cards?"

"What can I say? I wanted something in the fast lane."

She gestured to the holding area. "It doesn't get much faster than this."

"Honey, that's the truth."

"Don't call me honey."

"Darling? Sweetie pants?"

"I told you, this isn't going to work."

"It's the cloud of murder hanging over my head, right?"

"No, I already told you. The age difference."

"Oh," he yawned. "That."

"Look, let's stay on track here, all right? Can I get you something? Or is a detective going to offer you a sandwich and then play bad cop?"

"Honey, I have no idea. I've never been arrested before."

"Well," she said, "I'll go get you something to eat."

"Thanks, honey."

"Stop that."

Chapter Eight

"This is getting weirder and weirder. I mean, the evening just keeps topping itself."

"It's like adopting a dog," Scott said, glancing over her shoulder as she signed page after page. "Look at all the stuff you have to fill out! Is there anything there about me having all my shots?"

"Ho-ho. I don't know why I'm doing this."

"Because we're in lurrrrrrrv?"

Because she couldn't stand the thought of him in that grungy cell when she knew to her bones he was innocent. Because she wanted him to like her. Because she'd lost her fucking mind. Because his shirt was off.

Yep, he was standing there in his dark slacks and his shoes, but his bloody shirt had been taken as, she assumed, Exhibit A. His chest was exceedingly distracting: wide shoulders, a light fur of hair running between his nipples and down into his pants, flat stomach, nipples the size of quarters. Christ!

Focus focus focus.

"Have him back here at 1:00 P.M. tomorrow, Miss About."

Whew! Something to focus on besides Scott's nipples.

"That's 'Aboot'," she corrected the lady detective, whose name, she had since learned, was Hobbes.

"You're kidding."

"No."

"Okay."

"Aw," Scott said, rubbing his wrists where the cuffs had recently been removed. "I think it's cute."

"Shut your nipples, Scott."

"What?"

"Mouth. Shut your mouth." *Oh, God, I didn't just say that, did I?* "So, Detective Hobbes, you were saying—back here tomorrow afternoon?"

"Yes. And you were telling him to shut his—"

"Never mind. He'll be here. Guaranteed."

"Yes, I know," Hobbes said cheerfully, scooping up the ream of paperwork Julie Kay had just signed. "It's not like we can't track you down."

"So that's it? I can really leave?"

"As I said earlier, we don't have enough to hold you overnight. But we'll be chatting with you again tomorrow." Yes, the lady was weirdly cheerful for a murder cop. Maybe it came from being a redhead? "And between now and then we'll be conducting a number of interviews."

"You're thinking, if I have a super-secret motive, you'll find it."

The smile slipped off Hobbes's face. "Yes. That's what I'm thinking."

There was an awkward silence, and then Julie Kay tentatively touched Scott's bare shoulder. "Come on. Let's go."

"So, should I get a cab or do you mind giving me a lift back to my—"

"I promised your lawyer and the cops that I'd vouch for you showing up tomorrow."

"Great. So—"

"So, you're staying at my place."

"We are in lurrrrrrv!" he said delightedly.

"Shut up."

"Seriously, Julie Kay, thanks. You're a girl in a million."

"I haven't been a girl in twenty years, and shut up."

"I mean, most girls would have fled screaming into the night, not gone to the jail with me and got me released and promised to haul me back the next day."

"Most girls are smarter than me."

"Not hardly."

"Well, thanks, but there's got to be an explanation." *Besides his yummy nipples.* "I think I have a fever," she muttered, unlocking her car. Then, "Aren't you freezing? You look . . . uh, cold."

"Well, I am, a little. But it seemed kind of lame to complain. What's being cold compared to being dead?"

She rummaged around in her backseat and found another cardigan. He shrugged into it without complaint. It wouldn't button—he was too broad—so he just held it as closed as he could.

"Home, Jeeves," he mock-ordered, and she almost shuddered. She really had lost her mind. How was she ever going to *explain* all of this?

"You just better not be guilty, you perky-nippled son of a bitch."

"Have no fear. Drive on."

Chapter Nine

"Well, this is it." She tossed her keys on the kitchen counter. "Home sweet hell."

"It's nice," he commented, glancing around the small house she rented from her brother-in-law. "I used to live in Inver, back when I was a student at the U."

"Yeah, what, six weeks ago?"

"Oh, you're hilarious."

"I hate apartments. I always feel like a bee in a hive. So when my brother-in-law moved into a bigger place, he let me rent this one. It's worked out for everyone."

"Mmm." He was prowling around the living room and dining area like a big, brunet panther. "I have an apartment, and I know what you mean. But I'm almost never there."

"Where are you?"

"Work, usually. That's why I was really glad when you decided to go out with me. I mean, I have no social life."

"But you're so . . ." Gorgeous. Delicious. Fabulous. Tall. ". . . smart."

He shrugged. "I was always the tallest kid in my class, *and* the skinniest. But I was bad at sports. So who'd want to go out with a big gork like me?"

Oh, I dunno, anyone with half a brain?

"Uh, let me see if I can find something better than my old cardigan." She turned to go into her bedroom, but he came up behind her and put a hand on her shoulder, gently turning her around.

"It's fine," he said. "It's the least of my problems, believe me. What the hell am I going to do about that poor guy at the restaurant?"

"Uh . . . well, I . . . uh . . ." Blue eyes were filling her world, her universe. They were getting closer and closer. There was nothing else: no house, no living room, no cardigan, no dead guy.

She felt his lips on hers and put her arms around him—she could hardly reach, his shoulders were so broad. Her mouth opened beneath his and his tongue touched hers, tentatively and then with more assurance, licking her teeth and nibbling her lower lip. She pulled, and the cardigan was on the floor, and her hands were running across his fine chest, and . . .

(dead guy, dead guy!)

. . . she yanked herself away. "Stop that! This is totally inappropriate!"

"Hey, you kissed *me*."

"I did not!" Oh, wait. Maybe she did. "Well, it doesn't matter. This isn't the time or place."

"I *know.* That's why I didn't kiss you. Although, I have to say," he added cheerfully, "I've been dying to all night. But you're right, this isn't the right time. Bad sweetie."

"Oh, like you were really fighting it!"

"It seemed rude to give you the brush-off," he said, sounding wounded. "You know, me being a guest in your home and all."

"Well, never mind that. Let's stay focused. Put your sweater back on."

"I didn't take it off," he grumbled, but did as she asked.

"Let's figure this out. We have to be back there in fourteen hours. So, if you didn't kill the guy—"

"Charley Ferrin."

She gasped. "You know him?"

"No, no." He held his hands up, palm out. "Calm down, don't have a coronary."

"I'll have one if I damn well please!"

"It's not like that. Detective Hobbes told me his name. I swear, I have no idea who he is. The name meant nothing to me."

"Okay, okay." She forced herself to calm down. He was right, this was no time to burst a blood vessel. "So, if you didn't do it, who did? Who had a motive and could do it quick, and avoid the cops, and stick you with a murder charge?"

"Honey, I got nothin'. I've been trying to figure it out all night. I was minding my own business, waiting for you, and the next thing I know, I'm wearing handcuffs. And not in a good way."

She felt the blood rush to her face as she pictured him cuffed to her headboard. "All right. Did you overhear any arguments? See anybody fighting? Anything weird at all?"

"No."

"Come on. There must be something."

He shook his head. "No. And no, and no. I told the cops all this already."

"Well, now tell *me*," she snapped.

"Don't boss me!"

"I'll boss you if I like! If it wasn't for me you'd still be rotting in jail!"

"The hell. My lawyer would have vouched for me."

"Yeah, I could tell what a great job he did by the way it took him *hours* and *hours* to *not* show up."

"Listen—mmph!"

She had kissed him again. What was wrong with her?

"Not that I mind," he gasped, extricating himself from her grip, "but, again, don't you think this is a little inappropriate? Given the circumstances?"

She got up to pace. "Of course it's inappropriate—it's nine kinds of inappropriate! What the hell is wrong with me?"

He opened his mouth, but she beat him to the punch. "I'll tell you, it's this fucking holiday! It's killing me! It's making me act in ways I would never normally act! God, I hate it, I hate it, *I hate Valentine's Day!*"

"Take it easy," he said, and rose to cuddle her in his arms. Sulkily, she allowed it. "You've had a tough day."

"A terrible day."

"Yes, just awful. You poor baby."

"I never should have said yes when you asked me out. I like being single!"

"Aw, come on," he said to the top of her head. "And miss all this excitement?"

"Mmph." Her chin was resting in the middle of his chest and it was wonderful, thank you very much. They swayed together in her small living room, dancing slowly to unheard music. He was rubbing her back and she could feel his breath on the top of her—

On the top of her head.

She jerked out of his embrace. "You're really tall."

"Six-five. But it's not, you know, contagious or anything. Here, come back for another snuggle."

She resisted the snuggle command. "But the stains on your shirt . . . they were on your shoulder!"

He blinked. "Well, yeah. I think I got blood on me when I leaned down to roll the guy over, see if he was okay."

"But—think about this. If you'd stabbed him with your shrimp fork, don't you think—"

"The blood would be lower, given where he was stabbed, and where the stains were." His eyes widened. "Holy shit! And to think I hated being tall when I was a kid! It's just saved my ass!"

"We've got to tell Hobbes! They should be looking for someone shorter, not trying to pin it on you! And you know that's what they'll be doing . . . if they have a suspect, they try to make the puzzle fit around that suspect. They won't be looking for a new guy."

"How do you know that?"

"TV," she said. "Lots and lots of TV." She lunged for her cell phone, which beeped at her the moment she had it in her hand. She flipped it open and said, "Not now."

"But whodunit?" her sister asked breathlessly. "I've been waiting hours for you to call."

"We don't know."

"'We'?"

"But we know Scott didn't do it."

"But didn't you know that before?"

"Yes, but now we really, really know."

"Is he there? Is he with you? What's he like? Is he nice? He's nice, isn't he?"

"He's fine. Look—"

"Will you go out with him again?"

"One thing at a time," she said. "First I've got to clear him."

"You've got to clear him?"

"Long story. I have to go."

"Wait! When—"

She disconnected the call, then stopped. "What do I do? Do I dial 9-1-1 and ask for Detective Hobbes?"

"I think we better go back down to the station."

"But what if they arrest you again?"

He slapped his forehead. "Duh, we call my lawyer and tell him what we've figured out."

"Oh." She felt exquisitely stupid. "Right, of course."

"Don't feel bad," he said, correctly reading her expression. "It's different when it's real life."

"I'll say."

Chapter Ten

"You have the worst lawyer in the world."

"He's my dad's tax attorney," Scott explained apologetically.

"What! He didn't refer you to a criminal lawyer?"

"I don't think there was time."

"There would have been if you'd called him before asking to see me."

"Hey, the Minneapolis cops are really laid back. They didn't care how many phone calls I made."

"Okay, okay. Let's think about this. Your lawyer's not reachable. We're not keen on going back to the station—"

"Well, even if they arrest me again, once we tell them the new info, they won't hold me very long. Hell, even without the new info they didn't hold me very long."

"Yeah, but why take a chance? I know!" She seized her keys, then grabbed his hand and galloped out of the house. "Hobbes is probably at the restaurant, questioning everybody with her partner!"

"Oh, great. Back to the scene of the crime. Isn't that rule number one of things not to do when you're the chief suspect?"

"No, rule number one is get a lawyer who answers his phone. Come on."

* * *

"You know, I think you're really sweet."

"Shut up."

"And I totally get off on that grumpy exterior."

"It's not an exterior—it goes all the way down."

"The hell." He squirmed, trying to get comfortable in her bucket seat, and finally gave up. "If that was the case, you wouldn't be breaking speed records to get back to the restaurant, not to mention all the other stuff you've done for me."

"Scott, can we do this another time?"

"Well, no, because once you clear me, our date will be over and you probably won't go out with me again."

She snorted. "Probably?"

"You're hung up on the age thing."

"Other than working for a shitty greeting card company, name one thing we have in common."

"Well, we both like your cardigans."

"Scott, be serious."

"And we both like the way you kiss."

"Scott."

"And we both like to right wrongs, and play amateur detective. And we both like the collected works of Stephen King."

"How did you—oh. The bookshelf in my living room."

"Plus," he continued happily, "it's a huge turn-on, the way you can't keep your hands off me."

"That's because it's a weird night—don't let it go to your nipples. I mean, your head."

"Which one?" he asked innocently, and she scowled and smacked him on the leg.

"Finally," she muttered, seeing the sign for Tables of Content. With the ambulance gone, it looked a little less frightening, though there were still quite a few cars on the street. "Shit. No parking places."

"Park illegally. You are looking for a cop, right?"

"Oh. Good idea." She double-parked beside a nondescript sedan she hoped was an unmarked police car, and shut off the engine. "Okay, let's go find Hobbes and remind her that you're tall."

"Good plan, Holmes!"

"Shut up."

Chapter Eleven

"Excuse me," she said to the man in the dark suit. He was short, coming up to her shoulders, but impeccably dressed, although the red rose in his lapel was looking a little bedraggled. He was as smooth and bald as an egg, with dirt-colored eyes. "Are you the manager?"

"Yes, but I'm afraid the kitchen is closed. If you'd like to make a reservation, I can—"

"No, we're looking for Detective Hobbes."

"Who?"

"You know. The cop. About this tall . . ." Julie Kay held her hand up about an inch above her eyebrows. "Wearing a green, two-piece suit? Red hair, gun, badge? Weirdly cheerful?"

"I'm sorry, miss, there's no one here by that name."

Scott had been looking around the restaurant, where there wasn't a trace of crime-scene tape or fingerprint powder anywhere. But there were several people running vacuums and setting tables. "Uh, dude, I don't think you're supposed to clean up this fast."

"Clean up?"

"You're messing with a murder scene. And where did all the cops go?"

"What murder scene?"

Julie Kay gaped at the manager. She was totally at a loss. "You could go to *jail!* Interfering with a crime scene, or whatever it's called!"

"Miss, I don't know what you're talking about, but if you and your gentleman friend don't leave right now, I'm going to be forced to call the police."

"Great! Good! Call them! I'll call them! What are you doing? You can't cover this up! *Stop cleaning up,"* she shouted at the other workers.

"What's the problem?" Scott asked the manager, who had broken out into a light sweat. The lights made his forehead gleam like a star. "Afraid of getting a bad Zagat's review?"

"Sir, I don't know what you're talking about."

"But it'll be in the papers. Reporters check on this stuff all the time. You can't cover it up."

"I don't know what you're talking about," he said again.

"You're full of shit," Julie Kay told him.

"Atta girl. You should watch out," Scott told the manager. "She's got a mean side."

"You're standing there, all 'I don't know what you're talking about', and meanwhile, you've got a look on your face like you just bit into a rotten lime. So why don't you cut the shit?"

"Miss, do you want to make a reservation or not?"

"Did you do it? Is that why you're erasing evidence and pretending nothing happened? Did you kill—uh—" She looked at Scott.

"Charley Ferrin."

"Yeah, him. Did you do it?"

"We won't tell anyone," Scott assured him.

"I don't know what you're talking about. Now, please leave."

"Like hell!" she shouted.

"Okay," Scott said, and grabbed her by the elbow.

"Wha—? Scott! This guy's dirty! He knows something! He—mmph!"

This time *he* had kissed *her*. And, interestingly, was dragging her out of the restaurant at the same time. When he pulled his mouth away, he said cheerfully over her shoulder, "Young love and all that. Sorry to waste your time."

"Scott!" She was nearly apoplectic with rage. "What are you doing?"

"Getting you out of there," he muttered. They were on the sidewalk now, and he was looking around for a cop. "If he is dirty, I don't want you anywhere near him."

"But . . . we could get you off the suspect list."

"Yeah, but if he's rotten enough to stab somebody with a fork, he's rotten enough to tie up loose ends. Like some weird woman yelling at him about how she thinks he did the deed."

"But—"

"Forget it, Julie Kay. It's too risky. We'll figure something else out."

She hardly knew what to say. Her anger had melted and been replaced by . . . what? Gratitude? Sexual longing? Admiration? Annoyance? He was risking his own freedom to keep her safe, and that was just . . . well, so romantic. And dumb. But mostly romantic. No, mostly dumb.

"They must be done with the interviews," he observed.

"What?"

"Look around. There's, like, nobody on the street."

"Ugh. That means they've decided you did it. I bet that rotten, lying managerial son of a bitch was sooo helpful, too."

"Unfortunately, I didn't see any blood on him."

"Dark suit, though."

"Yeah, but still . . ." He trailed off doubtfully.

"Well, let's definitely not go to the police station now."

"But—"

Her phone beeped, and she remembered she'd shut the ringer off when they got to the restaurant. She flipped it open and hit the Missed Calls button.

"Oh," she said.

"What?"

She showed him. Bright blue letters flashed across the small white screen: Hobbes, Catherine A., Detective, Minneapolis Homicide, 612-592-3921.

"Shit."

"Think she wants me to come back?"

"I'm sure of it."

"Well," he pointed out, "there's not much we can do about that. You can't just not take me back."

"The hell."

"What?" She was already at the car, and he jogged after her. "What are you doing? Where are we going?"

"Back to my place until this dies down."

"But you have to take me back. Or at least return her phone call."

"No, I don't."

"Julie Kay, be reasonable."

"Never!"

"Come on, you can't not produce me."

"Watch me."

"Julie Kay!" he said sternly.

"Get your ass in this car," she told him.

"But you're planning on kidnapping me," he said, although he did, she was glad to see, climb into the passenger side.

"Yeah, but it's for your own good."

"The latest bad idea," he said, hiding his face in his hands, "in an evening full of them."

"Oh, shut up."

Chapter Twelve

She came out of the bathroom in time to hear him say, yet again, "You can't keep me."

"Ha!"

"Julie Kay, come on. Call her back. Find out what she wants."

"No. We're not talking to her, nobody talks to her. Not yet. Do you want some coffee or something?"

"No. I want you to see reason. This irrational, nutty side of you, while sexy, is unnerving as hell."

"I *am* seeing reason."

"Oh, I can't wait to hear this one."

"You have to stay away from the cops until we clear your name. Or they figure out that you couldn't have done it."

"But, honey, you're not sharing information with them. They're not telepaths, you know."

"Your lawyer will call them tomorrow. If he ever checks his fucking voice mail. Meanwhile, you're laying low."

"But you promised to bring me back."

"Well, I changed my mind!"

He rubbed his eyebrows and squinted at her. She got out a gallon of milk, poured herself a tumbler, and downed it in three gulps. "I don't know," he said at last, "whether to strangle you or kiss you."

"Well, while you're making up your mind, let me see if I can dig up a spare toothbrush."

"Julie Kay—take me back."

"No."

"Fine. I'll go myself."

"You don't have a car," she said smugly. "It's twenty miles to the police station."

"I'll call a cab."

"With what? I don't have a land line here—I use my cell phone for everything."

He swore under his breath. She knew he didn't have his on him—the cops had taken it. It was Exhibit B.

"Julie Kay . . ."

"Look, just accept the inevitable, will you?"

"Give me your phone, please."

"No."

"Julie Kay!"

"No!"

"Goddammit, give me your fucking phone!"

She shook her head. He yowled like a scalded cat and jumped on her, so quickly she couldn't get out of the way in time. They both hit the kitchen tile and she felt the breath leave her lungs.

"Sorry," he panted, groping in her pockets, "but this is for your own good. I don't want you to be booked as an accessory."

"Go fuck yourself," she gasped, kicking.

"Dammit, where is the fucking thing? I know it's not in your purse—you've been clipping it to your belt all night."

"You leave my belt alone," she warned. He was so close, his dark hair was brushing her face. She groped for his ribs and gave him a vicious pinch. He groaned, but kept feeling her belt.

"There's plenty more where that came from," she said, squirming like a grub on a hot plate.

"Sit still. And don't pinch me again—I'm already going to have a bruise the size of a grapefruit, dammit, *what* did you do with the—" His eyes widened and the fight went out of him; his forehead rested on her shoulder. "The bathroom. You went to the bathroom first."

"Yep."

"Oh, God. What did you do to it?"

"It's possible," she admitted, "that I flushed it."

"Christ."

"Repeatedly."

"You wrecked our only phone?"

"It was for your own good."

"Strangle you," he decided. "That's what I'll do. It was a toss-up before, but now I've made up my mind." He put his hands around her throat, gently, and pulled her up for a long kiss.

"That'll learn me," she gasped after a long moment. "Yep, I guess you showed me a thing or two."

"Oh, shut up," he murmured, and kissed her again.

Chapter Thirteen

If she hadn't been so out of her mind with lust, she would have been appalled at the stickiness of her linoleum. Well, that was a worry for another day. Right now she was concentrating on shedding her clothes and helping him shed his.

She was covering every part of him she could reach with wild kisses, and he was kissing her back and running his big hands over her body.

She reached down and felt him, long and ready for her, and cupped his testicles in her hands, marveling at their furry warmth. He groaned into her mouth and she straddled him, a knee coming down on either side of him. Her knees stuck, and she grimaced.

"Protection?" he managed, his hands covering her breasts, testing their weight, stroking them, even squeezing lightly.

"Birth control pills," she told him.

"Tremendous geek who never has sex," he replied.

"So, it's safe to say you're not riddled with disease." She giggled. She rose over him and he gobbled at her breasts as they swung near his face. She seized him with one hand and guided him into her, and he clutched her ass and slowly rose to meet her.

"Oh, Christ," he groaned, "you're so wet, how can you be so wet?"

"Hours of wanting to bone you," she replied, truthfully enough. "Oooooh, that's nice. Don't stop doing that."

"Never," he gasped.

From her position she could look at him all she liked, and loved what she saw. He had broken into a light sweat, and his crystal blue eyes were narrowed into slits. His hips flexed to meet hers and it was superb, it was heavenly, it was—

"Oh, boy," he managed. "I hope you're close."

"I'm not," she told him. "But you can make it up to me later."

"It's a date," he replied, and then shuddered beneath her, and she went down for a soft kiss, and rested her head on his chest for a long time.

Chapter Fourteen

"It's *not* a date," she told him later, after they had showered and he had pulled on an old, baggy sweatshirt of hers to wear with his boxers. The sweatshirt that dwarfed her and came to her knees was just this side of too small for him. "I told you. You're too young for me."

"Oh, who cares? Do you really think something like that matters? Do you think this sort of thing happens every day?"

"I have no idea," she said. "I like being single. I don't seek out dates."

"Well, you're going to now. With me." He jabbed a thumb at his chest. "You can't honestly say after tonight you're never going to see me again."

"My, my, don't we think a lot of our dick."

"I was referring," he said with great dignity, "to all the excitement earlier, but you've got a one-track mind, I must say."

"Shut up."

"I should get kidnapped every week," he commented, sitting down on the couch and pulling her down with him. She had changed into the sexiest nightwear she had, her green flannel gown. It made her look like an extra on *Little House on the Prairie,* but what the hell, Scott didn't seem to mind.

She snorted. "Sure."

"No, really. This has been the weirdest, scariest, coolest, sexiest, most amazing night of my life."

"Yeah, but you're still young."

"Oh, quit with that."

"But you are," she said, laughing. "You're a baby, an infant."

"A law-abiding infant. I can't believe you're going to get yourself in trouble in a misguided attempt to keep me out of jail."

"What can I say? V-Day makes me do weird things. Look at it this way: if I hadn't gone out with you, you wouldn't be in this mess."

"Worth it," he said, rubbing her shoulders.

"You dumb-ass."

"Flattery will get you laid again."

"You—" Her doorbell interrupted what was going to be a spectacular insult, and they both froze and looked at the clock. It was four o'clock in the morning.

"My sister," she decided, getting up. "She couldn't bear to wait for the gory details."

"Mmmm." He got off the couch as well. "You've got a peephole, right?"

"What, you think the killer tracked us down?" she joked. She went to the side door and pulled the shade. "See? No problem. It's—oh, shit!"

"It's worse than the killer," he observed, then thumbed the lock and pulled the door open. "Hi, Detective Hobbes."

Hobbes opened her mouth.

"Don't arrest him!" Julie Kay shrieked.

"She's all right," Scott said, grabbing her elbow and pulling her out of the way so Hobbes could come in. "Just stress, you know."

"Nice underwear," Hobbes commented. "Listen, I tried calling you, but—"

"Julie Kay accidentally dropped her phone in the toilet," Scott said helpfully. "Five or six times."

"Anyway—"

"He didn't do it! He's innocent! You don't have to take him, you just have to get ahold of his lawyer! Just call his lawyer!"

Hobbes rubbed her head. "Do you have to scream? It's been a long fucking night, pardon my French. You going to offer me a seat or just keep me standing here?"

"Sorry, sorry. Here, take the couch."

"We don't have to let her in," Julie Kay said frantically. "Where's your warrant? Where's your writ? Where's your—your—"

"Where's my Advil," Hobbes muttered, rummaging around in her bag. "Ah!"

"You want some milk with that? That's all we've got. Well, there's some orange juice that looks questionable, but—"

"Milk's fine."

"Scott, for crying out loud! Why don't you just go lie down in the back of her car and put the cuffs on yourself?"

"That's okay," Hobbes said cheerfully. "I had my date earlier."

Scott brought her a glass of milk and she gulped it down with three Advils. "Okay," she said, setting down the empty glass. "Like I was saying. I tried to call you earlier but couldn't get through, so I thought I'd stop by in person—I'm sorry for the late hour, but I didn't think you'd want to wait to hear—"

"He's too tall to be the killer!" Julie Kay blurted.

"Julie Kay, will you let the woman get a complete sentence out?"

"Scott, shut up and let me handle this. Detective, check his shirt! Check the dead guy's wound! They won't match. He's innocent!"

"Yes," Hobbes said, rubbing her temples. "We know. That's why I'm here. We got the guy. Once we figured out the stains didn't match up, we went out with our handy-dandy, police-issue tape measures and figured out how tall the killer was, then questioned him at the restaurant. He confessed. We got him. Stop screaming."

"You *got* him?" she yelled, completely taken by surprise.

Hobbes rolled her eyes. "Yes, that's what we do: catch bad guys."

"Did my lawyer get ahold of you?" Scott asked excitedly.

"No, Mr. Wythe, we figured it out all by our lonesome. It's not like the movies, you know. An amateur sleuth doesn't figure everything out and eventually enlighten the cops, who then gratefully see that justice is done and put the bad guy in jail. *We* enlighten *you.*"

"There's no need to be snotty about it," she muttered.

"There's all kinds of need," Hobbes retorted. She stood and slung her bag over her shoulder. "Anyway, since you were never charged, you don't have to come back for an arraignment or anything. Just wanted you to know you can skip your one o'clock appointment."

"Thanks."

"Yeah, uh, thanks, Detective."

"Don't mention it." Hobbes stepped to the door. "Or, if you do, mention it *quietly.*"

"Wait!"

Hobbes groaned.

"Sorry," Julie Kay continued, softly. "But who did it?"

"Oh. Gerald McDougal the Third. He—"

"—was the manager, right? Oh, I knew it! He was totally trying to cover it up. And he's completely wrecked your crime scene," Julie Kay added in a self-righteous tone.

"No. The manager is Gerald McDougal the Second. The killer—"

"Was his son?" Scott asked, an amazed expression on his face.

"Yes—second in line to take over the restaurant."

"Why'd he kill Charley?"

"Charley was a regular at Tables; they've known each other for a year. Tables is a real family operation—the coat-check girl is McDougal the Third's wife. Apparently Charley was having an affair with her."

"Oh, ouch," Scott said respectfully. "That's harsh."

"To put it mildly," Julie Kay added.

"Harsher: she picked tonight, of all nights, to confess. McDougal the Third took it badly."

"That sucks."

"And," Julie Kay added, "that would explain why he—McDougal the Second—was trying to cover everything up. Protecting the family name, or whatever."

"We arrested his son earlier, so I'm not sure what you're talking about when you said he's wrecked the—"

"He had cleaners and vacuums in there. Took down all your crime-scene tape. Like that."

"Oh." Hobbes looked unsurprised. "Well, I'll go back down there and book him for that, then. But I've seen it before. The mindset of the cover-up. He couldn't stop his kid from being arrested, or his daughter-in-law from screwing around, but he could protect the restaurant's reputation. Try, anyway. It never works. I don't know why they bother."

"That doesn't make sense," Scott commented.

"Love makes you do stupid things." Hobbes tipped them a two-finger salute. "Happy Valentine's Day."

She left.

Chapter Fifteen

"You didn't get that hysterical when the I.T. guys were ganging up on you," Scott commented, hours later after they were snuggled into her bed. "This bed blows, by the way."

"I live alone and I don't have a boyfriend. I don't need anything bigger than a twin," she pointed out.

"Remind me to get you a double bed for Easter."

"Getting a little ahead of ourselves, aren't we?"

"No. You lurrrrrrrrrrrv me! My God, I thought you were going to pop Hobbes right in the eye. I was torn between anxiety and sexual arousal."

"Pig. I just didn't want to see an innocent man go to jail," she grumbled.

"Suuuuuure. Total altruism on your part. Sweetie, you're a jingle writer, not a homicide detective, but you got yourself ass-deep in my problem, and how come? Because you lurrrrrrrrrv me."

"Stop saying that," she said, "or I'll pull off your testicles. I just thought it would be nice if, just once, V-Day wasn't the worst day of the year. Although, it sure as shit didn't start off too well . . ."

"Ah, but the ending." He stroked her thigh. "What are you doing tomorrow?"

"Working."

"Call in sick. Let's stay home and make love and buy something to drink besides milk."

"And miss a single day of my wonderful job? Just to stay home and have sex with you?"

"Well . . . yeah." He sounded uncomfortable . . . almost tentative? Like he wasn't sure she would want to?

"I'm teasing, dumb-ass. Of course I will. I'd much rather bone you than write get-well jingles."

"Oh, God," he sighed, pulling her on top of him. "That's so romantic."

"But you have to get older in a hurry. I'm not dating someone in his twenties. It's just . . . yech."

"Now you're just being annoying for the sake of being annoying."

"Yeah," she sighed happily, resting her forehead on his. "I guess you don't mind, though."

"I guess not. I overlook all kinds of bad behavior on Valentine's Day."

"Oh, shut up."

A "No Drama" Valentine's

Leslie Esdaile

Chapter One

At a little café on Twentieth and Chestnut Streets, Philadelphia, PA

Who needed a man on Valentine's Day? The species was more trouble than it was worth! Jocelyn Jefferson held up her wide-mouthed teacup and clinked it against three other mugs in the all-female soul-renewal fest. She glanced down at her chamomile tea, smiling as it almost sloshed on the table.

"This year," she announced to her three best friends, "we're gonna have a 'no drama' Valentine's!"

"I heard that!" Tina said, raking her fingers through her long braids and tossing her hair over her shoulders. "Look at us. We're all in graduate school; therefore we're all obviously trying to do something positive with our lives. All of us are under thirty, and not bad on the eyes," she added with a mischievous grin. "Don't have kids, have a future, and shouldn't have to put up with the 'Oh, baby, see, what had happened was,' rhetoric."

"No lie," Jacqui chimed in, talking with her hands as her rust-hued dreadlocks bobbed. "I am so sick of it. Every year it's the same thing. Disappointment, long stories about why he didn't come through. A bunch of la-la. And, I'm always scratching my head, wondering why it has to be all of this. Why the games?"

Freddie shook her head with disgust, making a profusion of shiny, onyx curls dance as she spoke. "Chile, pullease. I hear it all, working down at the Galley Mall. Brothers fall into the store, run game while buying their woman or wife perfume. Dawgs. Hear what I'm saying, ladies? Dawgs. And they think because I'm ringing a department store register that I don't have anything else going on in my life, so I was just waiting for them to come along and blow my mind."

"Right, that's what I'm talking about. Over at the supermarket, just because I'm in the checkout line ringing customers, they think I must be waiting on them to go to the Wizard to get a brain, okaaaay," Tina said, laughing. "I'm always like, man, if you don't get outta this sistah's face with that tired yang—"

"Oh, girl," Jacqui said quickly, "just because I'm at the library with a security guard's uniform on, they try to crack, thinking they have me all figured out, but when I drop on them that I'm currently in an engineering master's program, and just finished my law degree, they get all funny-acting and back up."

"That's because they can't deal with intelligent women who aren't needy," Jocelyn said decisively, her gaze narrowing as it shot around the quaint little vegetarian café and tea salon. "So, what are they going to do with an engineering lawyer who's blowing up the dean's list at Drexel University, huh, J? Or, one of the baddest designers I've ever known, rocking her thing over at The University of the Arts." She slapped Tina a high five. "You can't even take a brother to your fly-ass apartment that looks like something out of a Manhattan showroom. And I know they can't deal with Freddie—what, a Fox School of Business MBA who could probably run circles around Sir Donald, if she had some money? Once you get out of Temple U, sis, you're gonna shake up the business scene, for real. Pullease."

They all laughed.

"That's the point, chica," Freddie said. "Today, I can barely pay for my grilled vegetable salad. But tomorrow, when I graduate, I'ma show them what they should have been doing on *The Apprentice*—but I'll be playing for keeps. Shoot, they thought Omarosa was bad, but they haven't met me yet."

Companionable laughter erupted and kept their spirits buoyed. No, this didn't make any sense for them to all be good-looking, educated, young, but so very single. Jocelyn refused to allow herself to go down that slippery slope of depression. Nope. Not for a dreaded Hallmark holiday that was only a consumer-ruse-turned-nightmare created by the greeting card and floral industry, any ole way. As the conversation built to a male-bashing crescendo, Jocelyn honestly appraised her friends, quietly battling despair.

Jacqui was tall, regal, with a dark walnut complexion and slender, athletic build that commanded attention and respect as much as her no-nonsense personality did. Girlfriend was destined to be a judge, or maybe a top manufacturer's technical legal counsel, and she deserved a serious brother who could pull his own weight. That sister didn't have time for games, and shouldn't have had to be subjected to them.

Then there was Tina. The sister was artistically fly, unique, and her petite five-foot-four frame was that of a lithe dancer, but her effervescence gave her a pixie-like quality. Bottom line was, Tina was fun, culturally deep, and would one day be a force to be reckoned with, no doubt. Jocelyn could see her girlfriend on the cover of *Essence* magazine, or in there as *the designer* to the celebrity circuit, just like she could imagine Fredericka one day on the cover of *Black Enterprise* as one of the nation's top African American women in business. Freddie had the Midas touch when it came to entrepreneurial exploits, and from the time she'd known her, Freddie always had a moneymaking hustle going on the side of whatever else she was doing—plus, her girlfriend had the supermodel corporate looks to go with it. The fact that Freddie was still single gave Jocelyn serious pause.

But it wasn't just the concept of being single, or serial dating, that made Jocelyn and her girls feel so sad. She knew it was the long, dry spell for years that was probably giving them all a nervous tic. Just because they were very clear on their dating parameters, and had each vigilantly held the line, had put them in isolation. It wasn't fair. Yet they'd each made a vow not to denigrate themselves: No married men reduced the percentage of dates by fifty percent, right off the bat.

Then, by excluding roughneck homeboys who had prison records, nefarious business operations, and baby momma drama, cut that number by a third. Then, by employing the "no gay men" rule, also known as "no brothers on the down low," the odds got even slimmer that a sister could find a legitimate date. Instinctively she knew that the last parameter had cast them into the veritable dating desert: No polygamous philanderers who had five women at the same time. No potential STD, typhoid carriers. That was it. Game over. So, they sat together at a place where there were no available men to be found, trying to cheer each other up on the day before *the big one*.

"Listen, ladies," Jacqui said, taking the conversation hostage and holding court, "it's not about lowering one's standards. Think about it. They don't."

Tina nodded. "And I don't care what your female coworkers show you, all that glitters isn't gold."

Jocelyn sighed. "See, by working in telemarketing, I don't have to deal with jackasses approaching me in the street all day, but working with all women is a trip." She let out another weary breath. "It's like they're all in there secretly competing and trying to convince themselves that they're safe, just because some fool gave 'em a tennis bracelet or dropped some roses on their desk like a trophy. Every year it's the same ole mess. They show off their treasures like they'd won some kinda contest." Jocelyn wrinkled up her nose and made her voice squeaky. "Oh, girl, look, he brought me flowers." She put her hand out and brandished an invisible ring and bracelet. "Look what my baby brought me!"

Again, the table erupted into a hailstorm of hard laughter—but bitterness singed the edges of it.

"Oh, I know it must be *deep* on your job, Joce," Jacqui said, shaking her head. "All those married women and airheads in there? Girl, I don't know how you, a doctoral candidate working on a dissertation about social and economic injustice, can sit in a telemarketing pit with *them*? It's absurd. They've all allowed their power to be co-opted!"

"It's good research," Jocelyn said, forcing herself to laugh. "Everybody's crazy and is a candidate for a section in my paper. Consumerism and the buttons the system pushes to keep people spending what they don't have, is part of my dissertation. I'm going to devote a whole section to manufactured holidays."

"Yeah, but girl, how do you keep your sanity in there with the people on your job? I know they floss their Valentine's Day trinkets in your face to make themselves feel whole. Shoot, as pretty as you are, lady. The Bally gym body, honey-brown skin, hair might be in a bun to go to work, but it ain't acrylic when it drops to your shoulders—and smart? If you ever take off the horn-rimmed glasses and go to contacts, they'll be in trouble. So, I know they give you the blues," Jacqui argued, laughing. "Those women can't even begin to deal with you, much less any man—you need a heavy brother, and those are in short supply. Oh, where oh where has the black intelligentsia gone?"

Tina swooned at the table, showing off her hammered metal earrings, and mimicked the girls on Jocelyn's job.

"Girl, two karats—you know I've got him on lock," she said, teasing the group and pretending to have on huge diamond studs.

"It's a farce. One day a year to make the female species forget all the horrible things they've done to us for the other three hundred and sixty-four days. I say we boycott!" Jacqui shouted, suddenly raising her teacup, almost making the raspberry zinger in it christen the group. "Reparations!"

"That's right," Freddie agreed. "What is so romantic about a day that the mob wiped out a rival gang—I believe the St. Valentine's Day massacre comes to mind, hmmm? Absurd."

Again, hearty but weakening chuckles shot around the small huddle of women.

"Jacqui is right," Jocelyn said. "We need to take proactive action. I say, why sit around this Valentine's Day, watching a tearjerker chick flick, *alone*, wringing our hands, drinking wine, *alone*, and being morose? Why allow the lusty calls from cheating spouses or the O-T-O, one time only, booty call brothers who just wanna get their swerve on, disrupt our Zen and make us weak? We do not have to be victimized by this cultural insanity. Not for one freakin' night of the year."

"No justice, no peace!" Tina yelled, making heads turn in the vegetarian restaurant as her girlfriends screamed with laughter.

"Girl, you crazy, hush," Freddie said, laughing but glancing around. "You don't want people thinking they need to call Homeland Security on your behind."

"I ain't playing," Tina said, laughing so hard, tears came to her eyes. "I ain't had *none* in over a year, and I'm ready to jihad. It ain't right!"

Jacqui clasped a hand over Tina's mouth, almost falling out of her chair as she laughed harder. "TMI, girl. Way too much information!"

"It's the truth," Tina mumbled from behind Jacqui's hand.

"Oh, say it ain't so," Freddie giggled. "Don't start with the celibacy Olympic records, y'all, 'cause next thing ya know we'll be holding up number cards for the no-dick months. Ten! Nine-point-five! That's an eight-seven!"

Jocelyn laid her head on the table and covered it. "Shut up, girl, before you make me pee myself."

"Tell the truth. What's your number?" Freddie said, laughing harder as Jocelyn waved her away.

"I'ma need Depends if y'all don't cut it out," Jocelyn wheezed.

"Our American contender looks at the line, readying herself for the competition," Tina whispered like a sports announcer.

"She's a pro, been through many events," Jacqui said, going into character with Tina and leaning into the table, her voice low and serious as the others roared with laughter. Jacqui allowed her voice to gain in momentum as she moved silverware around an imaginary track. "The gun fires, and she's off, rounding the corner, taking out the girls on the job, has the lead, and her time is *unbelievable*! We might just have an abstinence record, folks! The judges are furiously calculating. We might even have a world record. Since she began graduate school . . . wait, wait, the numbers are coming in."

Jocelyn threw her head back, laughing, and did a victory dance in her chair. "Thirty-six-point-four! Yes!" When her girlfriends laughed so hard they nearly fell out of her chairs, Jocelyn donned an invisible ribbon, blotting at tears that weren't there. "First, I wanna give all honor to God. And, if it weren't for my mother . . . thanks, Mom!"

Jacqui spit out her tea in a laughing spray. Tina was coughing, and Freddie was hiccup-laughing so hard that her mascara was beginning to run.

"Girl, if you mess up this year and lose your mind, and take a booty call from some worthless male, we ain't gonna be mad at you. Dayum . . . that don't make no sense!" Jacqui dabbed her mouth with a napkin, and the table exploded with new rounds of mirth.

"No, see, girl, this is the thing. I'm not going out like that. One has to plan," Jocelyn said, shaping her curly Afro with her palms. "You only get victimized by the system when you don't understand it. So, this year, I propose that we do something different to end the cry-all-night-be-horny-all-night cycle."

"You got a plan, girl, then I'm down," Freddie said, her smile fading to a serious but curious expression.

"For real, I've already got a nervous tic every time I go into CVS to buy toiletries, and I see *the red aisle*," Tina said, laughing hard. "Styrofoam cupids and big paper hearts give me the shakes like a junkie. What's the plan?"

"I almost broke down last night for some fool, and y'all know I'm studying for the bar!" Jacqui shook her head. "Don't they have some drug that can just kill libido? I need a 'script, bad. What is wrong with modern medicine?"

"I might turn to cybersex before the night's out," Freddie said, wiping her brow. "But I'm trying to ignore my sister Brenda's advice—she's outta her danged mind."

"Stay strong," Tina said, giggling as she raised a power-to-the-people fist.

"All right," Jocelyn said, putting her hands flat on the table. "We do a Pollyanna. Get each other gifts, since women are better at picking out stuff than men, any ole way. Why sit up in our apartments waiting on some guy that isn't going to do that for us?"

"That's deep," Jacqui said, nodding her agreement with the others. "Go, Joce."

"Right," Jocelyn said, gaining confidence as the plan formed in her mind. "All the clubs and places to go out will be catering to the Valentine's Day groove, which will only be depressing. Couples, lovers, yada, yada, yada. The music alone will make us weak and all teary-eyed. Then, just watching folks all hugged up will bring on very dark thoughts of self-annihilation. So, we should make our own party."

"Like invite people? But who?" Freddie's expression was incredulous. "Everybody will be otherwise hooked up, so who will come to a party—"

"Us, girl," Jocelyn said with a weary sigh. "Look. They have these visit-your-house spa-party places that will come out to your home and beat your hair, give you a facial, do your toes and nails, liquefy you with a massage . . . that's what we're missing. Pampering. We must honor the goddess within. So, why not throw a pamper party, just for us?"

Astonished glances passed around the table. Mouths opened. Jaws went slack. Jocelyn had them, she knew it, and pressed on.

"We need it. We deserve it. And just because some guy doesn't have enough forethought, caring, or is too cheap to do that, hey. Why wait? Why deny ourselves sensual pleasures? We can get a lovely gourmet food platter from Fresh Grocer, where Tina works. We can use Freddie's eighteen-percent employee discount at the mall, to keep gifts for each other to a reasonable level. Jacqui could research on the fly at the library and find a great in-home spa service for us that has solid references. Since I'm on the telephones all day, I can coordinate it all and let my fingers do the walking . . . and tomorrow night, while every other woman in the city is either home alone weeping, with some man that ain't actin' right, or is on her cell phone, blowing up his, hollering into voice mail for her man to show up—we'll be sitting back, drinking wine, laughing, getting *done* by pampering professionals, eating good food, relaxing, kicking back, listening to great music, and opening presents."

"Damn, girl," Jacqui said in a reverent whisper. "That is scary brilliant."

"I'ma get snot-slinging toasted, right in the middle of the work week," Freddie declared. "I'm gonna come to work the next day, moving slow, dark shades on, and give the girls on the job something to really talk about! But I'll never divulge the trade secret of Miz Jocelyn's ancient Chinese secrets of Zen." She bowed slightly with both hands pressed together, giggling. "Master teacher, I shall grasp the stone of knowledge from your hand, and purge every errant male being from my black book, returning revived and renewed and pampered."

Jocelyn laughed and bowed toward Freddie. "And you will also receive the red rose of truth, grasshopper."

"You're gonna buy roses for us, too?" Tina squealed. "Yo go, gurl! Sho' you right!"

"We shall laugh," Jocelyn said in a phony Asian accent. "We shall dance! We shall dog every no-good male that has ever walked the planet. We shall have roses . . . to show them heifers on the job the next day," she added with a wink, and then changed her voice to the around-the-way patois designed to make them all hoot with laughter. "'Cause we ain't all metaphysical, now—sometimes ya gotta pull your blade, ladies."

Laughter rang out as the plan became manifest. High-fives passed as high-calorie dessert was ordered to seal the pact.

"Who's in?" Jocelyn asked, not needing to. Four friends simply giggled at their own mischief and hugged each other hard.

Chapter Two

This was precisely why he didn't do Valentine's Day. Drama. People were crazy.

Detective Mayfield cast a disgusted glance around The Round House. Police headquarters was bustling with a spike in the number of arrests. It was already starting, and it was only the day before what he called "the night of insanity." He knew that Valentine's Day eve drew out the crazies just like a full moon did. Domestic violence would be up, as spouses accused each other of infidelity. Stabbings, murders, jilted lovers putting bodies in ditches, bar fights, street brawls when two suitors came knocking at the same door.

Ladies' room incidents would be at an all-time high, cat fights in clubs, babies' mommas rolling up on their ex-men, firing off rounds. Hostages taken by ex-husbands suddenly wanting their families back—and ready to die trying, suicide watches, students walking on the ledges of building, unable to deal with failing exams and losing the loves of their lives on this night of all nights. Cars left running in sealed garages as midlife crises made normally reasonable men snap and inhale fumes. Illegal pharmacists would be working overtime to supply Ecstasy, barbs, or whatever people needed to get on, to stanch the pain.

The working girls would be serving single males all night long, and college frats would employ them at group rates rather than individually buy a bunch of freakin' roses for some co-ed. Go figure.

See, this is why he'd told his boys he'd work the overtime, and would rather get paid than get laid, if it had to be all of that. This pending Valentine's Day was killing him.

Raymond Mayfield kept walking through the station, just shaking his head. He didn't do romance, for this very reason. It was ludicrous. In fact, he'd sworn off the whole enterprise since last year. Women were treacherous; he'd seen enough on the vice beat to know that. Had personal experience in getting burned—and burned badly, too. All he'd needed to see was what he saw—his old girlfriend hugged up at a movie when she'd claimed having the flu. He was done. That was it. Real estate was a better option.

So, he'd just keep on buying buildings to rehab, creating a nice sideline income. This was just a job. How he'd made detective was a sheer case of being in the right place at the right time, he was so sure. He was next in line, had a stellar record, never missed a day at work—sometimes it was better to be lucky than good. He hadn't done bad for himself at thirty-five, being all by himself, no wife, no kids, no drama. One day he might even be able to quit the day gig and focus on watching economic trends and his paper moving on the stock market. But, for now, he'd committed to a double shift tomorrow night when temporary insanity would rock the city.

When his cell phone vibrated on his hip, he already had a pretty good idea of who it might be. He stared at the number and just sighed.

"Yo, Mayfield," his buddy Marcus said, laughing. "Listen, I met this chick, and she has a sister—"

"Nope. I'm working."

"Ray, man, she's fine."

"All of the women you tell me about are always fine,

dude. I'm working. Unlike you attorneys, my schedule ain't that flexible."

"They have you working vice *tomorrow night*? Aw, man," Marcus argued. "That is the night when even *your* surly ass can get—"

"Man, I told you," Ray said, becoming annoyed. "Even if I wasn't working, I'm not in the frame of mind to—"

"You gotta get over that Debra thing, brother. Listen, if you follow my lead, and play your cards right, you could be *the man.*" Marcus laughed hard into the cellular unit. "Like, today, I took out Barbara—since she's married and has to act like she knows on the big day. So, we did a little lunch down at Zanzibar's, had a little midday fun upstairs in the Bellevue, then I don't have to service that account again for maybe another week. Tomorrow afternoon, I'll take Wanda out for a late lunch—already dropped the roses, man. Then, whatever we eat will give me a stomachache, you feel me? . . . I'll need to go home, of course, alone. That's when I'll call Vivica—*she's fine*. Just met her on the Internet. And, her voice . . ."

Ray stared at his cell phone in disbelief. "Brother, you met some chick in cyberspace, and are gonna—"

"You should see her, brother."

"I don't have to see her, man. You're an attorney. You of all people should know better. The woman could be here in my vice squad records."

"That's why I'm calling you. I need a background check."

Ray sighed. "Have you lost your mind?"

"Baby got back, a double-D cup, face so pretty, legs—"

"I'ma ask you this again real slowly," Ray said. His friend's stupidity was making the muscle in his jaw jump. "Is she a working girl?"

"I don't exactly know, but, uh, could use a favor . . . since you work vice. Uh, if I give you some—"

"If I do this, look her up and let you know if she has a

record, you'll owe me, Marc. No questions, no hesitation, no 'I'll get back to you later.' If I ever—"

"Done. Just run her tags for me, man. This babe is so freakin' fine, and serves phone sex so damned good—man, I'm like, hell yeah, baby. Come on down from Jersey City, bring your sister, whateva. Just come."

Laughter filled Ray's cell phone. Again, he could only stare at it. This was TMI, over the top. Just because he and Marcus Dorchester went back to high school, didn't mean this fool wasn't getting on his last nerve.

"The girl looks like—"

"I don't need to know what she looks like," Ray snapped.

"Turn on your PC, I'll shoot you her pic—just in case she comes up on your visual radar. I hope she isn't one of the casino girls that occasionally cross into Philly to do a little condo work downtown?"

Ray shook his head, sat down at his desk hard, but complied, waiting for his tube to boot up.

"She told me her sister was about five-seven, like her, but with darker brown hair," Marcus went on. "I told her that my single buddy was all that . . . six-four, built, brown skin—you know they like the tall-dark-handsome type, has a good job, is well invested in real estate, no kids, no wife, no live-in problems, feel me? I wanted her to be comfortable with coming to Philly, not knowing me and everything, and figured a double date might coax her down. She said she'd be game, we could meet and all go to dinner, and if the chemistry was right, maybe we could go somewhere alone for a nightcap, you hearing me? So, see if you can get the blue flu for this one and—"

"Send the picture and the tag number," Ray said flatly, rubbing his close-cropped hair with his palm. He waited as his friend's booming chuckles continued to ripple through the phone. He kept his focus on his computer. He was not taking off from work, no matter what. One day, if his boy Marcus didn't stop the madness, he was either gonna wake up coughing and sick, shot by some woman's husband, or be found stabbed to death with a lady's stiletto in his chest.

"You get it yet?" Marcus asked anxiously.

"The jpeg is downloading now," Ray said, feeling self-conscious as his fellow officers walked by his desk and gave him nods of appreciation. The girl was fine, but still . . .

"If I lose my job," Ray muttered, "promise me I'll be able to work as a security guard in your office building."

"Did you get it?"

"Yeah," Ray said, his tone growing surlier as he pulled up a file of known prostitutes and studied the unnamed woman's photo beside it. She was fine indeed, but that wasn't the point. "Girlfriend is all pro, my brother," he finally said, pushing away from his desk. "Busted last year in the suburbs, Montgomery County, for porn movies with animals, then—"

"What!"

Ray couldn't help but chuckle as he stared at the honey-blond sister with the body that wouldn't quit.

"You're killin' me, Ray-Ray. Say it ain't so!"

Raymond laughed and began closing computer files. "Man, listen, you mess with her if ya wanna, but you might get hoof-and-mouth disease." He laughed harder as one of his older vice colleagues passed his desk, caught the comment, and slapped him five. His other buddy, Raul, was openly laughing and pounded his fist as he went for coffee.

"Tell your boy he might get his feeling hurt coming behind a stallion and a couple of Dobermans," Raul teased. "I know he thinks he's the baddest mutha in the valley and all, but hey. He ain't no Smarty Jones, last I checked—and this sister is into thoroughbred racers."

"The peanut gallery has weighed in," Raymond said, his mood much improved. "Case closed, man. But you still owe me for even considering doing a spot investigation. When you gonna learn, brother? Just take Wanda out, be cool, treat the sister right, get some, and go home. Why the intrigue, why the drama? Live the simple life and stay alive. Wanda's gonna cut you, one of these days."

His friend was laughing so hard that he had to be sure his cell phone wasn't on Speaker.

"I know, man," Marcus said, wheezing. "But it's just the dawg in me—the thrill of the hunt, the adrenaline of the chase—the not knowing the conclusion. Big game huntin' is just—"

"Suicidal, yo. So, I have things to do, you need to be prepping some poor client's case, and tomorrow, for me, is like a black hole in the universe. It doesn't exist. I'm working."

Tonight was the big night. Jocelyn cleaned her small loft apartment with the fervor of a woman on a mission. Music blared from her five-CD tabletop stereo system. Alicia Keyes, Myra, Jill Scott, all the divas were in the house. Power music. Women of substance. Yes!

It hadn't bothered her one bit that tennis bracelets had glinted off her coworker's wrists, or that flowers had shown up on blushing females' desks. She was impervious to the slings and arrows of outrageous misfortune. Their little digs at lunch didn't bother her one bit. Signifying sighs of bliss didn't break her down. Tonight, she and her posse of strong, sane, independent women were not going to allow Valentine's Day to kill their joy or self-esteem. Nope.

On her way home from work, she'd gone crazy, buying all sorts of pretty flowers to put in every room. Birds of paradise, roses, calla lilies, and large sunflowers made her place a veritable garden—Tina would most appreciate that. Candles were perched in lovely holders all around; even the bathroom had some. The Dollar Store was *her store*!

She'd found fresh Dollar Store towels and had laid them out on her bed, alongside inexpensive little silk robes that she'd practically stolen down in Chinatown for ten bucks each. But it was a necessity for each girlfriend with matching Chinese slippers, just so they could be pampered in style. Red would be for her, yellow for Jacqui, electric blue for Tina, and jade for Freddie.

Aromatherapy would add to their healing sanctuary, and she lit incense everywhere, spilling lavender and jasmine throughout her apartment. The platters she'd picked up at a discount from Tina's job looked so good she wanted to pinch off them rather than wait, but resisted.

Gourmet cheeses and fresh deli salads and fruits graced each platter. Hummus and star fruit and kiwi and strawberries with seeded black breads—see, men didn't think or know how to do! Dizzying desserts—cheesecake slices, cream-filled petit fours, and small mousse cups with decadent chocolate rims—almost broke her resolve to wait for the group. Chocolate-covered strawberries . . . hmmm . . . well, one was lost to the cause, but she'd closed in the hole and giggled as she did so. She couldn't remember being this happy on a Valentine's Day evening.

Black plates, again, courtesy her store, made it look like an expensive, high-class restaurant, with the lights low. A fondue pot sat readied and waiting. Spinach dip was already made and in the fridge. She'd light the candles later; for now, the liquor store called.

Yes, true, she'd gone over the limit, finding a bottle of wine for each friend—since they each liked something different. Jacqui was into zinfandels, Tina loved the artists' merlots, Freddie was a business-clean chardonnay, and she liked the heavier cabernet sauvignons—so the best compromise was to buy one of each. But champagne was the order of the day. At first she bought a magnum, then decided to get each of them a bottle. It was excessive, but hey, they were purging the demons of male inattention and ineptitude, and if one of them started crying about an old boyfriend, there needed to be plenty of hooch on the premises.

Quite pleased with herself, Jocelyn lugged her box of

booze up the four flights to her door. Student-living over in the Powelton Village area didn't come with the luxury of elevators, but that was okay. Tonight, she'd turned her small place into an all-female oasis. It was a spa for the lovelorn.

Dabbing the slight perspiration from her brow, she kicked open the door and shoved it closed behind her with her backside. She was so happy, she could have skipped across the floor, were her package not so heavy. And it had made her feel good that the ladies at the liquor store had asked her if she was having a party, and had given her high-fives and *Go, girls!* Yeah. That's right, she *was* having a party.

Jocelyn set down her box of booze with care and stripped off her faux lamb jacket, crossing the room with purpose to hang it up. It was seven P.M.—her girls would be there by eight, the pamper pros would be there by eight-thirty, everything was ready. She even had time for a quick shower.

As she glimpsed her phone and saw the light blinking, she giggled. No doubt her girls were getting anxious, too, and had called to squeal and check on last-minute details. She picked up the phone and scrolled through the missed calls on the digital display, glancing at the coffee table which had four little gifts, each wrapped in pretty, glistening silver paper with large gold bows. She casually munched on the mixed nuts that had been set out, and picked a slim chocolate mint out of a candy bowl as she made her way to the kitchen, juggling bottles of wine with the cordless phone to listen to each of her friends' messages.

But as she stood in the middle of the floor, she almost couldn't breathe as the first message rang in her ears. Jacqui was canceling? Jacqui! Miss, I don't need no man to complete my world?

Fury and hurt made tears come to Jocelyn's eyes as she replayed her friend's lame message.

"Joce, girl, listen, I know you're gonna feel some type of way about this, but Bill called . . . after months of miscommunication—and he wants to talk, reconcile, go to dinner, and try to figure out where we went wrong . . . girl, he sent *roses* to my job. Look, tomorrow, when he leaves, I'll call you, baby. All right? You know I love you, and give the girls a hug for me, but . . . Joce, you know you're my boo, right? Don't get all mad. Promise me? We'll do lunch tomorrow. 'Kay?"

Jocelyn stared at the telephone and had to set the wine down very slowly. If her girl didn't sound like a man making excuses to go on a booty call, she didn't know what! If it weren't for the fact that her telephone was a cheapie model that couldn't handle the abuse, she would have thrown it. But common sense told her not to press her luck with plastic.

"I cannot believe you!" Jocelyn shouted. "We made a pact! Oh, Lawd, give me strength." She erased the message, sure now that her other girlfriends were blowing up her line while she'd been out to fuss about this transgression. But to her amazement, Freddie . . . levelheaded, got-it-together Freddie had a long story, too?

"Girl," Freddie's voice was near shrill, breaking and hitching as her cell phone transmission sputtered into Jocelyn's voice mail, "see, what had happened was, I was minding my business, and this guy, an attorney, who comes in every day, just to cut through my store to get to his offices on the other side of the mall . . . well, the brother is fine—no, restatement, *fionne*, and uh, he came up on me at the end of the day, said he'd been watching me, but never approached, on account of the fact that he was waiting for his divorce to go through, respect, and uh, what had happened was, his papers came in earlier this week, and he was all messed up . . . said he just couldn't deal with doing Valentine's Day alone—girl, you shoulda seen the tears sitting up in his fine eyes—pretty lashes, all black and shiny and whatnot, and he asked me if I'd just have a drink and listen to some jazz with him, girl, you know what I mean, and uh, on the way to the jazz spot, he stopped at a vendor on the street and brought me flowers—*roses*, chile! I'm in the ladies' room at the club right now, trying to call you—*where you at*? Holla. Call me. I know you all gonna be mad, but this is a love 9-1-1, and y'all can't be mad at a sistah, for real. I love you, boo. I'm taking this one home tonight, so I'll call ya tomorrow—*peace*. I'm out!"

Jocelyn gripped the telephone so hard, her knuckles were turning white. When she saw Freddie, she was gonna kick her natural behind! "Oh! You and Jacqui are crazy! What a lame story! What a crock! That fool was plottin' on your booty since the day he saw you, girl! Arrrgggghhhh!"

Pacing, she erased Freddie's message, hitting the button so hard she almost broke a nail. "C'mon, T, don't you stand me up, too, girl . . . we go way back," Jocelyn yelled, listening to her last friend's message. "Somebody has to hold the line tonight!"

"Jo-ce-*lyn*, my sistah, *my sistah* . . ."

Jocelyn closed her eyes as she listened to Tina's voice mail message, knowing what was coming next—an excuse.

"It happened so fast—I was going on an internship run, trying to do some volunteer work for the Philly sports teams and children's foundations they work with . . . and this tall, fine, NFL brother walked in . . . girl, we got to talking, and uh, he's single, and uh, he was all caught up in the post season 'what-am-I-gonna-do-till-spring' thang, and liked my posters, and my t-shirt designs for the kids . . . and uh, he was like, whatchu doing tonight, and uh, I was like, me and my girls was supposed to be hanging out at uh, our friend's apartment, chillin', and uh, he asked me if I'd like to uh, maybe roll up to the Poconos with him, given it was Valentine's Day, and uh, he has a cabin in the woods, and broke up with his lady before the season, and was trying to stay away from drama so it wouldn't interfere with his game—girl, lemme just say, the man is six-six, two-eighty, built like, oh Lawd, ain't been with a woman since the season began, chile, see, so, I'ma have to make this run, but I got y'all's gifts, and tomorrow, or maybe later in the week, we'll catch up for dinner, you know I love y'all, right, but Joce, girl . . . Okay, look, he's coming back into the gym and uh, I gotta run. 'Bye. Luv ya. Don't be mad."

Jocelyn set the phone down in its cradle very precisely and put the wine and champagne in the fridge. She took out a platter and swiped off a fat, chocolate-covered strawberry, the best one on the tray and set the tray, down on the coffee table. Then she walked around her apartment, stoically lighting her candles, firing up some more incense, and then turned her music up very loud. Never again. She sat down calmly on the sofa, willing herself not to cry, and dialed The Pamper People.

Chapter Three

See, now, this was *exactly* why she didn't do Valentine's Day with any man, and from this point forward, with any female friend, either. Forever, this night would go down in infamy—banished from her vocabulary and thoughts. As the late, great Gil Scott Heron once said, 'The revolution will not be televised!'

Jocelyn sat on the sofa, thoroughly disgusted, eating everything she could get her hands on as she listened to the cool, professionally icy tone stating policy in her ear.

"While we can certainly understand your disappointment, at this late juncture I'm sure you can also understand that we will still have to charge your credit card with the full six-hundred-dollar balance, Ms. Jefferson. Our pamper crew is already en route, their time has been utilized, their transportation costs must be covered, and we could have easily slotted in another client that had firmer plans, had we known *earlier*. We try to be fair, and pride ourselves on working through customer issues until a satisfactory conclusion has been reached for both sides. But an hour before they are due to arrive, it is just not our policy to offer a full refund."

Jocelyn sighed. "Well, if you're gonna charge me anyway, you might as well send them."

"I'm so glad we came to terms," the salon owner cooed.

"You'll be able to experience the full range of their treatments with so much more attention, so, who knows? Perhaps this is really a blessing in disguise."

Jocelyn just looked at the telephone. Right about now, wine sounded like a good idea. A shower, some wine, and she'd put on her short little red kimono and matching mesh slippers and just let 'em do her.

"Yeah, whatever," Jocelyn finally muttered and hung up without even a civil good-bye.

By the time her doorbell rang, Jocelyn had polished off a bottle of wine and had begun pouring champagne into a pretty, long-stemmed flute. She weaved, set the glass down carefully, and went to the window to be sure she wasn't about to buzz in a burglar. She opened it with effort, and cold air slapped her cheeks as she peered down from the fourth floor. The ladies all seemed blurry as she stared at a group of women huddled against the cold on her building's steps.

"I'm in 4-D," Jocelyn yelled, weaving as she managed to coordinate sticking her head out of the window while reaching for her champagne.

The older ladies on the steps gave each other curious glances, swallowed away smiles, and entered the building.

Jocelyn didn't care what they thought of her. She was beyond words, too through. To let them know that, she slammed the window down, but spilled her champagne. This didn't make no kinda sense.

She was standing in front of her wide-open door by the time they all huffed up the stairs. Jocelyn surveyed them with disinterest. Each woman seemed to be in her late forties, maybe early fifties, and was carrying a huge, embroidered satchel with their company logo emblazoned upon it. Just her luck to have her home invaded by four Mary Poppins stunt doubles. Okay, so these were pampering pros. Fine. Their expressions seemed pleasant enough, and at least she wouldn't be spending the entire night alone. But six hundred bucks—Jeez.

"Might as well come on in," Jocelyn said with a weary sigh, turning to go back into her apartment. "Sorry about the steps. No elevator. Story of my life, doing things the hard way."

"We'll have fun, don't worry. The other ladies are gonna miss out. My name is Agnes," a tall, mahogany-hued woman said. She had pretty eyes, kind eyes that held a hint of mischief. Her skin was flawless, even at her age, although a slight thickening of her middle told on her a bit. She extended her hand with a gentle smile.

"I hope so," Jocelyn said in a dejected tone. "My girls stood me up."

"Not to worry. Their loss." Agnes glanced around the apartment and shook her head. "You went to so much trouble, too. Well, we'll make lemonade out of lemons, like my momma taught me. Okay?"

Jocelyn nodded, just to be polite. "You can hang your stuff up over there," she said flatly, pointing toward a wrought-iron coatrack. "Would you like some wine, or some tea? Maybe some food? I've got all this junk in here, and it'll go bad if we don't chow down."

"Maybe later, and thank you so much. But right now, our focus is you," Agnes said as she took off her heavy, raisin-colored cloth coat and carefully folded it over her arm, then set her bag down on the floor. She gave a slight nod to the other women to follow suit. "My specialty is skin care," she said proudly. "We'll start you off with a facial, hon. Then Mildred is gonna work the kinks out of your back with a full body massage," she added, gesturing toward a short blonde who had laugh lines around her cat-green eyes.

Mildred gave Jocelyn a little wave and a huge smile while taking off her navy pea coat. "I might be little, but I pack a punch," she said, chuckling. "I'll have you so loose we'll be able to pour you in a glass when I'm done."

To that, all the ladies laughed, and a shy, older Asian woman chuckled behind her hand.

"Let Sue-Lin do your feet last, because once she does, there's nothing to do but go to sleep," Agnes said, offering a slight bow of appreciation toward her colleague.

Sue-Lin waved with the tips of her fingers and glanced down at Jocelyn's feet. "You want designs? I brought air-brush, can make *very* pretty feet, especially big toe. Smooth, like baby's butt. You need pretty feet. All ladies must have pretty feet. Hands, too."

"Okay," Jocelyn said, laughing despite her mood. "Make it so, Ms. Sue-Lin."

"Now we talkin'," the youngest woman in the group said. She flipped off her white leather coat with flair, showing off a stunningly fit body that belied her age. "Girl, don't let this situation stress a sister, hear? I'ma have your head beat so tight when I get done, it'll cut 'em to the bone. Yeah, let your girlfriends know they missed gettin' their hair did by Kimika, 'kay? Call me Mika, though—I couldn't work with Kimberly, so I changed it. Every woman needs change, from time to time. We'll make this makeover night, since your girls weren't acting right. It'll be all right."

She strutted around in a tight circle as the other ladies laughed. Taking center stage in the middle of the apartment floor, she smoothed her hand over her slick Halle Berry cut that was a hue somewhere between strawberry blond and platinum, which offered an eclectic contrast to her almond-toned skin. "Now, if you want *color*—"

"No, no, no no, no," Jocelyn said quickly, imagining the possibilities. Maybe Ms. Kimberly, aka Kimika, could pull off Lil' Kim, but she wasn't ready for that dramatic a change. "Uh, if you could just make it a gradual transition."

Kimika laughed harder. "Oh, okay. The conservative type. My bad. But, uh, sis, we have got to lose the bun."

The older ladies smiled and nodded as Jocelyn's hand self-consciously reached up to feel the offending hairstyle.

"You have pretty eyes," Agnes said, going to the coatrack. "You ever consider contacts?"

"I'm a student," Jocelyn said with a chuckle, moving to the coffee table to offer each woman a glass.

"And? I don't follow," Mildred said with a shrug.

"Glasses are easier and don't dry out my eyes," Jocelyn fussed, remembering how her girlfriends had stayed on her about the same issue.

Agnes shook her head. "Uhm, uhm . . . gorgeous skin. You shouldn't hide it behind glasses. You'll see once I slough off all that dead skin and make you radiant again. I'll show you some makeup techniques, too. *This* is what I do."

"No offense," Jocelyn said, laughing as she began to hand out glasses, "but radiant . . . uh . . . I don't think so. Not because of skill, but you're gonna have to grow new skin in a lab petri dish to do that."

Kimika laughed and went right for the fridge. She pulled out a bottle of champagne. "Agnes can work wonders, chile. Radiant, like—after-you've-got-your-world-rocked-by-the-finest-man-on-the-planet radiant. Watch." She popped the cork as her crewmembers squealed.

"Kim!" Agnes yelled, laughing. "How you gonna just go into the woman's refrigerator like that?" She turned to Jocelyn. "Miss, I'm sorry," and she spun back to focus on her team member with a glare in her eyes. "You know it's not company policy to—"

"Aw'ight, relax," Kimika said, one hand over her ample breasts. "This is for Miss Jocelyn. Not me. I know she had to have the bubbly in here, given how she set up for her friends. Chill."

"It's really all right," Jocelyn said, not sure what to do. On one side she had a tall, very distraught-looking West Indian matron, on the other side a forty-something quasi-rap star with a South Philly grandmother, and in the middle, an Asian lady who looked like she wanted to die of shame. "Ladies, my offer stands, and please call me Jocelyn—

no, Miss Jocelyn, really. Let's eat, laugh, do the different treatments, and just all relax tonight. What do you say?" Trying to keep the peace, she went to the coffee table and selected a gift for each woman. "These are for you," she said, giving away the presents that her girlfriends never bothered to collect.

All eyes went toward Agnes, who finally smiled. "Well, if you insist."

"I do," Jocelyn said, making a beeline for the champagne so she could pour.

"Don't you wish all our clients were like this, Millie?" Agnes said. She peered down at the silver-wrapped gift. "This is . . . just . . . I don't know what to say."

"You know it. Got two ex-husbands and five boys," Mildred said with a scowl, "and not a one of those rat bastards ever did half as much as this young lady just did. Imagine, her girlfriends stood her up like this. Shameful."

"Oh . . . look how pretty," Sue-Lin said, turning the glasses to the light, and then bending to touch the little gifts on the coffee table. She shook her head, made a little tsking sound of annoyance with her tongue. "You such a nice young lady. One day a good man will see."

"This young sister is sweet—that's the problem," Kimika said, folding her arms. "Real genuine heart ready for the breaking. So, tonight, ladies, we're doing an old-fashioned, get Cinderella fly for the ball, bibbity-bobbity-boo on girlfriend. Gonna make heads turn when she rolls out of here to go to work tomorrow. Give her co-workers something to gossip about. Gonna make *the men all pause*, yeah," she said, slapping five as she passed each of her pamper team members like she was an NFL coach. "This ain't right. My feelin's is hurt for her. So, ladies, all champagne and whatnot aside, let's do our best work tonight on *this one*. She gets the special client treatment. I might even have to bust out and serve her wardrobe."

Jocelyn didn't say a word as the women murmured agreement. There was a fiery determination in their eyes that was almost frightening. It seemed as though each woman was remembering her own past personal hurts as they shared in hers, and she could tell by their lifted chins and straight backs that Kimika had ignited a quiet defiance in them—the ladies were on a mission. Once their glasses clinked, the secret, collective call to arms had gone out. One of their species was being dogged by friend and foe, so *it was on.*

Jocelyn hurried around the room, pouring champagne. "I have desserts, all sorts of good stuff." She made herself smile and become the perfect hostess. She wasn't sure why she was doing what she was doing—after all, she was paying six bills for the services yet to be rendered, but it was just something that had been drilled into her since conception. When people visited, you just did.

Before long, the tension eased with Jocelyn. The wall between professional service provider and client was crumbled. Huge tears rolled down her cheeks as sweet Ms. Agnes swathed her face in a warm, lavender-scented hot towel and plugged in a steam lamp. Someone kept refilling her glass, and each woman chimed in, telling her own tale of woe. Shaky spouses, no-good boyfriends, absent fathers, no card or flowers on the special day; it was a pity-fest in full effect.

Their stories made her weep, and Jocelyn even left her prone position on the sofa despite Agnes's complaints to give each woman a long-stemmed red rose. That brought the house down. Everybody was crying. Kimika blew her nose so hard that it sounded like a ship in the harbor.

"Oh, girl, just stop!" Kimika groaned, covering her face. "Why do you think I always work Valentine's Day? Lawd have mercy . . ."

Sue-Lin was snatching off rose petals to float in the foot whirlpool, sniffing. "No flowers. No candy. Just work! He never say, 'Wife, I think you pretty. Wife, how was your day? Wife, you mean world to me.' I know men dog. Rat!"

"Why do you think I became a bodybuilder?" Mildred said, downing her fifth glass of champagne and popping a miniature cannoli into her mouth behind it. "Met a massage therapist over in the gym—what can I say? Taught me everything I know, and then some, love. When Aggie is done, roll over, and I'll show you some stuff that'll make you putty, but never forget—women are tougher than them."

Kimika nodded and knocked back the last of the champagne in her glass. "I'ma tell you what. We should really make her night and have us a for-real party. I hate feeling like this!"

"Me, tooooo," Jocelyn wailed, sniffing hard. "You all shouldn't be working."

"Doll, this ain't work," Mildred said, and then glanced at Kimika. "Your cousin still go out with that cutie who works over at the club?"

Kimika nodded. "Yep, and I'ma call him. He should be off the poles by now," she said with a wink and then glanced at her watch.

Jocelyn barely lifted her head as Kimika began punching numbers on her shiny little cell phone. Did she say 'off the poles?' It wasn't election time, poll-watchers shouldn't . . . "Uh, Kimika, did I hear—"

"Shush," Kimika said, putting a long, Caribbean-orange talon against her ear and listening hard for a cell phone connection. "I've gotta go by a window. Reception sucks in here."

Feeling too mellow to double back on the question, Jocelyn sank against the sofa, allowing parts of her body to be stretched and pulled. Her face was so clear and radiant that she'd made Agnes laugh by asking if it were a trick mirror. Her feet felt like butter, her hands so pretty. Little red hearts covered frosted white polish, something she never in her life did. Her toenails were the reverse—white hearts on a wicked red background. If it weren't winter, she would have had to find open-toed shoes just to floss the pedicure.

She'd even gone for broke and had allowed Kimika to cut off an inch, add highlights, and practically hot-rod her hair into a curly, wild profusion. She felt like a million bucks. A sleepy million, maybe even a tipsy million, but it was good to be the queen.

When the doorbell rang, the ladies began laughing all over again. She stared at them, and then remembered, oh yeah, this was her apartment. Jocelyn stood with effort and staggered to the window.

"I got that," Kimika said, yanking the stubborn pane up. "You just got your nails done. Don't mess 'em up!"

"Yeah, right," Jocelyn said, fussing. "And I know those heifers didn't come here after wherever they were expecting to get done. See—"

Her words caught in her throat and she jerked her head back, holding Kimika by the arms. "It's the cops! Ohmigod. My neighbors hate loud music, and—" She ran to the stereo and clicked it off. "Okay, okay, okay, why would the cops be ringing my bell?"

Kimika shook her head, Agnes had her hands over her mouth, Mildred was laughing so hard she slid from the sofa to the floor, and Sue-Lin was rocking and giggling in a chair.

"Do you hear yourself, chile? You are looking around this apartment at some wine and champagne like we're in the middle of the Prohibition era. Girl, get a grip. Loud music?" She waltzed over to the stereo and flipped it back on. "You have on mellow jazz," she said with disdain, and then switched it from CD to tuner and found a hip-hop station. "This is loud music," Kimika announced, and then proceeded to crank the volume.

The doorbell rang again, and this time someone was leaning on it.

"Go on and let the man in, girl." Kimika stood wide-legged with both hands on hips. "Pullease!"

Jocelyn buzzed the buzzer and shut her eyes tightly. Why would the cops have to harass her tonight? Yeah, okay, mostly graduate students lived in the building—people with small children, a few old ladies—they had to be the culprits. She sighed and walked to the door when a loud banging began.

"Officer, listen," she said as calmly as possible, not trying to sound flippant. "There's no reason for you . . . to . . . Oh, my . . . God . . ."

The finest male specimen she'd ever seen had stepped around her, tossed his hat, and instinct kicked in—she knew exactly what Kimika had done. Jocelyn slammed the door, covered her mouth, and screamed with the other women in the room. A dashing, mega-white, cosmetic-dentist-manufactured smile greeted her. A two-hundred-pound bodybuilder frame ripped off a uniform top at the snaps, and she covered her face as a greased body strutted forward. When he made each nipple jump, Jocelyn began running, laughing all the way into her kitchen.

Body-blocking this ebony Adonis with a refrigerator door, she kept the metal between them as the pants went next. The music changed; Jocelyn looked down once and almost broke her nose on a shelf as she ducked behind the door. Never in her life had she seen a piece of thong hold that much beef. She covered her head and laughed harder. These ladies were insane.

Chants to the music were echoing behind her, the door was being pried from her fingers; cold blasts from the fridge were chasing her out of her holding pattern. Wild. On her feet in seconds, she plopped her butt onto a counter stool and considered making a dive for the other side of the built-in pass-through. A party tray and several glasses blocked the attempt. So she had to sit there while a strange but awesome male dry-humped her leg.

"Go get one of them—please!" Jocelyn said, dissolving into a fit of giggles. "Over the top, ladies—call him off!"

Kimika roared with laughter, and Mildred confessed bladder issues and dashed for the bathroom. Sue-Lin found her purse and waved a ten-dollar bill. Jocelyn just couldn't watch.

"I should call my nephew," Agnes said, wheezing. "By now, he should be off from work at the restaurant, and I know he and a few of his buddies said they don't like clubs because of all the fights. We could have some nice young people come here."

Kimika poured another round. "I'ma call my girls. Tell 'em to bring something you can serve straight, no chaser. You got rum in here, doll?"

Jocelyn's head pivoted like it was on a swivel. Mildred was coming out of the bathroom, laughing and waving two five-dollar bills.

"My Joey can bring some food from the deli—good kid, broke up with his girlfriend last year. She was a prissy little bitch. But I digress. He could bring some cheese steaks, ya know, and some beer. Cut the sandwiches up real nice," Mildred offered.

"I have girlfriend who has special business. Nice gifts for women. I call her," Sue-Lin said, standing quickly and dashing for her cell phone. "You will like. Very nice."

"But—" Jocelyn couldn't get the words out before the dancer cut her off.

" 'Mika, girl, you were right. She *is* a sweetheart," the exotic hunk said, his voice a pitch higher than Jocelyn expected. "Honey, now you listen to me. Even though I'm not speaking to Paul tonight, on account of the fact that he *knows* I have to work on Valentine's Day *every* year, but gets all pissy about it, I'll still call his evil ass and ask him to be nice and send some real dancers over." He strutted across the room, kissed the back of Jocelyn's hand, and began putting on his pants. "I have to get back down to Delaware Avenue, but you ladies crank up the music. I'll send some good dancers over here . . . at least you can get your boogie on with guys who can actually dance. Pullease."

Jocelyn opened and closed her mouth as she watched the

most handsome gay male she'd ever seen calmly put on his clothes. "Thank you," she said, too stunned to say much more.

"Now, girl, they might be into alternatives," Kimika said, "but the brothers can dance their fabulous behinds off—can't they, Tommie? Don't mind taking a sister for a spin on the floor. When's the last time a man actually danced with you in a club?"

"Uh . . ." Jocelyn glanced at the very tipsy women around her for support, but found none.

"That's my point," Tommie said, snapping his fingers as he tucked his shirt down over his perfect abdominal six-pack. "Dress well, listen, dance, have class, darling. Forget all that roughneck mess—leave that for us men. Y'all don't need that. True, you can't take them home and keep them, but just for a night of dancing on the town, there's options." He leaned down and tweaked Jocelyn's nose. "It's all about options and illusion, theater. Can't find a man when you have a desperation look in your eyes." He twirled around and looked at Kimika with his hands on his hips. "She's too young and sweet to be having that look in her eyes already. Y'all betta work tonight and get that look off that chile's face. Humph." With that, he blew Jocelyn a kiss and flounced out the door.

It had to be the combination of wine, champagne, and too much chocolate. Either she'd fallen asleep and gone into a chocolate coma, or she was hallucinating from the sugary substance. Pan did *not* just blow through her door as an exotic cop, and she was *not* surrounded by four drunken fairy godmothers who were now on a tear to throw a wild party in her apartment!

In her heart she knew that common sense had fled her brain the moment she didn't contest the call for liquor. She was about to challenge the merits of more food when the doorbell rang again. Sue-Lin had depressed the buzzer before she could be stopped, and another mild-mannered Asian woman appeared at Jocelyn's door.

Chapter Four

Jocelyn's mouth opened and remained that way when the most unassuming woman dropped a huge, red plastic bag on the floor, took off her plain black wool coat, and opened her satchel. The first thing she lifted out made Jocelyn squint, unable to close her mouth. This grandmom was standing in the middle of the floor with a very large vibrator, wearing a white restaurant smock, black slacks, a gray sweater, and penny loafers.

"You like? I have all colors."

Wide-eyed, Jocelyn stood transfixed with her hands over her mouth.

"Oooooh, girl, whatchu got in the bag?" Kamika said, sashaying over to it to peer down. "Whooo!"

"My friend Lily have all good things for women," Sue-Lin said proudly, ushering her friend to the coffee table. "She give discount. Good businesswoman. Nice."

Lily smiled and began unpacking her assortment of items as the women crowded in to see.

"This looks like it would be good for your skin," Agnes said, guffawing as she lifted out a jar of butter crème. "Smells divine."

Lily smiled. "Good to eat. You understand?"

The room exploded in gales of laughter.

"If he bad, spank him," Lily said, producing a black strap. "If he very good . . . hmmm . . . tickle him," she added, proudly displaying her feathery choices.

Her doorbell was ringing; a huge black rubber vibrator was on her coffee table. Products that she didn't even know what to do with were being set up on store display stands on her kitchen counter. The music was blaring.

Jocelyn dashed to the window. A tall, good-looking Italian guy was at the door balancing hot food packs. A Cadillac Escalade had pulled up, and several very fine but obviously gay men had swept out—the fur coats were fierce. Tommie hadn't lied. Two BMWs were not far behind it, and several well-dressed women stepped out, laughing and talking. A white panel-body truck was double-parked, and two brothers from 'round the way got out to begin bringing in cases of booze. What the hell had just happened?

He was not going on the street tonight. He'd do this shift as a paperwork-only type of thing. This was a good night to clear off his desk. Didn't want the hassle, didn't need the drama.

"Yo, Mayfield. Got a call that our boys Phatman and Smooth are on the move."

Raymond Mayfield lifted his head from his files and stared at Raul. "What time did they start moving?"

"Around midnight. Were in the clubs, but made a little house call over in the Powellton Village section."

"That's not their normal territory. Think they're planning a hit, or an expansion?"

"I don't know," Raul admitted. "Our boys in squad cars had been drive-by monitoring a wild apartment party over that way. Nothing out of the ordinary, just loud music, a couple of minor complaints, but it wasn't worth a hassle. They cruised by, figuring it was a frat party, students making noise, but spotted the car double-parked in the street—

that's when we got the tip-off." He let his breath out hard and sat down on the edge of Ray's desk. "Want the boys in blue to go pick 'em up, or wait till they leave to trail 'em?"

"If they pick 'em up for no reason, you know we're gonna have drama making whatever we find stick. A loud party isn't enough to book these two slimeballs." Ray rubbed his palms over his face.

"But if they were going to deliver a package, and we find it—"

"Unless it's serious weight, these guys have enough resources to beat a rap over a joint. Besides, then narcotics will own it. I wanna stick 'em on the vice side, too."

Raul nodded. "As hard as we worked on this case, and as long—I hear ya, man. We got the hot lead, found out about the major case elements, and now narcotics wants in and has the nerve to want to shut us down, like we didn't contribute. That's bull."

"Precisely. So, if they're just out on the town, let 'em walk. But tell our boys down on the street to keep their eyes open. If they hear anything unusual, see any drug activity, or any of our usual working girls and boys, take everybody in. I want a lot of witnesses and a lot of squeaky wheels when we haul their asses in. Understood?"

"Gotcha back, my brother."

Raul pounded Ray's fist and stood with a stretch. "Why does this night always seem like the longest night in the world?"

Jocelyn sniffed but kept walking. The incense was waaay heavier than she'd remembered, but then again, there were now close to fifty or sixty people in her tiny place—that she didn't even know! *But it was fun.* Great food, her blender was going, the music pumping—she hadn't laughed so hard since she could remember. Lily was making a mint and had set up shop on the kitchen counter. Someone had the foresight to bring plastic cups and plates. Agnes was dancing, and had even gotten her palm read. Sue-Lin was chowing down on sweets and booking appointments at the coffee table. Kimika was partying so hard that girlfriend's relaxer was about to wear off; her hair had gone from bone-straight to wet ringlets at the nape of her neck. Millie could dance, truly cut the rug, and her son spun her around as they both showed off old disco moves.

This was what it was all about, Jocelyn thought as she accepted another margarita from some anonymous hand. Why be sad, why be blue? The world was her oyster. Who cared if drinks splattered her Ikea rug? The hardwoods could be mopped in the morning. Chocolate didn't come out of fabric, but who cared? She'd buy a throw, but would remember this night for the rest of her life. The neighbors could kiss her butt. She never made noise, but tonight . . . what the hell!

Jocelyn danced her way through the crowd to open the door. Two very well-built police officers stood there, surveying the room.

"C'mon in, fellas!" she yelled over the music. "Join the paaaartaaay!"

"This your place, ma'am?" one said, glancing at his partner.

Jocelyn laughed, grabbed him by the belt, and yanked hard. "Sure is."

A hard, male grip clamped over her wrist. Jocelyn's drink sloshed on the floor.

"Hey, I just got that drink made to order, dude," she said, fussing through a giggle and looking into one pair of stoic hazel eyes, and then a pair of blue ones. "All right, lemme try it from the seams, bottoms up."

"Ma'am, I'm going to have to ask you to step outside."

When the officer didn't move, nor did his pants rip away with a snap, and her nosy, elderly neighbor shook her head from the hallway, and his partner unsnapped the holster on his gun, and the dance floor froze . . . *that's* when she knew she was in trouble. It all happened in slow motion, and then pandemonium broke out.

Her drink hit the floor with a splatter. Her body got slammed against the wall. Her glasses were gone. She could hear folks fleeing out the back fire escape. Suddenly the smell of marijuana separated from jasmine incense. Footfalls were running out of her bathroom and going toward her bedroom window. Angry voices were shouting, "Don't move!" Women were shrieking. Somebody was hollering for backup in a squawking radio. Someone cut the music. Sirens were blaring. Brakes squealed. Engines gunned. Her hands were tightly held behind her back by something hard.

Oh, God, she needed to throw up.

"The one hyperventilating in the chair. Red kimono," Raul said, nodding toward Jocelyn. "It was her house. Only found a coupla joints and a cute pair getting busy in her bathroom. But there were plenty of working girls and guys on premises, so, the guys in uniform made a call when they saw Phat go out on her back deck with a joint in his mouth and using his cell phone. They went in, and the chick was so blitzed she tried to strip Murphy." Raul chuckled. "Lucky SOB, she yanked his chain, good, if ya know what I mean." Raul laughed harder and shook his head.

"Damn, man, it's always the quiet-looking ones, right?" Ray stood and assessed Jocelyn from behind the two-way glass. "She looks like butter would melt in her mouth at ten paces."

"Cried all the way to the station in the squad car, hollering about her mother dying of a heart attack, then upchucked in the back of Murph's patrol car, and then apologized and asked for a rag to clean it up. Then she started bawling all over again about Valentine's Day killing her." Raul started laughing harder. "That good Catholic boy is so messed up right about now, you might have to talk to him. This was his first real collar."

Both men stared at the glass for a moment, laughing.

"I can understand it, though," Raul finally said. "Ray, brother, if she'd grabbed my crotch like Murph swore she did, I might have keeled over and had the heart attack for her momma . . . *she's fine.* Guilty as sin, but sheesh. All legs."

"Give her a blanket to put over that red kimono so I can interview her, man." Ray raked his fingers through his hair and set his jaw hard. His partner wasn't lying; guilty or not, this broad was awesome.

Jocelyn rocked in the chair with her eyes closed and kept her hands clutching her hair, restating the same panic-laden whisper over and over again. "Ohmigod, ohmigod, ohmigod, oh, Lord, ohmigod, ohmigod, oh dear God, help me."

She was gonna be fingerprinted, was in a police station, had been *arrested*? OH, GOD! She was a graduate student, a law-abiding citizen—Oh, God! She had grabbed a *real* cop's crotch, oh double God! Her momma was gonna die a thousand deaths. Her father was doing cartwheels in his grave. Her grandmother was in heaven, shrieking to be released by the angels to come down and strike her dead—Oh, God! She was already dead. A zombie. Her reputation was ruined. She'd lose her job. She'd be ousted from the university. Her professors would freak! Her career was no more. She was half naked. Where was the wastebasket—her stomach was roiling again.

"Miss Jefferson."

Her head snapped up so hard she nearly gave herself whiplash.

"Oh, God, oh, God, oh, God, sir, I can explain everything, I'll tell you how it all happened. I've never done anything like this in my life; I don't really know all these people. I didn't know there was actually weed in my house—oh, God, I'm a doctoral studies major at the university and am in the social justice program, oh, God—do I need a lawyer?

I can pee in a cup and prove I don't do drugs, oh, God. I've never, I swear, ever, I swear, really, I swear, it looks really bad, oh, God! But, see, ooooh . . . Jesus . . . Lord, for real, mister. I mean, officer, sir, I—I—I . . . can't breathe . . . and . . . have . . . to . . . throw . . . up, oh, God."

"Ma'am," Ray said coolly, backing up just in case she lost her lunch. "Take several deep breaths." He outstretched the blanket, but rather than put it around her shoulders, she buried her face in it and began sobbing.

Now, true, he'd seen a *lot* of perps in his life, and a whole lotta streetwalkers in his time, but there was something so unnerving about this one. Her rolling, run-on sentences sounded like nothing he'd ever seen drugs produce, and her wide brown eyes were puffy and red from tears and histrionics alone. He listened to her gasp in air, shiver, dry heave, and then fan her flushed face.

"Can I get you some water?"

"Huh?" she mumbled from the blanket at her face. "I can't hear without my glasses, oh, God, I'm blind—where's my glasses?"

Ray fought not to smile. He knew his partner was probably doubled over with laughter on the other side of the glass, so he took a deep breath and let it out through his nose. He sat on the edge of the desk and peered down at her silky, light brown hair. "Miss Jefferson, I'm going to get someone to bring you some water, but you have to calm down so we can sort all this out. Did you hear me?"

She nodded quickly, wiped her nose on the blanket, and clutched his hand with her eyes closed. "Sir, the room is spinning."

"Okay, in the wastebasket, all right?" He extracted his hand and quickly grabbed a waste can from the far corner of the room, and got it under her face just in time. He didn't move as she snatched it, practically put her head in it, and heaved, then slumped back in the chair.

"I normally only do red wine—what was I thinking to

have champagne and let Kimika give me a margarita? Oh, God . . ." She slung her forearm over her face to block the fluorescent glare. "So help me, I will never invite people I don't know into my house."

He watched two big tears stream down her face as her head hung back. Even with vomit in a wastepaper basket, her face puffy and red, clothes askew, and hair sitting up on top of her head like a squirrel, there was something so innocent about this chick that was making him process everything she had to say twice. He watched her chest rise and fall in shudders, like that of a frightened bird. Her red silk robe was stained . . . little mesh slippers scuffed and dirty . . . pretty feet must be cold, gooseflesh sitting up on her arms.

Ray nodded to the glass. "I'll get you another blanket and a cup of coffee—then we can talk, all right? Tell me where you met these people and under what circumstances, and maybe we can shorten your evening in here?"

She nodded, but didn't look at him. More tears slipped down her cheeks beneath her forearm.

It was the most convoluted story he'd ever heard. His partner stood behind the glass, scratching his head.

"Brother, either this chick is on a bad acid trip, or she's the most bold-faced liar I have ever seen. How is a gorgeous chick like that gonna make *anybody* believe she hasn't had a boyfriend, in what, three years? Nah, wrong answer! Save it for the jury."

"I know," Ray said, studying Jocelyn Jefferson through the glass as she meekly sipped her coffee with a blanket clutched around her. He touched the two-way mirror with one finger. "She doesn't come up on radar as a working girl, though. That's the thing. Everything we've asked her checks out, down to no driving violations. I see what I see through this glass, know what Murph and the fellas brought in, but this chick's alibis are airtight. She's offering everything without a struggle—DNA, urine, fingerprints, birth certificates, phone numbers, addresses to all her hangouts—it's crazy. She's even told us to come to her house and dust every surface, to even check out the sheets, and keeps claiming not to know Phat and Smooth. So, either she's the best liar we've run across, or . . ." He snatched his hand away from the glass and made a fist. "I hate not being a hundred percent in my gut."

"I know. We called that professor she said to call, and sure enough, dude was home, he comes up as legit faculty on the university Web site. Chances are, this chick is registered there as a student—easy enough to determine. But it ain't like we haven't had grad students that work a neat circuit before."

"Yeah, but not like this one," Ray said, beginning to pace. "Something ain't right. It sticks in my craw. If what she says happened the way it did, I'd hate to ruin this chick's life. By the same token, though, she's fine enough to be Phat's woman, or a top-rung pick—know what I mean?"

"I feel you," Raul said, his eyes never leaving the two-way mirror. "Besides, you think women get all that upset about a stupid holiday? I mean, to . . . you know . . . throw a party for their girlfriends, and then other people start filling in the gaps, and whatever? I mean, Ray, man, you see the evidence bags?" Raul shook his head. "Some of that equipment was scary . . . I mean, size-wise, just saying."

Ray smiled. "We talking about the case or the fact that you forgot to buy roses again this year?"

Raul chuckled. "I'm so far in the doghouse brother, you might as well throw away my leash. Won't need it. Tomorrow morning I'll be at the pound."

"You just answered your own question, and maybe a few of mine . . . but, I just don't know. Loud music, a joint on the back deck, and some exotic products is no reason to completely ruin a woman's life. However, I'm not about to let crocodile tears, a long, crazy story, and a pretty face be the reason I missed a key informant or witness."

"That ain't the kinda crap to lose a badge or shield for, man." Raul pounded Ray's fist. "Whatchu wanna do? Your call."

Ray let his breath out hard, thinking out loud as he spoke. "I'ma call my boy, Marcus. Ask him to do me a favor, since he owes me one, and have him give girlfriend some legal advice, since she's a most likely broke coed, then let her go and follow her. Her bank accounts show up real slim digits, no real big credit, no flashy car, modest apartment, low-key day gig, but that doesn't mean she doesn't have a secret stash." Ray rubbed his chin. "If Phat circles back in a few days, or she goes to him, and I can't imagine him staying away from her long . . . at least she'll have representation—will know what she's up against, then me and Marc can work on cutting an information deal. I'm just mad that the bastard slipped down the back fire escape and got away with his boy."

"That's crossing the line, man," Raul said carefully. "The *providing an attorney* part."

All previous mirth had dissipated. Both men stood shoulder to shoulder and stared forward at the nervous woman who couldn't see them.

Ray nodded, watching Jocelyn take tiny sips of coffee as her pretty hands trembled. "I know. But the thing I hate most about seeing young women get hooked up with these roughnecks is them not realizing their legal position. They have no clue that just because their man is doing illegal crap, even if they aren't directly, they can go up the river for a very long time. That's why I want my boy to talk to her, get into her head, and make her think about the ramifications of staying with one of these guys. Marcus knows his shit, cold. Is excellent at what he does, so she won't get no jackleg advice. This one has a brain, is too intelligent, and seems like she comes from a decent family that would flatline if they knew she was caught up in any of this. Hopefully, after she starts thinking, figures out how precarious her situation is, and all that she has to lose . . ."

"Man, you're dreaming. You know it doesn't work like that. They go for the bling bling, the money. They're also scared to death of retaliation and won't talk, which you *know* is real." Raul chuckled sadly. "Besides, trying to save this one might get your boy killed. Marc ain't gonna be able to help himself; he'll push up on this one for sure—a damsel in distress, too?" Raul walked away from the window and held the doorknob. "Plus, you know he won't violate attorney-client privilege, even for you, if you're angling for inside—"

"I'm not, and that wouldn't hold up under any judge. I want this one to have a shot at getting untangled, if she's innocent."

"Can't save 'em all, man," Raul said quietly. "Can't fix what happened to Sharon . . . or your sister. It wasn't your fault."

Raymond didn't answer.

Raul opened the door. "But I can tell your mind is already made up. Got that look in your eye. Jaw muscle's jumpin'. Okaaaay, partner. You sure your mind is set?"

"Yeah. It is. Marcus owes me."

Chapter Five

Her mouth felt yucky, like a wad of nasty cotton had been shoved into it. She was freezing cold; goose bumps covered her arms and set her teeth on edge. Her eyes were puffing and felt like sandpaper had replaced the insides of her lids. She was sure that her hair was standing on top of her head, and knew her face looked a fright. *Bone-weary* didn't come close to describing it as she made her way out of the interrogation room, down a long, ugly greenish-gray corridor, under glaring fluorescent lights.

No money in her pockets—how was she going to get home, on a SEPTA bus, with no coat, in the dead of winter, wearing what looked like a hooker's outfit? Logistics and new realities pummeled Jocelyn's already embattled brain. She had no purse, no ID, no keys to even get back into her apartment, were she to find a way there. Hitchhike? Not. And wind up back in the slammer for soliciting? Pullease. Every friend she had was AWOL, not that she had a cell phone on her, and if she did take the cops up on a phone call offer, who would she be able to reach?

Calling her mother was out of the question—that's all she needed, was for her mother to have a heart attack at the station's front desk. Althea Jefferson would fall out, dead away, from a horror stroke. The woman would literally have a cow.

However, the lure of freedom from incarceration made Jocelyn step up her pace. At least the kind officer had half listened to her story, even though he'd been a hard ass. Imagine, *her*, of all people, supposedly dating some drug-thug kingpin? It was too insane. Maybe instead of writing her dissertation she could write an action-adventure novel, given that her career was probably in shreds by now.

Jocelyn froze when the large double doors opened and her professor stood before her, nervously shifting from foot to foot in his tweed wool coat. If she could have disappeared into the toes of her red mesh slippers, she would have—and she seriously considered clicking her heels three time to wake up back in Kansas. Oh, God . . . Professor Benjamin Bryant, perhaps the most dignified black man she knew, outside of her dad, could not be standing in the outer lobby of a police station, waiting for her! She blinked twice, hoping he was a mere hysteria-induced mirage. But he was there, all right, standing tall and proud, his shoulders back, his warm brown eyes holding a hundred questions, his jaw locked, chin thrust up in pure disgust as he smoothed his palm over his perfectly barbered, salt-and-pepper hair.

Without much ado, he used his tightly clasped brown leather gloves to motion that they should leave. Jocelyn simply nodded, too mortified even to utter a thank-you, and she followed him out to the front lot.

"When they called me to verify your claims that you were, indeed, one of my students," he said in a fatherly, disappointed tone, "I could not believe my ears. I came down to see for myself. I knew there had to be some mistake." He flung open the passenger door of his Volvo and shook his head as Jocelyn climbed into the seat. "Here," he said, extracting a coat from the backseat. "The detective told me you weren't properly robed for the weather. That's when I knew I had to come downtown."

Jocelyn kept her lips firmly sealed as a warm, luxurious mink coat flowed over her legs. She peered down at it, and then up at the professor. *Mink*?

"It was my wife's," he said curtly, and slid into the driver's seat, gunned the engine, and careened away.

She wasn't sure if it was outrage at the hour, the situation, or the indignity of being anywhere near a police station that made this normally staid professor drive like he was auditioning for NASCAR . . . maybe it was a combination of everything, so she kept her mouth shut until he pulled into a parking space before her building.

"Professor Bryant," she said quietly, "I can't even begin to explain all this, but it's not what it looks like."

His eyes were fixed on some unknown point beyond the windshield. His jaw pulsed. Not a good sign.

"You were my most promising student. I thought you had your head together. I am beyond disappointed. *Devastated* would be a better description."

She hated the way he wouldn't look at her, and the tone of his voice. It cut to the bone. He spoke in the past tense—*were*. She was no longer his promising student, and her career was over, just as she'd imagined. Her father's face flashed before her eyes, disappointment looming in his expression, and suddenly her voice felt shaky.

Jocelyn smoothed the sleek fur on her lap and delicately folded it and drew a long breath. "I am so sorry, but I am none of the things I may appear to be, sir. Thank you, more than words can say, for coming to my rescue tonight. Maybe, one day, you'll let me explain it all, but I certainly understand your position." With that she reached for the door and unlocked it.

"Where are you going?" Professor Bryant's attention snapped toward her and he turned in his seat to study her with a frown.

Jocelyn froze and just looked at him for a moment. "Inside."

"Alone? Are you insane? Your doors have been left open all night. This is an urban environment—I wouldn't even do that in Chestnut Hill, let alone down here." He shook his head, thrust the coat back toward her, and got out of the car in a huff. "Surely you need someone to go through your place and check it out. There could be intruders. Not to mention, you should list anything, immediately, that is missing. These unsavory friends of yours could have doubled back to rob you blind!"

He began walking ahead of her. She followed him, stunned. That part of this whole drama had never occurred to her.

Jocelyn's heart was pounding so hard she thought a rib might crack. As she got to the door, the only person she knew would probably be awake was her nosy neighbor, Mrs. Schwartz. The old bat was probably also the one who'd called the cops, so it would serve her right to have to buzz her in.

They waited as the crotchety voice filled the intercom. When Mrs. Schwartz began to fuss, Jocelyn lost her cool.

"Haven't you done enough already?" Jocelyn shouted. "My keys are in my apartment, my professor is out here in the cold, and I got hauled down to the station for a party—because you called the cops—so the least you could do is let me in out of the February cold to a place where I pay rent each month!"

The buzzer sounded and Jocelyn leaned on the door, furious. Professor Ben Bryant followed her up the steps but insisted on taking the lead once they reached the top landing. He bent and found her glasses on the floor and handed them to her.

"You stand in the hallway with your neighbor, and if it's all clear, then come in. If you hear voices, call 9-1-1. All right?"

Jocelyn nodded, but glared at Mrs. Schwartz, who was hanging on the professor's every word. It seemed like the old lady was taking unusual delight in the living stage play happening right before her in the hall.

Too angry to move, and not trusting herself not to reach out and snatch the old buzzard by her throat, Jocelyn set her crooked glasses upon the bridge of her nose and folded her arms, wearing the mink like a very expensive cape. She would not say a mumbling word to the old goat who remained defiant and triumphant beside her in the hall, her flowered housecoat and fuzzy pink slippers and oily old scarf covering blue-white hair and pink rollers. Nope. It would degrade to a screaming match. When Mrs. Schwartz neared her to touch the coat, Jocelyn almost growled, and the old woman wisely backed off with a shrug.

"You didn't do too bad for yourself tonight," Mrs. Schwartz said, admiring the coat with a yellowed-denture grin. "He's not bad, either. A little old for you, but a looker."

Jocelyn kept her eyes forward and affixed to the open apartment door. Assault and battery was not out of the question if the old bird didn't stop.

"All clear," Professor Bryant said, his normal calm returning to his voice. He gave Mrs. Schwartz a dismissive glare and opened the door wider for Jocelyn to enter, and then abruptly shut the door.

"Begin at the beginning, Jocelyn," he said evenly, and began removing his coat as he sat down on her sofa.

She briefly closed her eyes, removed the mink coat cape, and laid it beside him. "How about if I make some tea as I talk? You do deserve an explanation." She accepted his slight nod as a yes, and watched him scan her apartment from the corner of her eye while she slipped into the kitchen.

"If you hand me some plastic wrap and a garbage bag, I can help begin to get this ruination in order."

"You've done enough, already, sir. Let me—"

"I need to walk and think as you talk. You know that's my teaching style, anyway."

He smiled, but it didn't hold as much venom as his tone had earlier. She was glad he was calming down enough to listen, because she certainly didn't have the energy to argue. She handed him a box of cling-wrap through the kitchen pass-through and a big, black trash bag, and then began talking a mile a minute as she found tea, put on hot water, and located both sugar and honey.

She kept her back to him as she explained. She didn't want to see the man's face—didn't want to see pity or disbelief in it, or worse, pure disgust. She'd been through enough humiliation for a lifetime. So, she just spilled her guts and cleaned up the kitchen, and waited for the water to boil.

When she returned to the room, he'd taken off his coat and was sitting on the sofa, his gaze going out the window.

"Wow. You did all that, *that* fast?" It was nothing short of amazing. The man had dumped everything, glasses and all; food was gone, platters, everything, but the room was much improved.

He chuckled. "I used to be in the military, and have a penchant for removing clutter." He accepted her tea with grace and sipped it slowly, glimpsing her over the top of his horn-rimmed glasses. "But now I understand what happened here."

She let her breath out in a rush, and almost spilled her tea. "Professor Bry—"

"Ben," he said in a low, warm tone. "I guess we're friends now that I've retrieved you from the police station."

She laughed and sipped her tea. "That does remove some formality, doesn't it?"

He nodded, but his smile was just a half-smile, and his eyes searched hers. The gaze was penetrating, and it set off internal alarm bells. Was she imagining things or was there some type of male vibe happening? True, she'd been through a lot, might be reading things wrong, but as she replayed the timbre of his voice and the expression on his face . . . aw, Lawd . . . no . . .

"Jocelyn, I was worried out of my mind," he said quietly, setting his tea down on the coffee table. "Then I became angry, because the brightest, most promising woman I've encountered since my wife passed away five years ago had, on first glance, done something outrageously foolish that could have jeopardized her entire life." He smiled sadly and glanced at the trash bag. "But as a widower for five years . . . I do understand what momentary bouts of loneliness can do to an individual."

Jocelyn's cup hung midair between her mouth and the table. Her eyes went to the trash bag. Then down to the coffee table, where the last thing she'd remembered on it was a very kinky product display. Then she instantly remembered hearing the man move the sofa as he tossed things—oh no!

"That stuff wasn't mine—really. It was, a—"

"I make no judgments and cast no aspersions," he said, with mischief tugging at his mouth. "You're a very attractive woman, Jocelyn Jefferson. I have kept my professional distance because it is prudent, and you definitely deserve respect. But if you were not my doctoral fellow, I would have asked you to dinner a long time ago. Since I've been the recipient of much too much information tonight, it only seems fair that I also come clean with you. So," he added with a sigh, "shall we be honest with each other, since a lot has been revealed between us?"

She opened her mouth and then closed it quickly. Her hands were practically shaking as she brought the tea to her lips. This man was at least fifty-something. Like, twice her age—not that she was prejudiced, but it hadn't occurred to her, really. He was handsome, but . . . she felt like a crazy woman—why did she tell a man who had been a self-proclaimed celibate widower that she'd been dateless for three years? The kimono suddenly felt too revealing. She slurped her tea to help keep her voice from squeaking.

"I respect the hell out of you, Professor," she said, and then immediately wished she could swallow away the poor choice of phrase. "I mean, you're awesome. Uh, and a real knight in shining armor, like nobody ever would believe this madness, and uh, truly I totally appreciate you leaving your home, getting involved in all this nonsense, and for not thinking the worst, uh, but, uh." Lordy-Miss-Claudy. "Thank you?"

He laughed. The tone of his rich, ebullient voice flowed over her as he stood and collected his tweed coat. She watched him, thinking hard about the very generous dinner offer. Benjamin Bryant was fit, athletic, and intelligent, and she liked his laid-back, gentleman's gentleman style. He had a way of even making his navy-and-rust herringbone jacket with elbow patches and a pair of corduroy slacks with penny loafers look like a decorated Marine's uniform.

It made her wonder what he'd look like in a theater tux—probably like a White House diplomat. That fantasy cascaded into snapshot mental images as she tried to fit him into her life's frame of reference and herself into what she imagined his to be. But the images were a tad askew, and they really didn't work: her friends, his friends . . . hmmm . . . their interests, not sure she was feeling it. She had never paid full attention to him as a possible suitor, but he honestly resembled a darker-hued Colin Powell . . . and he did exude a quiet charisma that was something to be reckoned with. If the saliva hadn't burned away from her mouth, she would have gulped when he reached out a hand to bid her to stand.

She got up slowly, and then suddenly covered her mouth. "I threw up at the station," she shrieked, and dashed from the room.

Baritone laughter echoed down the hall behind her as she snatched up her toothbrush and squeezed a glob of toothpaste on it. From the corner of her eye a dark presence filled the hallway, and she nearly bumped her head on the mirror as her head jerked up.

"How about if we go back to casual knowledge of each

other until your nerves become steadier?" His smile made crinkles form at the corners of his eyes. "I didn't mean to alarm you, and wasn't about to kiss you . . . I was going to invite you to the theater tomorrow night, however . . ." He glanced around the apartment hallway and wrecked bathroom. "You may need a few days to collect yourself. The offer stands. But I promise to be discreet and not do anything that you might feel uncomfortable with. You set the pace. Is that fair?"

Jocelyn bobbed her head up and down while scrubbing her teeth into a lather.

"I'll see myself out. Lock the door, and get your locks changed tomorrow, in case someone made off with your keys."

Again, she didn't speak, just mumbled agreement through frothing white paste. As soon as the front door slammed, she collapsed against the bathroom wall and took a very long look at herself in the mirror. She looked absolutely rabid.

Immediately peals of laughter echoed in the bathroom. Her hair was in wiry spikes, dark rings were under her eyes, she was literally foaming at the mouth—had almost been locked up, and now her professor wanted to date her? Oh, what a night!

Jocelyn paced to the living room, chewing on a toothbrush, but became very, very still as she glanced at the sofa. A five-figure mink coat was still slung over the arm of the furniture, and obviously not left there by accident.

Chapter Six

Morning entered her consciousness like a sledgehammer. The alarm dug knives behind her eyeballs and gouged at limp gray matter that lay dormant within her skull. Jocelyn slapped the offending buzzer with such force that the clock radio fell off the nightstand. But she had to get up. Even with a splitting headache, she was well aware that her job didn't allow for too much sick time, and she'd used up most of it during the semester for lectures and important research meetings.

She pulled herself to the side of the bed and sat up, groaning and holding her head in a vise between both palms. All right, she had to suck it up, pop some painkillers, and take this crap like a woman. First order of business, call a locksmith. Get that guy out of there while inhaling black coffee, and get dressed. Put on something understated and tasteful to go visit the professor, only to take his dead wife's mink back to him—was the man crazy? *Were all men crazy*? Why, for the love of God, would she want to sashay around in a dead woman's coat?

In the cold light of day, the gift seemed ludicrous, if not offensive. But she decided to keep her thoughts on the positive side, and would just assume that he'd meant it as a sentimental gesture—and that's how she would return it.

Jocelyn strode to the closet; just thinking about the glaring lights in the bathroom delayed her efforts. She'd put on her little pink mohair sweater that Miss Kimmie suggested, and a little pleated black skirt, with some boots, understated silver stud earrings . . . yeah, she thought, snatching the items off hangers. This way, she'd look like a student, but wouldn't mortify her professor by showing up in his office looking like the hoochie she'd appeared to be last night. This was a brand new day. Good riddance to Valentine's disasters.

Within the hour, the emergency locksmith had arrived and changed her dead bolts on the front door and back door that led to the deck and side fire escape. All SOS messages to her AWOL female crew had been succinctly left and their cell phones and home voice mails, to no avail. Whatever. Tylenol was kicking in, so was black coffee. The only thing she had to do now was get on public transportation and make it downtown to work.

Sure, she'd be a little late, but at least she hadn't called out. From this point forward, given the shaky state of affairs her academic career was in, she would be mindful of all the rules of her job. Now, she had to—especially since it seemed probable that this was the only career she had left.

Jocelyn thrust her body into a short, black pea coat, tugged on a sassy woolen cap and cocked it to the side, put on her lip gloss, and draped the expensive fur over her arm. She was on a mission. The sun was out, it wasn't snowing, and she would not be denied.

As she sorted through the new tangle of keys, the phone rang and she dashed for it. If it was one of her girls, even though late for work, she had enough time to give her a good piece of her mind. But as she drew a breath to begin her tirade, a deep, male voice entered her ear.

"Marcus Dorchester, Esquire, here, from Dorchester, Upland, and Johnson. A mutual friend suggested I call you—am I speaking to Miss Jocelyn Jefferson?"

"Yes, but—"

"Good. I normally only take clients upon referral, and do not have a lot of time today—but can squeeze you in at eleven-thirty. Does that work?"

Stunned, it took a moment for all the tumblers to fall into place within her mind and engage her vocal cords. Either her best friend Jacqui had heard her SOS, thought she needed representation—in which case, she did, if Jacqui had pulled out the heavy artillery—or Professor Bryant could have sent the guy, also a good source of knowledge. Rather than give the arrogant voice on the phone the flip-off, Jocelyn mellowed her response.

"Okay. I can do that. But I only get a half-hour for lunch, and I'm already late, so how far—"

"I'll meet you in the lobby at your job, you can download your version of what happened to me then, and I'll be on my way. Thank you. See you at eleven-thirty, Miss Jefferson."

The connection clicked off and Jocelyn stared at the telephone receiver. If a friend had sent this guy, and he already knew where she worked, then whoever called him must have thought it was worse than she'd imagined.

"Look, Ray," Marcus barked into his cell phone. "I don't have time to go around Philly visiting some chicken-head, ghetto-fabulous little—"

"You owe me, Dorchester," Ray shouted back. "She's not a chicken-head, just a sister that got turned around in a situation. I'm calling in my marker."

A long sigh entered the phone, and Raymond Mayfield flipped it shut.

By the time she got to work, it was already nine-thirty A.M. She knew the boss would be breathing fire; she hated her floor manager. Jocelyn strode off the eleventh-floor elevator with her head held high. Today she would not be cowed. After the police station, what could some bleached-blond shrew with dark roots say to her, or do to her, that would engender fear? An attorney had called her house; this had to be serious. Today, the words, *You're fired,* would only make her laugh. Margaret was not Sir Donald!

She pushed through the double glass doors of their telemarketing suite and tried to smile at the receptionist.

"Hey, Gail. I know the boss is probably having a coronary, but I had a mini-emergency this morning." Jocelyn lifted the expensive fur. "Can you put this in the locked closet for a sister?"

"Sheeit," Gail said, standing and almost toppling her coffee. She snatched off her headset and let the phone console light up with waiting calls. "Gurl! I'da been late, too, suga." She accepted the coat, held it out, and then pressed it up against her short, plump frame. "Oooooh, chile! Let Miss Thang be mad, plus he sent you roses this morning, too? Whatcha work on that man, mojo? Humph!"

"What?" Jocelyn shook her head and laughed. "This was left at my house by accident—I can't accept the gift, long story, and—"

"You lost your mind?"

Gail was so indignant that she thrust her chubby arms into the coat and twirled around, making Jocelyn laugh harder, despite the headache. It swept the floor, looking like a huge rug on Gail's four-foot-eleven frame.

"All I know is, he sent flowers, too—so whatever you did, girl, was da bomb." Gail strutted over to her wide, walnut reception desk, still wearing the coat, and handed Jocelyn a crystal vase.

Jocelyn whipped off the already opened card.

"Girl, read it," Gail said, giggling. "It says, 'Thank you for an adventurous, delightful evening.' " She did a little dance in the coat. "Now, I don't know about you, but I wanna know what you did that rocked a man's world where you came out holding mink and roses in the morning? Tell me, whatchu do?"

Jocelyn closed her eyes, threw her head back, and laughed. "I didn't do anything but nearly get arrested."

"You had him screaming that loud, or was it you that made the neighbors call the cops? Daaayum, chile, you was wurkin' it, wasn't ya?"

"Well, *somebody* around here should be working," a tight voice said from the hall leading to the cubicles. "The front-desk boards are going crazy, as am I!" The office manager strode forward, her mouth a tight line of fury. "You are so late and so docked, Miss Jefferson. This goes on your record, you are written up—because a family emergency was obviously a lie. The coat and roses tell it all. Do you think we're here to play games, or that your job is some kind of joke? We do not pay you to strut in here late and disrupt the flow of our activities because you had some sort of wild night on the town. You have two minutes to be at your desk, with your headset on, and dialing for dollars."

The storm came and went so quickly that Gail and Jocelyn had barely blinked. Gail took the coat off quickly, and yanked open the closet, but hung it up with care.

"Somebody obviously didn't get laid for V-Day," Gail whispered, and then winked at Jocelyn, rushed over to her, and gave her a discreet high-five. "But my gurl did!"

They both covered their mouths and laughed as Jocelyn ran away from the reception area, not bothering to take the flowers with her. Why rub salt in the wound? The professor's note was kind, but really pushing the borders of laid-back casual. Now she would have to root in the bag of garbage he'd collected, just to see what had blown that older brother's mind. Then again, don't ask, don't tell was also a good policy. She did not wanna know, oh!

* * *

Two hours slipped by in an uneventful haze. The normal suspects who would have approached her desk, showing off diamonds and flowers, said nary a word. Nods of respect greeted her as she'd passed cubicles. How odd. How twisted. This made no sense. As she worked, Jocelyn allowed her eyes to scan the desks. Soon, she understood how this very sick game was played. She had *roses* in the lobby. Roses, with a capital R. Huge, blood-red, long stemmed beauties separated by fern, baby's breath, and swathed in crystal, and with a big red bow, whereas the others had cutesy mini-sprays or bunches delivered with no vase. Then she realized that full-length mink worth twenty-grand-large beat any tennis bracelet or one-karat studs, any day.

It was so sick. She began scribbling notes to herself in the borders of her computer call list. This was a weird female phenomenon created by male-dominated industries. Yes, she would use this as a lab experiment. She had been in the control group before; now, a variable toxin was added, a new materialistic drug . . . hmmm . . . and the pathology that spun off of that was truly insane.

Doodling away, she rattled off the spiel that she knew by heart, no longer needing the script. But when she saw Gail racing down the aisle, she hurriedly clicked off the next call.

"Gurrrllll . . . . Ohmigod, you didn't say how fine he was! Oh, chile, Lord have mercy, I can't breathe—you were on the phone, so couldn't buzz ya, but he's in the lobby, standing six-something, cold-blooded gray chesterfield, briefcase, Lawd, the man has a job—and, oh, girl, he smells like a million bucks! Where'd you find him?"

"My attorney—oh, shoot, I'm late!"

"He's an attorney—you snagged a lawya, ohmigod!"

Heads pivoted, necks craned, Jocelyn was on her feet in seconds racing for the lobby. But she came to a dead stop when she spied what Gail had seen, and she grabbed Gail's arm and dodged into an empty cubicle.

"Ohmigod, ohmigod, ohmigod, he's fine—Gail, ohmigod, what should I do?"

Gail was shaking her by both arms and whispering through her teeth. "Do what you did last night, girlfriend, and knock him dead—rock his world, lose your job—he can get you another one or can pay your bills!"

"No, no, no, you don't understand—"

"Oh, right, yes I do—not too much, string him out. That's how you got him to fall by for lunch. He's looking at his watch." Gail dipped her head out and huddled back to Jocelyn. "He's on the phone. Tapping his wrist. Dude wants some more bad, brother is out there jonsin like a crack addict—just—"

"Not another word," Jocelyn hissed. "Cover me with Margaret and I'll owe ya for life."

"Done!" Gail said, and then skipped out to the lobby. She slid behind her desk and into her chair with a wide smile. "Mr. Dorchester, she'll be with you in a moment."

Marcus Dorchester snapped his cell phone closed. This was why he hated doing charity cases. People who got everything for free had no sense of time, or what time was worth. If he and Raymond hadn't gone back to the old days together, this appointment would never have made his Palm Pilot. In fact, screw old ties; he didn't have it in him today to wait on some airhead drug-dealer's girlfriend. He didn't even take cases like this!

Beyond words, he picked up his briefcase, about to tell the receptionist he had to leave and to simply flip her a business card, when he looked up, stopped, and set his briefcase down very slowly. Good Lord in Heaven . . . he'd owe his boy, Ray-Ray, until the end of time. No wonder the man couldn't lock her in a cell and throw away the key. Jesus . . . an angel had appeared in the lobby. He tried to keep a professional expression on his face, but her skin just asked to be scanned . . . honey-butter-almond, big doe-brown eyes, black silky lashes, hair like shoulder-length velvet, hiding behind a pair of conservative glasses that made the little pink sweater she wore all the more sexy . . . like the hot-pink bra strap with little white hearts peeking out at the shoulder did . . . all the way down to her long, curvaceous, black-tight-clad legs, sneaking thigh beyond the hem of a black pleated micro-mini. All legs. *Just slap him.*

"Why, hello," Marcus Dorchester said, extending his hand.

"Hi," Jocelyn said, shyly. "Thanks for coming here, and I'm sorry it took me a moment to get away from my desk."

"No problem," he said. "We should do this over lunch, anyway."

Jocelyn glanced at the clock and at Gail's wide-eyed signals to go for it. "I only have a half-hour."

Marcus Dorchester flipped open his phone and speed-dialed his office. "Linda, clear my appointments for the next two hours." He flipped his phone shut.

Gail covered her mouth and ducked her head down to stare at the phone lines that weren't being answered. Jocelyn's eyes widened.

"Either your future is important to you, or it isn't," Marcus said with authority. "Tell your boss an emergency came up, because it did. Client-attorney privilege. I keep a table down at Twenty-One a few blocks up. Let's sit where we can talk, and do this right."

Gail let out a stifled squeal that made Marcus and Jocelyn simply look at her.

"Oh, *I'll tell her*, Jocelyn," Gail said with a broad smile. "Go to lunch, and act like you know."

Jocelyn returned to the lobby, half angry, and half floating on air. She had never been lectured to so hard in all her life! The nerve! Oh, what a windbag. Fine, debonair, intelligent, clearly wealthy, with panache, but a *complete* jerk. She was losing faith in the species by leaps and bounds.

Half of her wanted to just jump his bones, just to see what being wined and dined by a man like that would be like—the other half of her was like: Get a grip—not!

Besides, she'd read enough women's magazines to know that a guy who was so clearly into himself would not be a good lover, because he was into himself. Du-uh. Period. She'd read and heard all the horror stories, plus sat shiva with enough girlfriends explaining about their lackluster experiences with professional guys, athletes, music icons . . . well, groupie status didn't count, because you knew what you'd get if you went to bed with a drunk, high, self-absorbed fool, but still, it was more fodder for her already overworked mind.

However, the reaction she got when she returned to work was almost laughable. Her boss was so angry the woman seemed ready to levitate, but her coworkers looked like they were about to lift her to their shoulders and do a Superbowl victory dance . . . albeit, while cutting her heart out.

Five o'clock couldn't come soon enough!

Ray drummed his fingers on his steering wheel as he sat in his unmarked Crown Victoria on Seventeenth and Market. In all his born days, he'd never heard Marcus Dorchester sound like he had on the phone. He stared at the hands-free unit in utter disbelief as his friend took a cool, distant tone with him. Marc?

"Like I said, Mayfield, this one isn't for the whole penal process. I'm serious, man. I thoroughly interviewed her at lunch, down at Twenty-One, and if you boys need a case-breaker, she isn't it. You back the hell off, or I'll go deep into my personal-favor bag of tricks and pull out a silver bullet. We clear?"

For a moment, Ray couldn't answer. "You feeling all right, man? Everything cool down at the firm?"

"I am fine. I am very lucid at the moment. What about what I said don't you understand?"

Silence strangled the airwaves between them for a moment, and then Ray found a chuckle bubbling within him. "She ain't no chicken-head, is she?"

A long whistle filled the vehicle through the speakerphone.

"Definitely not," Marcus said. "She's . . ."

"She blew your mind, is what she did." Raymond chuckled and put his gears in drive. Mirth dissipated as he watched Jocelyn Jefferson leave the building with a mink coat draped over her arm. Damn, he knew it! Guilty as sin. She was stashing payoff gifts at, of all places, her job.

"In a word, yes." Marcus said, after a moment.

"Well, all that notwithstanding, I still have to be sure she's not involved. If not, play on, my brother. If so, she's going down to turn up the heat on Phat."

"She's not involved," Marcus argued, his tone becoming brittle through the mounted receiver. "And, I'm not playing," he added. "Maybe for the first time in my life, I'm not running game."

"Neither am I," Ray said, merging with rush-hour traffic. "Then I guess we both have to do what we have to do."

Chapter Seven

He hated his job. Conflict wore on him hard as he pulled his vehicle up to the bus stop and depressed the automatic windows. "Miss Jefferson, would it be possible to have a word with you?" When she squinted and acted like she couldn't make out who he was, he flashed his badge, which got her attention—along with everyone else's waiting for the bus.

She dashed toward his car and jumped in before the light changed, holding the coat to her breast like a child would hold a rag doll. "What's wrong now? Am I in trouble again? This lawyer came to my job and said all this stuff could happen to me if I was in cahoots with some underworld figure, but I'm not!"

"Talk to me about the coat, Miss Jefferson. Off the record." He wished he hadn't added that last qualifier, because whatever she said might have to go down as evidence.

"Oh, this?" she said, laughing and looking down at it as though she'd forgotten she was holding it. "It's my professor's dead wife's coat."

"Are you implying that you and he are involved in a murder, as well as—"

"Oh my God!" Jocelyn flung the coat on the dashboard and it slipped to the floor. "Murder?" she squeaked. "Professor Bryant killed his wife? Oh shit!"

"No, no, I didn't say he killed his wife. I'm asking you if you are trying to tell me—"

"What, you think I killed somebody?" She snatched up the coat, fury blazing in her eyes, replacing all innocence. "I have never in my life been so utterly—let me out. I have an attorney. I am going to walk back to—"

"I'm sorry. It's my job to ask questions and assume nothing."

She folded her arms over her chest with the coat wedged between them and her breasts. "Since the moment you saw me, you assumed everything!" She shot a hot gaze out of the window. "Take me to campus, walk me into Professor Bryant's office, and you will see that he came to collect me from the station last night, because I was wearing—oh, you know what I was wearing. He found a coat in his closet for me to put on—probably because it was the first thing he grabbed, and the poor man obviously had this in his house because he couldn't bear to part with it—then saw me safely inside my apartment, because the police were too stupid to lock my door, so he was concerned that while being unnecessarily questioned, my apartment could have been burglarized, and today, I took it to work so I could just drop it off on the way home and say thank-you to the man who, by the way, got out of his bed at no o'clock in the morning and saw me home—*that* is a *gentleman*. You guys at The Round House would put an innocent woman with no clothes, no coat, no money out in the—"

"I'm sorry," Ray said, rubbing his palms down his face as the light turned red. Every time he encountered this woman, she turned what seemed perfectly logical around into something that sounded crazy, and everything that sounded crazy, coming from her, made perfect sense.

"Well, you should be!" Jocelyn said loudly, inching closer to the door. "I am fit to be tied! I just cannot understand why you people keep harassing me!" She spun on him and looked at him hard. "Racial profiling? Gender profiling? What is it? A conspiracy?"

He fought not to smile. "Would you like me to drop you off on campus?"

"Yes. Thank you," she said curtly.

"Since we didn't provide a ride last night, I could provide one today as a good-faith gesture . . . I don't mind waiting to drop you home."

"Fine."

He watched her from the corner of his eye as he drove. She so reminded him of his younger sister who once had a fiery spirit. But it broke his heart to see that fire snuffed out before its time. The streets had claimed his baby sis—messing with the wrong thug had put her behind bars; now the streets had her again with drugs wringing the life out of her, and his nieces and nephews were being raised by grandmom.

Taking the back way up to Temple University, by Spring Garden, then up Sixteenth through the residential badlands that expressway drivers never saw, Ray stared out the front window, wondering how something so good could turn so bad so fast. Same thing happened with Sharon, the first girlfriend he ever had. She was young, impressionable, foolish, just as anyone is at that age. A smooth brother with a wad of bills in his pocket and a nice car had siphoned her away from his side, only to have her accidentally riding in the wrong car on the wrong day. Gone at fifteen. A stray bullet owed no one an explanation. Both of them wept along with her family at the funeral.

Raymond turned the corner and double-parked on Montgomery Avenue. "I should walk you in—not because I don't trust you, but it's dark, you have a fur in your arms, and I don't trust the streets."

He watched her begin to protest, ready-made attitude just waiting to leap from her mouth, but then he saw her pause, glance out the window, and then over to him.

"All right," she said quietly. "But this is a delicate delivery. Okay?"

He cocked his head to the side, not quite sure what she meant.

She sighed. "My professor is a really nice man," she said, stroking the coat. "Very lonely, very nice, respectable. But, he's not my type, and I can't keep something that is so expensive and obviously means so much to him, or was given to someone that meant a lot to him—it isn't right." She looked up at him, her pretty eyes catching streetlights. "I don't want him to feel embarrassed by your presence, or like I'm trying to strut in there with some guy, even though you're a cop . . . or have him think that you made me return this. I don't know what I'm trying to say—all I know is that everyone deserves to have their dignity respected, especially when they went out on a limb, put their feelings out there, and didn't get the response they'd hoped for . . . what I'm trying to say is . . ."

"I understand. It's cool. I'll walk you to the building entrance and get back in the car. I'll wait for you and drop you off. All right?"

She nodded and slipped out of the car, not waiting for him to come around and open the door. That he was about to do that gave him pause. This wasn't a date, wasn't a thing . . . this was just a gesture of apology for hotly pursuing a wrong lead, which may have inconvenienced her.

But as he walked her to the building doors and then watched them close behind her, it took him a moment to pull himself away from the glass panes. She waved and offered him a little smile, and then disappeared onto the elevator.

Everything about her made him return to his vehicle slowly. His eyes had told him the woman was a fraud; now something deeper that he couldn't place his finger on told him the woman was legit. Had a heart of gold. The average sister would have worked the man out of a full-length fur, or done whatever she had to in order to put investment protection around it, using her body as a deposit. The way Jocelyn Jefferson spoke blew him away. He smiled just thinking about how her crazy, long, unpunctuated sentences rolled out when she was in a tizzy. But the soft, gentle sound of her near-whisper when she was calm and introspective in his car made his stomach clench. She cared about people's feelings, even some old dude who was vulnerable . . . whom she could have probably worked to get good grades.

Raymond Mayfield looked at his shoes. He didn't like feeling like this—out of sorts. He liked sure bets. Hard evidence in hand. Hated not knowing and having judged wrong. He understood Dorchester's dilemma. This was the kind of woman who made men fight for her, or die trying. But that thought was absurd. There was no fight to be had. Jocelyn Jefferson wasn't playing games, pitting men against each other in some gift-giving scheme, wasn't working a soul . . . except every man who accidentally came in contact with her, by just being who she was.

He looked up when he heard footfalls coming in his direction. Odd, but he could pick hers out from all the other pedestrian students walking by. He hadn't bothered getting into his car. What was the point? He needed to open the door for her this time. It was cold outside, but he really didn't feel it. Maybe she'd like a cup of coffee before she went home, though?

Words were failing him as he watched her let out a long exhale, rake her gloved fingers through her mane, and stride toward him. Her lovely eyes were lowered, as if she'd just gone to a funeral. The chilly night had added a rose tinge to her butter-soft cheeks. Her gorgeous legs seemed even longer in her black hose and boots . . . a thoroughbred stride, disciplined, smooth, graceful, head up and back straight . . . wind taking her hair over her shoulders, putting glistening tears in her eyes. He opened the door on reflex, like a limo driver.

"It's cold out. You need a cup of coffee," he said, then could have kicked himself. It was supposed to be a request, not a command like he was talking to a junior officer. What was wrong with him?

She nodded and sniffed and closed her eyes. He watched her as he rounded the vehicle and slid into his seat, and shut the door.

"Everything cool?" He waited, his heart racing, and he wasn't sure why.

She leaned her head back and didn't open her eyes. "He was a real gentleman—took it well, but he was so disappointed. I feel awful."

He couldn't respond. He was too elated that she'd passed up the offer, too spellbound by the calm compassion she exuded, and too blown away by the serene acceptance on her face . . . the way her hair spilled across his headrest . . . the timing of the sigh ran all through him. Her scent filled the inside of his car. Something was happening that wasn't even supposed to go down like this. He started his ignition. He knew it already—he and his boy Marcus might fall out over this one till the end of time.

"Don't feel bad," he finally said, as gently as possible, trying desperately to focus on the traffic. "He's a man, and men are used to rejection." Ray inwardly cringed. The statement didn't quite come out the way he'd meant it.

She looked at him with an expression of utter disbelief. "Men have feelings—don't you?"

She'd rendered him temporarily speechless.

"Uh, yeah, but . . . what I'm saying is—"

"The man has been widowed for five years, and hasn't dated a soul." She folded her arms over her chest, sat up straighter, and stared at him hard, occasionally adjusting her seat belt strap with nervous agitation. "He's looking for companionship, friendship, someone who shares his same interests and dreams, and to laugh with on a pillow at night . . . someone he can share the trials and tribulations of his job with, someone who will have his back when he feels pushed against the wall, and he thought maybe I could do that. He's devastated. You don't just give a woman a *twenty-thousand-dollar* coat on a professor's salary and think nothing of it. I can only imagine what he's going through . . . I haven't dated in years, and I know . . ." She suddenly pursed her lips and looked out the window.

A wave of conflicting emotions rushed through his system. Irrational jealousy dominated for a second, and he jettisoned it away. What was wrong with him? Why did he care that her prof had a thing for her? It wasn't his business or his concern. Then instant confusion gave way to a resounding *oh yeah*—he could definitely dig where the man was coming from—five years! He was feeling more than a year real bad right now himself; five would have made him a lunatic.

Then whatever was rippling through him flipped and changed into a sudden awareness that this woman had just spilled her guts in his car. Hope was sending very crazy messages to the rusty dating synapses in his brain . . . did *she* say *years*? This fine, smart, misfit angel hadn't gone out in years? She'd told him that back at the station, but he didn't believe it, then. Oh, Jesus . . . what was wrong in America? Had the brothers lost their minds?

She wanted to leap from his car and run shrieking into the night. Why had she just told this very handsome cop all of her personal business in one run-on sentence? Was she crazy? He'd already seen her at her worst, thought she was a felon, a prostitute, then an arms-, drugs-, and flesh-peddling ringleader's woman. Now she had openly admitted to possibly being a university charity case, with a professor who was on her, which would make the man surely question her validity for even holding a doctoral seat in a class. All she could do was stare out the window and take in very small sips of air.

"I hear you," Ray said quietly. "I didn't mean to come

off with the cold comment. You're right. Men *do* feel, so I can only imagine what the brother is going through. Might take him a while, but eventually, he'll be all right."

She peeped at the man driving the car. His mellow response made him seem like so much more than just a cop, Five-O.

"It would be easier if you didn't have to see him all the time, but you do. You'll feel funny, all weirded out when you bump into him; he'll be feeling some type of way . . . carrying a torch and yet having to play it cool. The hard part is when there's a heavy chemical attraction, the woman is gorgeous like you, and you just have to watch her from afar and know somebody else is with her."

Jocelyn turned her body around in her seat and gave Detective Mayfield her full attention. "Sounds like the voice of experience," she said quietly. "How'd you deal with it?"

He stopped suddenly at the yellow light, not trusting his reflexes to blow through it. They both lurched forward. Her question had thrown him for a loop.

"I didn't say I had direct experience like that, just could speculate on what that would be like."

"Oh," she said, her eyes scanning the side of his face. "It just sounded so realistically accurate that I figured only a person who'd gone through something like that could relate."

He kept his eyes on the light. Her voice was like a low-intensity interrogation lamp, making him begin to sweat. He didn't want to talk about Debra, ever. What went down was wrong, and still a tender wound.

"Happened on my job," he said flatly when the light changed. He forced a chuckle; he had to laugh. His mouth was on autopilot for no reason under the moon, but telling this woman the truth seemed like the only thing to do right now. "On Valentine's Day. I had to work; she was off. I begged my partner to ride shotgun with another officer, and to allow one of the rookies to switch with me, just for a few hours, because I couldn't wait to get home early to see her. It was gonna be a surprise. Boy, was I the one who walked in and got a surprise."

Ray let his breath out hard when she said nothing, but simply listened. "I was standing there with flowers in one hand and champagne in the other. Had to talk to myself and just turn around and walk. Still had my gun on me—it could not have ended well. So, he'll get over it. You didn't take him there, and were very, very cool with how you handled it—did it with class. Wish they all did it like that."

She still hadn't spoken, but the look in her eyes said it all. It wasn't pity, just understanding, a gentle knowing that said she hurt as he told her that story.

"So," he said, making his voice take an upbeat turn, "from that day forward, I have always worked Valentine's Day. Every Hallmark holiday, you can find a brother at work."

"Since how long?" she asked, her voice so soft that he'd barely heard her.

"I don't know," he said offhandedly. "A year or two—I lost track."

She pulled her gaze away from his face, and sent it out the window to process what she'd just heard. This tall, handsome, built brother with the deep, sexy voice has been off the market for years because some chick on his job burned him? What was wrong in America? This was a travesty. Her heart was pounding hard, but she wasn't exactly sure why.

"You don't still bump into her, do you?" Jocelyn asked, her tone a shy probe, not wanting to offend—but shoot, she needed info!

"Yeah," he hedged. "From time to time. Since I got promoted, I don't run into her as much. I don't see her the same way I used to, either—I mean, it doesn't mess me up." He shrugged and turned a corner. "Was a time when one glimpse and I'd be done, jacked around, for the rest of the day. Then, one day, I ran into her, and I spoke, she spoke, I walked, and I was cured. Don't ask me how that happens, but that's why I'm saying your professor will live."

She smiled. "I wasn't trying to be an egomaniac, thinking—"

"I know, girl," he said, laughing, "I wasn't taking it that way."

Did he say *girl*, in the I'm-getting-so-comfortable-in-your-presence-that-I-can-drop-the-professional-formality-and-kick-it-with-you-like-we're-from-around-the-same-neighborhood girl? The tone wasn't the same one that would have made her haul any other man's butt into court over a workplace violation. No . . . this was code familiar. Old Philly neighborhood connection stuff. Jocelyn almost slid out of her seat.

"Aw'ight," she countered. "Just so you don't go around thinking I have a big head."

He laughed harder. Did she just slip into comfortable, 'round the way slang on him? This woman was gonna make him stop breathing.

"Listen, we need to start over. I had you collared, brought downtown, run through the wringer, and let you freeze in a silk robe. Can I at least buy you a cheese steak, or a basic dinner and a beer and get you to call me Ray instead of Detective Mayfield—since you just got all in my bizness?" He smiled as she shyly glanced down at her black gloves, and was very pleased that his easy slip into neighborhood patois had made her blush. This woman was something else—a conflict, a dilemma, and a wonderful one at that.

"I'lln't know," she said, keeping the game alive by playfully displaying her colloquial dexterity.

Her bright smile and hearty giggle did him in. Her eyes flashed with mischief. Her mouth was full and lush . . . her teeth perfect. God, she was beautiful. Her warm humor made the smile form inside his chest and work its way back up to his lips.

"They call me Detective when I'm working. Right now, I'm not working. I wanted to give you a ride, *aw'ight, sis*?" he said, adding inflection to the words to make her gorgeous smile widen.

She chuckled. "Then you believe my story that I hate Valentine's Day, and why?"

He extended his fist for her to pound. "I've sworn off of it."

She pounded his fist and laughed harder. "Oh, me, too! I'm done. I almost got arrested on V-Day, okaaaay?"

He shook his head and banged it on the steering wheel. It was absurd. "Can I call you Jocelyn, and apologize, righteous?"

"Hmmm . . . I don't know," she said, putting one finger to her lips. "Had me outside, walking with my tail between my legs, getting read the Riot Act by my professor—who I had to show to the door later in a hurry, when it was all said and done. Then on my job, there's all this follow-up drama to contend with. It might cost you some *scrimps*."

Ray threw his head back and laughed even harder. She had mangled the word *shrimp* to tease him further, saying it like she knew he'd once thought she would. But she'd taken the whole ordeal with such good humor; it only turned him on more . . . a brilliant woman who wasn't stuck-up, had made him bare his soul, who he had run through every acid test and come out with flying colors . . . a caring, kind, sweet beauty who could laugh at life, even the most bizarre aspects of it, and who had a forgiving soul. And packaged like she was packaged, too? Oh, yeah, he'd almost stopped breathing and had to laugh to play it off.

"Scrimps it is, then. There's a Mexican place on Lancaster that does shrimp to the max, or if you want a whole pile of fried, coconut-battered decadence—Chili's is around the corner. Your call?"

Oh . . . the man's voice was awesome when he laughed . . . and his eyes, so intense, but held fun. Some out-of-her-mind sister had thrown him back into the availability pool? Please God, don't let her make a fool of herself. Please! He was stop-your-heart-good-looking . . . seemed honorable, didn't like games. Wasn't arrogant, had a very self-deprecating brand of humor, could be from around the way, and the next moment the quintessence of professional—she'd seen that no-nonsense side under dubious circumstances, true, but he delivered an on-the-job cool without all the mess that went with it. Didn't seem to think he was God's gift to women, had a heart, or why would he have gone underground for years? Her Momma ain't raise no fool.

This brother was upwardly mobile, had a work ethic, had been promoted, and the torch was waning for this chick. Hmmm . . . No. What was she thinking? He could have issues, be secretly gay, have anger-management problems; besides, why would he even think of her as anything more than a potential suspect?

"Wanna go to Zocalo?" she asked, hedging, testing, and hoping he'd want to do the little Mexican restaurant that was quieter and more intimate.

Chapter Eight

He settled back in his chair and sipped a Corona with a lime from the bottle, totally disinterested in the shrimp being prepared. Soft light framed her, hugged her close like her delicate pink sweater hugged every curve. No wonder his boy had lost professional distance—was it possible to maintain such a thing in Jocelyn Jefferson's presence? Yet there was something so classy about her that a man had to take his time and be very careful not to offend. It was almost too disorienting to watch her take dainty sips from a beer bottle, too. Everything about her was disorienting.

He'd also seen too much, as well . . . her hair tussled all over her head, a flaming red silk kimono precariously wrapped around her body. He watched her fingers clasp the bottle . . . little pink hearts drew his attention and made him remember her red pedicure with the reverse pattern on her smooth, pretty toes. He could also remember her hyperventilating, but definitely had to shake that sound out of his head—sounded too close to something that was waaay too early to consider. But as he listened to her light banter, and as her voice coated his insides, the more he felt the years of no affection making him stupid.

Then they messed up and brought the plates. She'd selected a spicy concoction of shrimp in a black bean sauce, and he had to watch her eat it and lick the oozing gravy from her full mouth . . . dip her finger in the corner of it to pick out a shrimp, toss her hair out of the way and bite it over her plate to spare her pastel pink top. That's when he stopped breathing, for real. His fork was moving from his plate to his mouth on automatic, but as good as the food was, he couldn't taste a thing. Wasn't sure what he'd even ordered. He was just glad he had a napkin in his lap.

She knew she was talking too much, just running her mouth a mile a minute, a nervous habit she'd had ever since she was a kid. She'd become so flustered watching his intense, dark-brown eyes and the slow, methodical way he brought his fork up to his sexy mouth that she'd forgotten her table manners completely—just swiped a shrimp from the edge of her plate! Have mercy.

Maybe it was the way the muscles moved in his arm under his sweater; she had to make her eyes stop scanning his broad shoulders and the tight bicep bulge created when the fork left the plate and moved toward his mouth . . . what a mouth . . . even, white teeth, a hint of a gap, moist but not wet. She had to stop getting mesmerized and then going into a breathless, bungling, run-on account of her crazy life experiences. This man didn't care about her entire life from grade school to grandmom . . . she had to breathe, she had to breathe, she had to breathe; a sip of Corona helped, but not much.

"So, tell me about you," she finally said, refusing to blow this evening by being a chatterbox.

"Not much to tell," he said, smiling around the mouth of his beer bottle.

She could barely find the table to set her beer down; her eyes wouldn't leave his face. Couldn't. She watched his Adam's apple bob in his throat . . . three years of no male attention was making her fray at the seams. "C'mon," she said, her voice working its way out in an unwanted plea. "I've been going on and on this whole dinner."

He set his bottle down very carefully and twirled it slowly at the edge of the table. "There's really not much to tell, other than our families are a lot alike. My pop passed away early, like yours did, although I had a bunch of brothers and sisters—but our mothers are the same, both strict." He smiled. "There's no big secrets, or anything like that." He looked at her intensely. "But I was thoroughly enjoying hearing your voice. You'll make a good social policy activist, Dr. Jefferson." He raised his bottle and clinked it against hers. "Takes heart and a lot of discipline to make it as far as you did, as fast. I admire that."

All she could do was stare at him. No other man she'd ever met had made such a simple but profound admission. She saw genuine pride and respect in his eyes, and needed to pinch herself to be sure she wasn't dreaming. His acceptance didn't seem laced with fraud, or insecurity, or any yang that could cause relationship terminal illness . . . and when her mind had made the quantum leap from a mere apology date to a relationship, she wasn't sure, but was very sure at the moment how much that didn't matter.

However, there was such a thing as protocol. If she wanted him to stay around, then it seemed unwise to just jump the man's bones tonight—though, if he'd asked . . . She straightened herself with a smile, clinked his bottle in return, and murmured, "Thank you." It was supposed to come out casual and upbeat, but she'd breathed the words, and was about to die.

But the response really wasn't her fault. This man was awesome. Was so laid-back cool, no pressure, respectful, and seemed to be a good sport about all her madcap drama surrounding his career-case. Her hands fell away from the bottle she was clutching and she folded them neatly in her lap.

If she wasn't such a lady, he would have called for the check and just boldly asked her to come back to his place. If Jocelyn Jefferson breathed another sexy statement, they'd have to mop him up off the floor. But since she was a lady, a classy one at that . . . and since he wanted more than that from her, he wasn't gonna act a fool.

"You want some coffee, an espresso, some dessert, uh, maybe an after-dinner liqueur?" He was babbling, had to regain his composure. She shook her head as a polite decline. He had to back up and not press her for more of her time. But if she'd allow him to, he'd soak it all up tonight. He'd gotten lucky; she'd agreed to come along with him this far. Cool had long since gone. She was drop-dead, smack yo' Momma fine. She had told him her life story with those big, innocent brown eyes, no games, just laughing easy and talking sweet. And then something struck her, and she felt it—he saw it, the same current that ran down his spine.

How could he speak, remember the past, and string together coherent sentences when she made him feel this way? How in the hell did he know what he liked, did as a kid, music, huh, sports, oh yeah, b-ball, sisters' and brothers' names—not sure right through here, favorite what? Irrelevant, he'd tell her later. But oh, man, her eyes. That was his favorite thing right now—happened real fast, too.

She had gotten this look on her face that, for a fleeting second, told him the wild thought of passion had run through her mind. He was a contender. Her eyes told him that. She was considering next moves. It was written all over her face, or was it only his wishful thinking? But how did a brother read the signs and know for sure? She got all nervous, couldn't look at him for a moment, cheeks flushed. Oh dear God, don't let him make a wrong move, or not make the right movc when it could be made. Then again, he wasn't just trying to make a move or play some game—she was a keeper.

"If you want something else, I might dip my fork into the edge of yours, though."

"Huh?" Dazed, he felt like lightning had struck him. "I mean, sure." His hands were practically trembling as he grabbed the dessert menu and studied it real hard. "Chocolate mousse, cheesecake, uh, what do you like—I'll share, but don't want to eat it all myself." He was babbling again—no woman had ever just robbed his cool like this.

He slid the menu toward her, and her warm hand brushed his as she accepted it, leaving a burn in its wake. She hesitated, glanced up and held his line of vision. "Are you really hungry?"

He looked at her without blinking, his mind processing a hundred responses at once. Did she mean what her voice sounded like she meant, or was she asking whether or not he was digestively challenged? Okay, okay, okay, man, be cool.

"If you want something, I'm down," he said with a shrug. He let the statement hang in the air between them.

He'd made the comment with such a low, sensual resonance that she almost shuddered. Did he mean what his voice sounded like he meant, or was he being polite and asking her about her choice of desserts? Okay okay, okay, remember what your momma taught you—be a lady at all times and do not grab this man by the front of his sweater and put your tongue down his throat.

"I confess, Officer. Chocolate is my weakness." She laughed and pushed the menu back across the table.

Was she flirting with him? Did she just drop her guard and make a tender offer—or did the woman want the mousse? He hailed the waiter, not sure what was politically correct right now, and placed their order. But there must have been something in the thick vibe surrounding them that made the waiter return with one dish and two spoons.

They both stared at the silverware and the delicate dessert between them. The challenge was going to be establishing the right protocol of sharing a dessert with a new person without making the consumption seem too sexy, too forward, but just sexy enough to let it be known there was definite chemistry.

"It looks real good," he murmured, not looking at the dessert, but staring at her.

"It does, doesn't it?" She released a sigh and picked up her spoon, allowing it to hover over the small bowl of pudding-like substance without taking her eyes from his. "It's so pretty, so perfect, I'm not sure where to begin. I'd hate to mess it up." She allowed the tip of her spoon to drag along some of the raspberry sauce, hitting the mint leaf and coming to rest against the swirl of whipped cream topping.

He swallowed hard. "Plunge right in. It's gonna be good going down and be messed up when we're all done, anyway."

She swallowed hard. "I like to pick around the edges, though . . . just break off a little of the dark chocolate cup. There's an art to eating good chocolate."

His lids lowered by a fraction, and all he could do was nod, pick up his spoon, and break the side of the cup. "This edge is broke down bad, now." He motioned with his spoon toward the decimated side of the dessert and smiled. "If you don't hurry up, all the good stuff is gonna ooze out."

He watched her smile and lower her eyes, then take a small dip of the mousse with her spoon. Her graceful hand had a slight tremor to it that ran all through him. When she placed her spoon in her mouth, closed her eyes, and released a satisfied sound, he almost lost it. Oh, yeah, he might have to act foolish tonight.

"You have to try this," she murmured.

He wasn't sure how to respond, and hesitated.

"Don't you like chocolate?" she pressed now, seeming concerned.

"Love it," he said, low in his throat.

"Then have some," she said with a warm smile, taking a more liberal amount on her spoon. "C'mon," she teased. "Don't you want some?"

"I definitely want some, but I'm trying to be a gentleman and let you get yours first."

They both stared at each other for a moment. She swallowed away a smile. He saw it; she knew he saw it. Until she smiled, he wasn't sure if the loaded statement had crossed the line. Okay, now what?

She set her spoon down and chuckled. "You're missing out, brother. And I do appreciate the chivalrous stance, but chocolate is chocolate. Just dip your spoon in and enjoy before I eat it all and leave you hanging."

He laughed, and a much-needed release of tension wafted through him as he put a huge glob on his spoon and shoved it into his mouth. "See, I warned you. I know me. I'm an extremist—once I get started, you'll have to go for what you know."

She leaned in and scooped a huge glob onto her spoon and laughed, covering her mouth. "I'm an only child and selfish. Oh, I'll get mine. Not to worry." She dodged his spoon, shot-blocking it with hers, and dipped hers under it. "Strategy, patience—see what I mean?" she said, placing another spoonful in her mouth.

By the time they'd finished, they were laughing like little kids, fighting over the remains and spoon-battling with each other. He couldn't remember laughing that hard with a woman and yet being so turned on at the same time. Her mouth was sticky, her fingers gooey from snatching at melting shavings to best him in the challenge. His were all messy, too, and they laughed out loud as she glanced over her shoulder like a thief, and quickly sucked the chocolate off her fingers.

That was it, the thing that made him call for the check. He didn't care. She didn't seem too appalled by the move. His car was right out front by a meter; her place was around the corner. His boy Marcus could go to hell; he'd seen her first, had called his friend in to keep her out of harm's way. Marc even had first shot—and blew it at a fancy lunch, talking rhetoric. The fact remained, she was holding onto *his* arm, laughing her way out of the restaurant and licking her fingers . . . all from a reasonable dinner at an out-of-the-way joint. Women, go figure, but he wasn't trying to go home alone tonight.

Of all the possible hookups in the world, of all the craziest collisions of chance meetings, she would never in a hundred years have expected this. She was laughing to keep from crying. Had to lick her fingers as a poor substitute for the fantastic, rock-hard, semisweet chocolate that was escorting her to his car. Momma never told her there'd be days like this, or nights when three fine, eligible bachelors would rush her for a little affection. But hey, what was a girl to do?

As she climbed into the navy-blue Crown Victoria, she suddenly became aware of just how good the man smelled. It was something beyond the earthy cologne . . . something all male that made her fight the urge to snuggle up next to him and breathe him in.

"Thank you so much for a great time, even though you *are* a cop."

He laughed and gave her a jaunty wink. "I'm off duty, remember?"

"Yeah," she said with a satisfied sigh. "Since I'm no longer a suspect . . . would you like to come up for a coffee?"

Now they both knew good and well that they'd just left a restaurant where every coffee imaginable was served. So it stood to reason that more than coffee was being offered. He just wasn't sure how much or how far, but he was definitely down to find out. Just one kiss would be enough, right now, and he was fairly certain that she wasn't ready for the main course . . . she didn't strike him that way. So, he wouldn't push her like that. But he wouldn't mind seeing her space, coming away with a kiss or two, a date for tomorrow night, a chance to move a little closer to the next level . . . God, she was blowing his mind.

"Yeah . . ." he said slowly, his smile feeling too wide as it spread on his face from her heat. He looked at his sticky fingers. "And I probably need to wash my hands."

They both laughed.

Chapter Nine

She dropped her keys twice, fumbling with the door. Dating etiquette raced through her mind. What was protocol, and according to whom? She tried not to seem nervous and to keep her conversation light and airy as she opened her door and they went up the steps. *It had been more than three years*. There had to be some clemency in that. The dating pundits would have to forgive her, because this man had her dangerously on the edge of propriety.

But she would be cool, she told herself. She tried not to wig as he crossed her threshold. She hadn't had a man in her apartment *for years*. What was the procedure? The magazines were at odds—the more racy articles suggested just letting the inner tigress out. The more conservative ones said, not on the first date. Her momma's advice went out with high-button shoes, but did it? Her girlfriends were no help; they even contradicted themselves.

"Okay, this is it," she announced.

The look on his face was somewhere between sucker-punched and open desire. When his full lips parted and he began inhaling through his mouth at the same time his eyes went to half-mast, she knew she had to clarify fast.

"My humble little abode," she quickly corrected. She did a comical pirouette in the middle of the floor, thoroughly flustered that he'd taken what she'd said the wrong way—or maybe the right way; either way, it came out a little too direct. "You can hang your coat there, the kitchen is that way, or if you want to wash your hands in the bathroom, it's that way. Oh, let me take your coat. You hungry—no, we just ate. Uh, coffee. Right. Coffee."

She watched him slowly unzip his bomber jacket and lower his head as though trying not to burst out laughing.

"Jocelyn, coffee is fine. I can find my way to the bathroom."

"Good!" she said too loudly. "I'll make coffee, okay?"

He nodded, chuckled softly, and walked through her living room. She almost passed out when he left the room, and she grabbed onto the coatrack to keep from falling down. Idiot! How could she sound so lame?

She snatched off her coat and flung it on the rack, tugged her sweater down, and made a mad dash for the kitchen. Where was her coffee? She yanked open cabinets, frantically searching in them like she'd been robbed. Jocelyn froze. This could not be happening. The post-party recovery had exhausted her supply. Supply—oh, Lawd . . . she had no supplies in case of emergency . . . If this tall hunk busted a romantic move and swept her off her feet, her medicine cabinet was bare. No birth control! Everything had gone in the trash with the last bogus boyfriend and was history. Ancient history.

Anything that might have been salvaged from Sue-Lin's erotic product dealer had been either taken downtown for evidence, or thrown in a garbage bag by her professor. She almost groaned out loud.

Jocelyn peered at the two huge black bags tied up and leaning against the lower cabinets by the trash, and cringed. A small part of her had momentarily considered ripping through the carnage to salvage a prewrapped condom, but she counted to ten and got her mind right. Now how would that look? Digging through post-party refuse like a drug addict for supplies just to get with this absolutely fabulous man? Her hands were shaking; she wrapped her arms about herself. She was not going there. But her eyes never left the trash. Would she? No. Definitely not protocol. Three years . . . Maybe. No, Jocelyn Jefferson, where is your pride?

When he walked back into the living room, she almost jumped out of her skin. She didn't know what to do, and an awkward apology stumbled to her lips.

"I'm so, so, so sorry," she said, half ready to laugh, half ready to cry. Unwittingly, she began wringing her hands and peering at him through the pass-through. "See, what had happened was, I thought I had something in here, and I don't. I . . . it's been so long—coffee was on my market list—but I didn't expect to have company, and uh . . . uh, I'm—"

"Jocelyn," he said gently. "It's all right. You weren't expecting me to just fall by, and I understand." His smile was warm and friendly, but his eyes burned with a silent intensity. "This was spur of the moment, and happened kinda fast. Neither one of us is prepared."

She closed her eyes, trying to stop the ringing in her ears. She'd heard him loud and clear, both the spoken and unspoken message contained in his meaning. Although it was disappointing, it was so very endearing to know that he wasn't the kind of guy that just kept a stash in his wallet. Oh, yeah, big brownie points. This man was nice, on top of it all. Charming, to make matters worse. A real gentleman, which oddly cut her heart out and made her want him all the more. Her father had to be looking down from heaven, laughing his natural behind off.

Jocelyn wrapped her arms around herself again and stared at the floor. She couldn't get this whole dating game thing down to save her life. She'd never be a domestic diva like her mother, a carefree sex kitten like Tina, or a sultry temptress like Freddie, and forget ever holding a candle to Jacqui, the love goddess. Four older fairy godmothers had even tried to come to her rescue, and all she'd managed to do was get arrested.

Ray's tall figure cast a shadow in the kitchen doorframe; the only saving grace was the man seemed to take her kookiness in stride and had the decency to still have a gentle smile on his face. When he neared her, he placed a finger under her chin and made her look up. No "date" had ever done something that tender, and so easily, to her in all her life.

He didn't know where to begin. He wasn't sure what he could say to help her relax. He'd been so overwhelmed by her presence that he hadn't even taken off his firearm, which now weighed heavily in its shoulder harness. He was blowing this whole thing with her, big-time. Hadn't dated in so long that he wasn't sure what the rules of engagement were anymore. It was clear this whole thing was moving too fast when he'd reentered the room and she'd looked like a deer caught in the headlights. And why that meant so much to him, he wasn't even sure. But it did. Just as her clumsy way of telling him she'd changed her mind and was out of coffee made all the difference in the world.

It drew him to her from a place well above his belt buckle, and made his arms enfold her . . . made his eyes slide closed, and the sensation of her warmth tilted his head so that he could rest his cheek on the top of her head. "We'll get coffee, maybe if you feel like it, the next time we go out. Cool?" He felt her body begin to relax and her arms slowly unfold as she nodded.

"I thought I had coffee in here, you know, and then . . . I didn't."

He kissed the crown of her head. Couldn't help himself, and her hair smelled so good. Was dark honey velvet, just as he'd imagined. "It's all right. I can wait till later."

He was rewarded by her warmth that molded against him in a perfect fit.

"Really?" she whispered. "You're not disappointed?"

He looked at her and shook his head no, devastated by what she offered instead that was so much more than just her body. "Uh-uh. Not at all."

"I really like you," she said quietly, touching the side of his face with the tips of her fingers. "I hope you'll come back for coffee soon."

"I really do like you, too, Jocelyn Jefferson," he murmured. "You're a rare find. I'll be back for that—soon, if you want me to . . . trust me."

He waited, let her find his mouth, not pressuring her, and allowing her to decide. She took his mouth with such a tender question in her eyes that he offered his return kiss to her softly and let her slowly explore it, not demanding. But as her tongue timidly tangled with his, and found soft tissue that hadn't yielded to another's for so long, her gentle ministrations sent a shudder through him that heaven and earth couldn't have stopped.

His hands ached to slide down her shoulders and find that dip in her back that gave rise to her luscious bottom. Only a thin thread of restraint kept him from pulling out of the kiss, deeply inhaling her hair, and running his fingers all through it. She felt so good against him, a burning, handcrafted fit. Her skin was so soft, he could only imagine the heat of it belly to belly. When her breasts pressed against his chest, he could feel every texture beneath her fuzzy pink sweater down to her pouting nipples, and it made his sting, fired the entire surface of his skin with need, and stole his breath.

Her skirt was hitching up on the zipper of his pants as she leaned against him, still stealing his breath, making it almost impossible to focus on walking out the door. He wanted to move against her in a rhythm denied for too long, but he tried not to offend, or drive himself insane by starting what he wasn't going to finish. However, her kiss was unraveling his intentions and stifling a moan as her pelvis swept across the throbbing ache within his. He had to go.

He gently pulled back but held her upper arms firmly. "I should probably go . . . and I'll bring coffee the next time I come over, or we go out. Cool?"

She nodded, breathing hard, which was really messing with his mind. He didn't want to leave, but definitely couldn't stay—not in this condition. He was no longer making sense.

"I'll have coffee the next time you come over, I promise." She raked her fingers through her hair and closed her eyes. "Count on it."

He remained frozen where he stood. The look on her face was making it impossible to leave. "I can run out and get some, and come back . . . if you want me to?"

She stared up at him for what felt like a long time. The pained expression on his face was doing something to the rational side of her brain. The man was speaking in jags and halts, but had backed up. He'd felt like hot concrete against her, and she didn't want even a sliver of cold air to come between them to stop the sensation. Her mouth ached for want of the lost kiss. Common sense dictated that a decision had to be made. He held a plea in his eyes, the same one that had imploded between her thighs and strummed an argument to hurry up and go get coffee—black, strong, no sugar.

"There's a 7-Eleven around the corner."

He nodded. "I'll take out your trash on the way out, and will be back in a minute."

This man was gonna take out her trash? Oh, this one was a keeper.

"Take out my trash," she whispered with a low chuckle, "and I'll be forced to marry you."

He brushed her mouth with a kiss, and reached for the filled bags resting against the lower cabinets. "I'll be back . . . with coffee for the morning."

Ohmigod, did he mean morning, as in, he'd be back tomorrow? Or, morning as in, baby-I'll-rock-your-world-all-night-until-we-need-coffee-in-the-morning? She couldn't breathe. She was about to hyperventilate. Raymond Mayfield had better get his butt back here in five minutes, or she'd die.

Jocelyn closed her eyes, leaned against the wall, and only listened as he crossed the room, set the heavy bags down, and put on his coat. She couldn't watch his body move anymore, too painful; 7-Eleven felt like it was in Russia somewhere. When the door slammed, she clutched her stomach. Her mind was on one track, processing the vibration from the hard jar that sent a tremor through the plaster into her spine as a touch.

It took her a few moments to push herself away from the counter and begin walking toward the bedroom. She flipped on the stereo and selected her most evocative CDs. They were both past the point of no return; she'd have to figure out the error of her ways tomorrow. But one thing for sure—she had to keep moving to work off the nervous energy he produced.

She glanced at the telephone as she passed it. The message light was blinking an omen, but she already knew who'd called. Her AWOL girlfriends had finally made contact. Her mother would be on the line thanking her for the flower delivery as a ruse to grill her about her Valentine's exploits and to offer a healthy dose of guilt. They would *all* have to wait. Semisweet dark chocolate was about to be delivered in a package that she'd only dreamt of. The bow around it was awesome, and she'd enjoy unwrapping it very slowly. Death by chocolate—she could live with that.

The doorbell sounded, and she literally ran for the intercom, breathless. She didn't even ask the standard 'who is it' question. Her body was on fire.

Jocelyn depressed the buzzer with her eyes closed and dabbed the thin sheen of perspiration that had formed on her brow. She ignored the telephone as it began to ring—not tonight. Her girls could wait, so could her momma. When the buzzer sounded a second time, she leaned on it. This man *had* to come back and finish what he'd started.

This woman had entered his nervous system so hard and so fast that he might as well have been in a prizefight with no headgear on. He was taking out her trash, ready to put down roots and turn in his bachelor's badge for good. Sucker-punched, he was down for the count, tasting canvas, was seeing double and still had a buzz ringing in his ears. This was *the one*. Happened just like that. Knew all he needed to know about this woman, who was as beautiful on the inside as she was on the outside. A man was not a complex being—didn't women know that? Basic. But it was too crazy that the only woman he'd trusted like this was the only one he'd arrested. The irony was not lost on him at all.

Ray walked to the side of the building with effort and dropped the bags. The buzz was getting louder, just like his need to be in Jocelyn's arms was getting stronger every second that passed. He hauled the bags into the Dumpster and tried to shake the incessant buzzing out of his head. Damn, he'd never experienced anything like this. Jocelyn Jefferson almost made him propose with two bags of garbage in his fists. Whew! He had to get it together.

He straightened his back and breathed in the cold night air. When he returned to her apartment, he needed to be cool. Take it slow, not just drop a box on her nightstand and go for broke. But she'd produced vertigo, had made him ache so badly that he could barely walk. Yet, there was something buzzing . . . and it wasn't coming from inside his head.

Raymond glanced around and then followed the sound. Against his better judgment, he pushed the Dumpster out a bit with a grunt, and listened. He stooped and reached out his hand and began clearing away a few pieces of stray paper on top of dirty snow, following the sound, and his hand came in contact with vibrating, icy metal. Police instinct kicked in. He used a glove to pick up the object and then peered up at Jocelyn's back deck and over to the attached fire escape. A very bad feeling worked him.

A cell phone. He groaned at the find. True, it was just what he and his partner needed, but not as much as he needed Jocelyn at the moment. His hip was vibrating and he glanced down at the incoming call.

"Yeah, Raul. What's up, man?"

"The four old dolls checked out. They weren't in it. Just came over to do a pamper party, like they'd said. So, we know a friend of a friend that these ladies didn't know must have invited Phat and Smooth to the mêlée. Maybe one of their girlfriends came by, just wanted a ride to wherever, and they musta fell by to pick up their women only because it was Valentine's Day—but I don't think there's a connection."

Ray stood and looked down at the telephone. Valentine's Day was killing him. While that was great news, *the timing sucked*. "Cool," he said flatly.

"You don't sound excited, Holmes," Raul said, laughing. "I catch you at a bad time?"

"Yeah. Real bad time."

"Thought you didn't do the whole Valentine's Day thing."

"It's the day after, man, listen . . . I'm kinda in a hurry, but I found a cell phone dropped behind a Dumpster." Raymond glanced up at the trajectory, trying to wrest back his detective logic. "Seems like in the flight from our boys in uniform at the front door, somebody lost or tossed a phone and kept moving. But the fact that it keeps ringing leads me to believe that they lost it, and they aren't sure where it is. If it was an intentional ditch, they'd have a new one by now, would have told their inside contacts not to call it, and the phone would be dead metal, feel me?"

"You need to bring that piece of gold in pronto, man. We can get our boys in Forensics to dust it, break down the code, and pull everything off it—calls, speed-dial numbers, and—"

"I know, I know," Ray muttered, looking up at Jocelyn's window, ready to bay at it.

"Where'd you find it?"

Ray closed his eyes. "Off the fire escape behind Jocelyn Jefferson's building."

"Then definitely bring that home to Poppa, man. Hopefully it'll help clear those ladies and lead us to anybody who's been in regular contact with our boyz."

"I'm on my way," Raymond said in a weary tone. "I just have to make a call first."

Jocelyn stood with the door open and her jaw slack. It took a moment for her mind to sync up with the image standing before her. Wrong man, right attitude. Oh, no!

"Professor Bryant?"

"Jocelyn, I thought about what you said, and just . . . I just . . ." He handed her a bunch of wildflowers that had been held so tightly, the stems were crushed and sweaty.

Her doorbell sounded and she absently depressed the buzzer to let Ray in. A second set of footfalls made her and Ben Bryant both turn around. She blinked twice and opened her mouth. An attorney was standing in her doorway with a bottle of champagne in his grip.

"I'm sorry. I tried to call first," Marcus said, scowling at Benjamin Bryant. "I didn't realize you had company, or that your father had stopped by." He extended his hand toward the professor. "Marcus Dorchester, sir. Attorney at law."

The professor looked down at the extended hand but didn't shake it. "I'm not her father, Mr. Dorchester. And you definitely should have called first."

She watched in utter horror as the two men bristled, instantly understood but misunderstood, and stepped back from each other like gunfighters.

"Oh," Marcus said curtly, and then thrust the bottle toward Jocelyn. "I see. Next time I will definitely be sure to call, make voice contact, and arrange for *an appointment*. Have a good night." He turned on his heels before she could say a word, and was gone.

Professor Bryant looked her up and down with a glare. "All you had to do was be honest with me, Jocelyn. I thought we both shared enough respect for each other not to play games. If you had some young suitor and preferred a purely carnal liaison, that's all you had to say." With that, he thrust the flowers at her, waiting until she accepted them, and turned on his heels and left, slamming the door.

Her phone was ringing off the hook, but she couldn't move. She glanced at her watch. Raymond should have been back by now—7-Eleven was a five-minute spin around the corner, and at this time of night, traffic was nonexistent. Twenty minutes had elapsed since he'd left on a mission. She closed her eyes and dropped the flowers on the coffee table and set the bottle of bubbly down very slowly. He saw them, had to, but didn't understand, and all she had was his work number—and he was definitely not there.

Jocelyn flopped down on the sofa and grabbed the phone. Just as she suspected, her girlfriends' voice mail messages prattled on. Apology after apology filled her ear, but she wasn't listening. Jacqui was having a post-date pity party—things didn't go well when the guy didn't call the next morning. Jocelyn skipped to the next message. Freddie was having an emotional meltdown because—the guy didn't call the next day. Jocelyn sighed and fast-forwarded. Tina hadn't called, which meant maybe one of her girls had gotten lucky. Her mother's voice felt like fingernails down a blackboard, but for some unknown reason, she felt like calling her mother back.

She stopped the message retrieval, knowing that she'd only hear the professor's forlorn voice, maybe a panting attorney, and her last girlfriend, who was still out in the wind. As she dialed her mother's number, it annoyed her no end that not one of her friends had heard her very real SOS, acknowledged her pamper-party blues—except to say that, in hindsight, they should have come there, given the circumstances of their dates. That wasn't the point! They should have honored the friendship, and come regardless.

The only quirky silver lining to the whole cloudy fiasco had been meeting Raymond Mayfield. But now even he was history. The rest of the messages could wait till morning, or maybe even until she came home from work. They'd made *her* wait, so now *they* could wait. By the time she connected with her mother's voice, Jocelyn was grinding her teeth.

"The flowers were beautiful, honey," her mother cooed. "You always remember."

"I love you, Mom," she said, staring out the window, waiting for the familiar turn of conversation.

"When I didn't hear from you last night, I got hopeful," her mother said, singsonging the word *hopeful*.

"It was a wild night, Ma. What can I tell you?"

There was a pause. Jocelyn sighed. She hadn't meant her tone to sound so acidic, but her mind and body were still trying to process significant disappointment, and her mom was getting on her last nerve.

"Oh, well, that's a very different story than you normally tell me," her mother said, her voice containing a mixture of curiosity and admonishment. "I hope he treats you nice and with respect, and showed you––"

"Here's the details," Jocelyn said, cutting her mother off as she stood and walked with the telephone. "I met him at a Valentine's Day party, but have known him a long time—almost three years. Last night I got a mink coat, the next day a dozen roses, was taken to lunch at an expensive restaurant, and then to dinner tonight. He came back here for coffee, but left like a gentleman."

"What!" her mother shrieked excitedly. "What does he do for a living?"

"He's a professor, and a man with a law degree, and works downtown as a detective hunting drug dealers. He's tall, dark, and very, very handsome. He has a baritone voice that runs all through me. But I haven't been to bed with him. He's kind, considerate, and respectful, and wears a gun to his job. Can you deal with that, Mom?"

"Oh dear Lord, child! Marry that man!"

Jocelyn chuckled and shook her head. The blend of three staved off her mother's probing Inquisition. "He just left—I have to go lie down before I fall down. My virtue is intact, but my mind is blown, okay? I just wanted to call to say I love you, and so you wouldn't worry. But I really can't talk about this anymore right now, all right?"

"Oh, baby, I understand," her mother cooed. "You just go on and lie down and rest your mind and your nerves. Make some tea and keep your resolve, and he'll be back time and again, and will marry you—I promise. That's just how it happened for me and your father."

Jocelyn just looked at the telephone.

Chapter Ten

Jocelyn walked into the job so mean and so irritable that she barely even muttered *good morning* to Gail. She hadn't slept a wink, had tossed and turned all night over a man who was definitely gone for good. Stupid! The only thing that made up for it was a devilish thing she couldn't resist doing. It was a childish prank, bad form, but they all got on her nerves.

So God would just have to forgive her for e-mailing Professor Bryant a nice picture of Jacqui. And Jacqui would just have to forgive her for sending a 2 A.M. message with a handsome professor's pic from a campus event along with some sage insight into the man's character . . . just like Freddie would have to just give her a friendship pass on the insanity that had attacked her brain when she sent a photo of a fine attorney off his Web site to her. Sending Freddie's pic to him seemed like a good thing to do at the time, too. But now that it was morning, it was ridiculous. All she knew was, she wanted all these drama kings and queens off her phone, out of her hair, and to back off. Even her mom . . . especially her mom.

"Whooo-weee!" Gail whispered and gave Jocelyn the eye as she passed her desk. "Look what the cat dragged in. Gurl, you look fried."

"I'm beat. Don't start."

"He rocked your world good again, didn't he?"

Jocelyn let her breath out hard and began walking.

"Don't you want your flowers, though?"

"No," Jocelyn said, glancing at the huge spray of orchids, irises, and exotic ferns.

Gail was on her feet. "Chile, are you nuts? Read this card!"

Jocelyn had to laugh, even through her evilness. There was something about Gail that just radiated mischievous sunshine. "Tell me what's in my card that you've already opened, then."

"Listen," Gail said in a conspiratorial tone. "This one's got it bad. It says, 'Dear Jocelyn, Thank you for the best time I've had in years. I'm sorry about what happened. Tried to call, but understand why you might not want to talk. I couldn't help it. I had to leave after things came up so fast and messed up our flow. I'll make it up to you tonight, if you'll let me. We'll start over and take it slow. I'll bring coffee for the morning, if you still want me to.'"

Jocelyn stood very, very still.

"Gurl," Gail said, coming in close and squeezing her arm and talking under her breath a mile a minute. "You cannot blame the man for getting overly passionate and having a premature ejaculation after you whipped the wild thing down on him and blew his mind! Take it as a compliment, especially when he sends flowers the next day to apologize!" She looked over her shoulder as though a SWAT team was about to barge into their conversation. "Call the man and be nice!"

Jocelyn's hand covered her mouth. She nodded without explaining the confusion to Gail and raced for her desk. Her headset was on before her boss got to her desk. She nodded at Margaret and prayed she'd simply pass by. The other ladies were giving her thumbs-up from behind gray, padded panels. Her fingers were speed-dialing without the aid of technology. She listened intently to the messages on her home phone and closed her eyes. He'd called!

Raymond paced behind his desk like a caged tiger. He had to get out from this processing bull and go down to Seventeenth and Market, or lose his mind. She hadn't called. Hadn't acknowledged the flowers. Criminals were in lockup, but he was the one who felt caged.

"You all right, man?" Raul asked, holding two cups of coffee. "Maybe you'd better switch to orange juice in the mornings."

Ray stared at the cup of abandoned java on the edge of his desk . . . Everything reminded him of her. Coffee . . . extra sweet, a dash of cream. "Man, is Cap done with us yet? I mean, I have to run an errand."

His partner just looked at him. "You know the drill. Probably won't be done with the initial processing till noon, then we have to powwow with the DA, and—"

"Yeah, yeah, like about two o'clock, this should be a wrap, right?"

"Brother, you look like—"

"I know what I look like," Raymond shouted, making heads turn. He mellowed his next response. "I'm just tired, haven't slept all night. We were out in the streets till almost four, and I need some head-space, feel me?"

Raul just smiled. "How about if I handle the paperwork and see if we can get the DA to move up the meeting by a coupla hours?"

When the reception desk buzzed her, Jocelyn pushed away from her desk with a grunt. All attempts to contact Detective Ray Mayfield had rolled over to damnable voice mail. But she kept calling it and hanging up, just to hear his wonderful voice intermittently throughout the morning.

She trudged down the narrow aisle toward the lobby. If Gail had only buzzed, it wasn't a 9-1-1 male emergency, and probably just one of her girls who had come for lunch to fuss at her or cry in her cappuccino.

But as she neared the entrance to the lobby, she could see the profile on Gail's face. Her receptionist buddy was looking forward, eyes wide, mouth hanging open. Jocelyn sped up her pace, and then stopped.

A very clean-shaven Raymond Mayfield was standing there, oozing the essence of fine. He'd changed, had on a thick, winter-white, cable knit sweater beneath his brown leather bomber jacket, and charcoal slacks with a crease in them so sharp it could have cut a sister. She could catch the faint drift of an expensive men's cologne from where she stood, and had to fight with her knees, willing them not to buckle. Under his arm was a large, oblong white box that said *roses*, loud and clear. Serious florist roses, not from the stand I just happened to pass by, roses. He wasn't wearing a weapon, either.

"I, uh, didn't know if you had plans for lunch, and shouldn't have presumed," he said quietly, "but things got messed up, and was wondering, even if you didn't have time for a full lunch, maybe you'd put these in some water and have coffee with me?" His eyes held hers for a moment, and then he looked at the flowers that had not been collected from the reception desk. "But I can't blame you if you don't want to," he said, carefully sliding the box of roses onto the receptionist's desk.

"Oh, she's going to lunch," Gail said, jumping into the middle of things. "These were only left up here because our cubes in the back aren't big enough to properly display them, hon. I was enjoying them till she took them home, but she needs a ride home to take all these beautiful flowers with her—the bus ain't gonna work, maybe you could give her a lift?"

"Gail, please, girl—"

"I'd be happy to take her home," he said, his eyes holding Jocelyn for ransom. "Any time she wants to go."

Gail shook her head. "Chile, get your coat. I got Margaret covered."

This time, Jocelyn didn't argue. She got her coat, said nary a word, and kept walking until she was by Raymond's side. He didn't say a word as he opened the door for her and pressed the elevator button. A strong arm slipped around her waist when the door closed. Quiet nestled between them as the elevator filled floor by floor with the lunchtime crowd. She had heard his long messages, each one becoming a little more intense in explanation.

"I got your messages," he murmured as they exited on the first floor. "Seems things always look one way but are another when it comes to you and me, huh?"

She nodded and smiled as she looked at his navy-blue Crown Victoria that was double-parked haphazardly, in the middle of the day, blocking a lane of traffic on Market street, flashers on, official business shield in the window. Oh, yeah, this was a 9-1-1 emergency.

"Coffee, my place?" she asked, breathing the question as he opened the door and she slid into the seat.

"Thought you'd never ask, but brought some with me just in case."

She gripped the oblong box of flowers as her gaze remained fastened beyond the window. Buildings and pedestrians seemed to blur by while he maneuvered his car through the thick midday traffic as though on the way to a crime scene. How could she look at him, really, once she'd spied a sheer plastic drugstore bag on the back seat filled with a can of coffee, a small box of sugar, some Half-n-Half, and a discreetly double-bagged package of condoms? His line of vision was straight ahead—a man on an obvious mission.

By the time he'd pulled into a parking space near her building, she'd almost dented the box from clutching it so tightly. Her voice failed her as he turned in his seat and gazed at her for a moment before speaking. The intensity in his eyes told her what words could never convey. His question left the decision up to her, but his spine-melting gaze didn't.

"You wanna go for lunch," he murmured softly, "or coffee?"

She glanced at the package in the backseat. He held his breath.

"Coffee."

He let out his breath and closed his eyes. "Okay. I brought some."

His hands were gripping the steering wheel so tightly that all she could do was reach out and cover one of them with a gentle touch. His glanced at her with an expression so pained that it seemed like her touch had burned him.

"You wanna go upstairs so I can put these in water while we wait for the coffee to brew?" Her question came out as a breathless whisper.

He just nodded and turned off the engine and opened his door.

It wasn't that she was expecting him to round the vehicle and open her door for her or anything; her legs had simply turned to jelly for a moment. However, as he opened the passenger-side door and offered her his hand, just looking up at him, allowing her gaze to lazily travel up his body to his face, produced vertigo. Oh, yeah, she definitely needed to hold onto something. His hand worked . . . as did the thick arm that instantly threaded around her waist when her feet met the curb.

She wasn't sure how he did it, but he'd managed to collect his backset parcel, her, and close the door in several deft moves, not letting her break contact with his side. This man was trouble for sure. Her fate was sealed and she was possibly soon to be unemployed—because if he could make moves like that curbside, going back to the office this afternoon was unlikely.

Rather than just melt in full public view of any nosy neighbors, she clutched her flowers and purse to her chest and tried to put one foot in front of the other, and then fumbled at the door for her keys like a maniac.

If she didn't find her keys in the next five seconds, he was ready to put a shoulder to the apartment building door. Never in his life had a woman made him feel like this. He was trying to be cool, act nonchalant, but the wondrous scent of her poured all over him . . . just like her smoky eyes were a magnet. The feel of her hugged in close to him created a level of delirium that bordered on the ridiculous. Her soft touch in the car had almost produced a gasp. Jocelyn's hands felt like satin. He could only imagine what the rest of her felt like.

Trying not to seem too anxious, he stared at her hair as she worked on the locks . . . had to be velvet. Then she opened the door, temporarily broke the trance, began walking ahead of him, and had him completely hypnotized by her shapely legs and perfect behind sashaying up endless flights of steps ahead of him. Good Lord.

He was tempted to take the stairs two at a time. Throwing her over his shoulder to get to the top and be done with logistics was not beyond him at this point, but he thought better of it. Just one more door . . .

The moment she stepped over the threshold, he thought he'd pass out. It was the way she'd entered her apartment, backed up a bit, turned to stare at him, dropping the box of roses. He dropped the bag and kick-shut the door behind them.

She started to bend to pick up the fallen flowers and then simply let her purse fall. "You want coff—"

His thumb gently stopped her words. "Yeah," he said, and then took her mouth. That's when he lost track of time, but not purpose. He was a goner.

Layers of clothes peeled away, but her sweet, coffee-lacquered mouth never left his. Her buttery skin was the definition of liquid sucrose, and when her hands ran under his sweater, the only acknowledgment he could offer was a deep moan. Coats lay abandoned on the floor. Shoes got kicked off and left idle wherever they fell. He had to break the kiss to get his sweater off, and fought with the decision until he felt her beginning to remove some article of clothing over her head. Only then did he give in to allow his eyes the full feast that his mouth had experienced.

God *Almighty*, coffee never tasted so good . . . or looked so deep dear, rich-flavor-roasted-to-brown-perfection fine . . . she couldn't catch her breath. Never had it had such an adrenaline kick to it either. She was addicted to the substance for life. Forget herbal tea. Yet he seemed just as quietly stunned as she was.

The separation from the kiss had only been seconds. How her clothes got shed was still an unsolved mystery, but she didn't care . . . just as long as he didn't stop kissing her . . . kept his warm, wonderful touch sending swirls of ecstasy through her. A glance toward the fallen drugstore bag was all it took. As though reading her mind, he'd swept it up, grabbed her by the hand, and was headed toward the room where things could really brew.

A gentle tug pulled her, and somehow she was in the hallway against the wall. Sculpted sinew covered and flattened her. His hot skin burned the length of her. Choked baritone released from his throat, his voice a low rumble of desire eliciting her gasp that became a soft moan . . . the bedroom seemed so far away. Stumbling together a few feet, they reconnected every two steps. It was a crazy dance of want all the way down the short corridor. The plastic bag hit her side, a deep voice begged apology and made up for it by a slow drag of palm over her hip to cover the offense. Strong, male hands were tangled in her hair, her name tangled on his tongue, muffled by her kiss and her strangled whimper. Jesus, it had been so long, and it had *never* been like this.

Her bed wasn't even made, but who cared? They fell against it, the contents of the bag strewn amid the jumbled linens. He was her blanket . . . a hard, hot blanket that slowly slid down her body, finding points along her throat, breasts, and belly that brought tears to her eyes. Passion-heated hands spread her hot thighs, her arch suddenly quenched by a well-placed kiss turned to a maddening suckle. Her eyes crossed beneath her tightly shut lids as one hand frantically patted the bed in search of the illusive box. Coffee was *definitely* ready. "Oh . . . God . . ."

His hand found the box, and she couldn't even open her eyes as she heard the paper rip—but she had to. She weakly lifted her head, gaping, half from the need to breathe through her mouth, and half from sheer astonishment. The man was hung like a horse. She almost sobbed as she watched him sheath himself . . . *God was good.* Immediate warmth covered her. A tremble was her initial response. For a moment, that was all she could offer until a slow entry made her voice rend the air with her man's name embedded in it.

Her shudder connected to his, fluid motion became deep, penetrating liquid fire, soft caresses turned into a feral grip, cool exterior transformed into sweat-drenched skin—tender kisses broke with his head thrown back, eyes closed tight, a staccato pant keeping time and yet blocking it out . . . her name became, "Oh, baby."

Lights danced beneath her shut lids, the sun gave the splintered darkness a golden haze, her hands slid up and down slicked back skin, broad, thick shoulders worked in unison with clenching and releasing muscles in sculpted buttocks that her calves gladly embraced . . . she arched so hard that she was sure her spine would snap . . . like her mind had. The pending seizure swept through her so suddenly that all she could do was weep.

The moment she tumbled over the edge, he lost his mind. Forgot all about the precarious nature of latex, taking it slow, or whatever else he was supposed to be thinking about. Jocelyn . . . Jesus, it had been so long. He hit the pleasure wall, convulsed so hard that he was seeing stars. His body wouldn't stop twitching . . . and he had messed around and had fallen in love.

He peered down at her, the sated expression on her face so serene that hot moisture filled his eyes. He gently kissed the bridge of her nose and she looked up at him, her hand cupping his cheek. Oh, yeah, he was a goner and had to make coffee in the morning, the afternoon, and at night a permanent part of his life.

"Tell me you don't have to go back to work this afternoon," he whispered, still breathing hard.

She smiled tenderly and shook her head. "No . . . I still have to make us that coffee. The job can wait."

He closed his eyes and dropped his head to her shoulder. "Good . . . 'cause so can mine."

One year later . . .

"I can't believe you're getting married on Valentine's Day, girl," Jacqui sniffed, her rose bouquet bobbing as she removed her mink coat and came in close for a hug.

Tina dissolved into tears and hugged her, mussing her deep red velvet dress with the crush. "Oh, girl, this is soooo romantic!" She patted her protruding belly, and laughed. "I can't believe you're letting my wide behind walk down the aisle with you—but thank you."

Jocelyn kissed Tina's cheek. "One of you had to be my matron of honor, and since you got married first," she added, laughing through the tears, "it doesn't matter under whatever conditions, you'll always be my girl."

Freddie extended her huge, four-karat ring and sighed. "Marcus just gave this to me this morning," she whispered thickly. " It's catching. How can I ever thank you, lady?"

"Just be happy," Jocelyn said, as butterflies swept

through her stomach. She glanced at her mother, who had tears standing in her eyes.

Kimika grabbed Jocelyn's hand and just stared down. "You young girls know how to get the rocks that don't stop. Have mercy." She dropped Jocelyn's hand and chuckled. "You sure you don't need a crane supervisor on site up at the altar to help lift your hand when he puts the second band on there? Gotta be five or six karats, flossing single solitaire in platinum—we should be taking lessons from you, doll!"

"Oh, gurrrllll . . ." Gail sobbed, hugging Jocelyn and falling apart so badly that the four pamper ladies shooed her away. "I can't believe you let *me* be in *your* wedding!"

"Do not get makeup on her gown, honey," Agnes fussed.

Kimika fluffed Jocelyn's veil while Sue-Lin fretted over her bouquet and Mildred poufed out her train.

"This is it, Cinderella," Agnes said with a sniff. "Our job is done. The music is playing, now the rest is up to you. Enjoy the ball."

"My baby girl," her mother said, weeping, and then hugged Jocelyn so hard she could hardly breathe. "Now you remember everything that I told you?"

Jocelyn laughed, sniffing, then smoothed back her mother's hair, and nodded. "Momma, everything you told me was right. I love you."

Her mother let go with a sniff and then chuckled. "You were right, too. Your professor's friend is . . . well, never mind. He's a very nice man."

"I can't believe I'm standing here next to you like this, Holmes," Raul said, raking his fingers through his hair. "Never thought I'd see it happen."

Raymond smiled but kept his eyes toward the back of the church, waiting. "Me, either, man. You have no idea."

All his brothers were assembled at his flank. Flowers littered the sanctuary. Friends had squeezed into the pews like sardines. His mother and sisters sat on the front row, crying. But he saw none of it. When the music started in earnest, he blocked it out and got tunnel vision.

She floated down the aisle like a vision, her professor holding her arm. A sheer, pearl-beaded veil covered her beautiful face, shimmering at the edges like it had been dipped in sugar. Her coffee-and-cream shoulders were bare, framed in a winter-white scoop that gave modest rise to her bosom. Blood-red roses trailing ivy and small white buds trembled ever so slightly with each step she took. Sudden moisture stung his eyes and gave her an angelic haze as she neared him. The winged collar shirt beneath his black, cutaway tux felt like it was strangling him, but he knew better; the sight of her did that. Always did, always would . . . just like Valentine's Day had just become more than a holiday. It was sacred . . . and the wait for Jocelyn Jefferson, soon to be Mrs. Jefferson-Mayfield, to walk down the aisle, was killing him.

VALENTINE SURVIVOR

Susanna Carr

To my twin sister, Jennifer,
the ultimate Valentine survivor.

Chapter One

T minus 87 hours

Shanna Murphy hopped off the bus. "This is going to be the best Valentine's Day ever!" she announced as she raised her fists above her head. Excitement fizzed through her veins as she tilted her face toward gray Seattle rain clouds.

"You say that every year," Heather pointed out as she wearily hooked her backpack over one shoulder. "Come on, I'm chilled to the bone."

Shanna didn't know what her sister was talking about. She wasn't the least bit cold. "This year is going to be different!"

"You've said that each year, too."

She ignored Heather's comment. No one was going to dampen her spirits. Shanna waited too long for the perfect V-Day and she was almost there. Eighty-seven hours and everything was in place! Nothing could—or would—go wrong. She'd made sure of it.

The certainty was unlike anything Shanna had felt before. She wanted to burst with joy. She wanted to squeal. Do a Mary Tyler Moore hat toss and twirl. Her body language must have given her away, because Heather grabbed her by the arm and pulled her along.

"This year *will* be different." She fell in step with Heather as they followed the crowd to the office buildings. "And do you know why?"

"I don't want to know." Her sister determinedly kept her gaze straight ahead.

"I'll tell you why. Because I have a fail-proof plan." Just saying it aloud made her jittery. She felt like a kid the week before Christmas. A virtuous kid who knew she was getting a good payoff from Santa.

Heather spared a sideways glance. "If it's anything like last year's 'contingency plan' . . ." She curled her fingers in quotation marks.

Shanna winced and her spirits took a tiny dip as she remembered last year. That had to be the worst V-day. Ever. And for someone who had never had a good Valentine's Day—not even a date on February 14 during her long and, uh, illustrious dating career—that was saying a lot.

"Okay, last year's plans didn't work," Shanna admitted, "but I really hadn't been expecting a natural disaster."

"Maybe I should define 'contingency plan' for you."

She swatted at Heather's hands. "Enough about that." She hated when people did quotation marks at her. Twin sisters, especially. "Last year was a dress rehearsal. Just like all the other years. But they were also learning experiences."

Heather rolled her eyes. "Apparently you haven't learned enough, because you're still excited about Valentine's Day."

"But don't you see?" She didn't know exactly why, but Shanna needed to convince Heather. Which was ridiculous—not to mention impossible—since her sister missed out on the romantic gene altogether. "I'm approaching this holiday in a different direction. I've pared down."

"You?" Heather stopped abruptly on the sidewalk corner and almost got run over by another pedestrian. "Pared down? Do I need to define that, too?"

"I want the perfect V-Day. A quintessential February 14. That means boiling it down to its very essence."

"This does not sound good," Heather muttered under her breath as they crossed the street.

"I even made a list." Shanna unzipped her purse and hurriedly shuffled through the trash.

"Yep." Heather rubbed her fingertips against her forehead. "Not good at all."

"See?" She pulled out a sheet of paper, slightly crumpled from constant viewing. "I'm concentrating on the basics."

"Give me that." Her sister snatched it from her fingers and read it aloud.

THE LIST

1. Receive a dozen long-stemmed red roses. At work. In front of everyone.
2. Dinner at the most romantic restaurant in downtown Seattle. Champagne optional, but would gain bonus points.
3. A date with someone who knows where my G-spot is without asking for directions. And knows what to do with it.

"So?" Shanna prodded, anticipation buzzing inside her again. "What do you think? Good, huh?"

Heather pressed her lips together and shook her head slightly. She wordlessly returned the list.

"Knock it off." Shanna reverently folded the paper and slipped it back into her purse. "You have to admit that this list is fail-proof."

Heather's forehead crinkled. "Are you kidding? *Everything* will go wrong."

"You wanna bet?" She already regretted showing her sister the list.

"Sure. Let's look at your dinner requirement. What do you consider the most romantic restaurant in Seattle?"

"Swish." She hadn't actually been there, but it had topped the ten most romantic restaurants for the past three years. For all she knew, they could serve macrobiotic junk. Who cared, as long as they did it with a romantic flair?

"Oh, sure. Swish." Heather scoffed at the idea. "Like you're going to get in there. I hear that they take reservations a year in advance."

Shanna didn't say anything, but she knew she was gloating. The best kind of gloat, as long as you weren't on the receiving end. The smirk tugged at her pursed lips. She felt the pull of her eyebrows as she tried not to waggle them.

"You didn't."

"Didn't what?" she asked innocently.

"You made reservations a year in advance." The way Heather said it made it sound like an accusation. "Without even having a boyfriend on the horizon."

The smile she tried to contain broke through. "Yep. I decided I was not going to suffer through another bad Valentine's Day. On February 15 of last year, I called Swish and made reservations. I got a table for two by the window overlooking Elliot Bay."

"Lovely." Sarcasm shimmered through the single word. "Too bad the second seat in your dinner for two is going to be empty."

"Not necessarily." She felt her eyebrows waggling.

"I'm not eating dinner with you."

Shanna tilted her chin up. "You're not invited."

"Are you telling me you have a date in mind?"

Pure pleasure kicked into her veins. "I sure do."

For the first time that morning Heather showed a spark of enthusiasm. "You and Calder?"

Calder. Calder Smith. Her breath hitched in her throat as her ex-boyfriend's image slammed into her brain.

His pitch-black hair was cropped close against his skull. Tanned, weathered skin stretched over his lean, angular face. Lines fanned from his gleaming brown eyes and bracketed his stern mouth. And every once in a while, a slow, almost shy smile that made her heart tumble.

She used to think that Calder had been almost too tall for her. So tall that she felt delicate next to him. Or maybe it was his harsh masculinity that made her feel fragile and ultrafeminine. Whatever it was, Shanna still shivered at the memory of his earthy sensuality.

She swallowed roughly and tried to clear her suddenly swollen throat. "Heather, you know the rule," she reminded her in a hoarse whisper. "Do not speak his name in front of me." It was bad enough she had to see him almost every day because they worked for the same computer software company.

"Okay, fine. But He-Who-Shall-Not-Be-Named should be on that checklist." She shook a finger at Shanna. "That would be the perfect V-Day you're searching for."

Like she didn't know that already. She didn't want to think about it. Shanna tried to push the image aside, but the tingling of her skin remained. She had to forget about him and not let any what-might-have-beens get in the way of her goal.

"So who's your date?"

She wasn't too sure if she wanted to share any more information, but she knew her sister wouldn't let the topic rest until she found out. "Dominic."

"Dominic? Who's Domi—no!" She grabbed Shanna's arm and pulled her to a stop. "Not . . ."

"Yep, that's the one."

Heather's eyes widened with dismay. "He's a *slut*."

"I think the term you're looking for is 'serial dater'." Even though she hated it, Shanna did the quote thing with her fingers. Just because she could.

"For future reference, anytime you use the word 'serial' to describe a guy, it's not going to be good."

Damn if her sister didn't use the quote move again. "I'll remember that."

Heather covered her face with her hands. "Dominic. Why-y-y?" She wailed and stomped one foot after the other. "Why him? He's not going to send you flowers."

"Yes, he is." If the subliminal messages didn't work, the full-frontal request could not have been misunderstood.

Heather dropped her hands from her face and glared with suspicion. "Shanna, tell me the truth. Did you order and pay for the flowers in advance?"

"No!" Her mouth dropped open in shock. Outrage. "I would never do that. That's pathetic! I can't believe you would even think I'd consider it."

Her sister's jaw slid to one side and she arched a knowing eyebrow. "Shanna."

"Okay, the idea crossed my mind," she admitted, as she and Heather jaywalked through a parking lot, "but I rejected it. I know the minute I did that, all my bitchy coworkers would sniff out the truth."

"Yeah, you would never live that one down." She shuddered at the possibilities.

"Anyway, the whole point of the exercise is having a *guy* send me a bouquet at work. A dozen red roses, to be exact. I will accept no substitutes."

"Why do you think Dominic is going to send you flowers?"

"He will if he wants to find my G-spot on Friday." Shanna knew the motivation didn't sound the least bit romantic, but it would all work out in the end.

"Do *you* know where it is?"

"It hasn't made itself known for the past three months," she said with a shrug, "but that doesn't mean it changed addresses on me."

"And you think it's going to head the welcome committee for Dominic?" Heather exhaled long and hard. "Of all the men you could have picked. Couldn't it have been anyone else?"

"Heather, think about it." It wasn't like she had randomly picked Dominic. He fitted her requirements for the night. "How many guys can you name who knows what a G-spot is, let alone what to do with it?"

"There's me," the familiar, rough voice said from right behind her.

Shanna stumbled to a halt and forgot to breathe altogether as Calder steadied her. His fingers spanning against the curve of her hip made her knees melt. She trembled as his heat washed over her. And, if she wasn't mistaken, her G-spot just announced that the hibernation season was officially over.

Calder's fingers flexed against Shanna, but he restrained himself before curling her against his side. He felt the void—ached with it—but he had to be patient.

"Calder." Her breathless whisper made his body tighten.

"Shanna." He reluctantly allowed his hand to drop as she took a cautious step back. His gaze roamed her face, his heart squeezing tight at the exquisite beauty. He could never get tired of her sassy pink mouth or the constellation of freckles scattering across the bridge of her nose.

Wishing he could look into her pale blue eyes without scaring her off, Calder allowed his attention to wander. His mouth straightened into a stern line as he noticed her trim, athletic body hidden under her shapeless brown sweater and faded jeans.

He forgot all about her clothes as she nervously hooked her long red hair behind her ears. He bunched his fingers into fists before he did the task for her and turned to Shanna's twin. "Hi, Heather."

It was a wonder how the two could even be related. They

might share the flame-red Murphy hair—Shanna's long and flowing hair begged to be touched while Heather's short, spiky hair reminded him of a porcupine—and that was where the similarities ended. They were like yin and yang. While one was romantic and yielding, the other one was brash and sharp. One cried over sappy commercials. The other was the anti-Cupid.

Heather's eyes sparkled with mischief. "Hey, He-Who-Shall-Not."

"Heather." Shanna gave a warning glare at her sister. He felt the unspoken communication arcing over them. Some things never changed.

Her sister paused and smiled sweetly. It was a scary sight. "Sorry, Calder. You don't make the cut for this list."

What list? Oh, yeah. The G-spot-hunter list. "Why not?" He didn't care if he sounded gruff.

"We're talking about a Valentine hunt for the G-spot," Heather explained. From the corner of his eye, Calder could see Shanna bristling. "Kind of like hunting Easter eggs, but on February 14."

Hell, not the whole Valentine thing. Again. Anything but that. Calder felt his temper flaring. "Why does the date make the hunt different?"

For the first time that day, Shanna met his gaze. Too bad it was to glare at him. "It just does," she said through clenched teeth. She pivoted on her heel and marched away.

"Oh, good answer," Heather called out to her as she clapped her hands. "Brilliant comeback."

Shanna whirled around, her blue eyes flashing. "How many people go looking for eggs on days other than Easter?"

Calder felt his eyebrow arch. "So you're saying that Valentine sex is different from any other kind of sex?" Because he didn't have any qualms reminding her of a few encounters they shared that made the average day special.

"You wouldn't by any chance have a case-by-case-analysis on this argument?" Heather asked.

Shanna folded her arms across her chest and huffed. "I wouldn't share it with you because I've wasted enough time trying to convert you nonbelievers."

"Yeah, you are never going to convert me," Calder admitted with brutal honesty as he held the door open for them to enter the office building. "I don't need a calendar telling me when to give flowers to the woman in my life."

"Yes, I can believe that," Shanna said as she bestowed a brittle, closed-mouth smile. "A calendar would be useless, considering that the last time you gave flowers to someone was in the second grade. And that was a Mother's Day assignment for school."

She had him there. He didn't feel bad about it, but that was the last time he allowed his mother loose with the family scrapbooks.

Shanna snapped her fingers and looked at the other side of the lobby. "That reminds me, I need to get some flowers."

Heather let out a long-suffering groan. "Come on, Shanna. Why not wait until Dominic gives you some for Valentine's Day?"

Dominic? Heavy stillness came over Calder. Who the hell was Dominic?

A hectic flush crawled up Shanna's neck and flooded her pale cheeks. "My other bouquet won't last that long," she explained in a mumble.

A bouquet from *Dominic*? Why hadn't he heard about this guy? How did his competition slip under his guard?

"You guys go on ahead," Shanna suggested as she backed away. Each guilty step ate at him. "See you after work, Heather."

" 'Bye, Shanna." He said it low and rough, but he knew it would get her attention.

Shanna turned around and tripped, her tennis shoes squeaking on the floor. "Yeah, okay. 'Bye!" she said, flustered and avoiding eye contact before she darted away.

That's it. He'd been patient long enough. Calder watched

the crowd swallow Shanna up before he turned to Heather. "What do you know about this Dominic?"

"That depends." Her sister hooked an arm through his. Her smile chilled his blood as she asked, "What's it worth to you?"

Shanna hurriedly crossed the lobby without giving a backward glance to Calder. She felt like she had just run a marathon. Breathe in . . . breathe out . . . breathe in . . .

He and Heather could make fun all they wanted to, but they never had to deal with a bad Valentine's Day. Okay, maybe Heather hated being required to make mailboxes and give cards to classmates in elementary school, but she survived.

And as far as Shanna knew, Calder hadn't had any traumatic V-Day experiences. No floral delivery truck accidents or chocolate tragedy in his past. No Valentine date gone awry. She would definitely have heard about it by now.

Even if he had slapped a lawsuit on the Valentine card industry for a paper cut, she wouldn't let his opinion change hers. She was used to people showing little appreciation about the most romantic holiday of the year. Of course, it was more difficult when the most important people in her life felt that way. But she wasn't going to let that sway her from what she wanted.

Shanna squared her shoulders back and threaded through the long lines at the coffee bar to get to the flower cart. She determinedly ignored the dark-roast scent that always beckoned her in the morning. A couple more days and she could indulge in her caffeine habit.

Most of her coworkers thought she gave up her morning coffee as a New Year's Resolution. Shanna was more than willing to let them think that when the real reason was she used her java money for a bouquet of flowers every week.

Of all the preplanning she had done for this holiday, Shanna realized the flower preparations were a mistake. She knew well enough to bring in the crystal vase at work around the beginning of the year. Any later than that, and she might as well advertise her Valentine expectations with neon lights.

But next time she wouldn't buy such a big vase. Great idea in theory, but it sucked buying jumbo bouquets. And, even though they came in a wide array of unnatural colors, she was getting tired of carnations.

Approaching the flower cart, Shanna nodded to the shop girl and bypassed the roses. The sweet, heady scent curled around and enveloped her, but she wasn't going to look at them. Roses, in her humble opinion, should not be bought, but given. By a man.

And it didn't have to be a man in love, Shanna decided, as she browsed the pale tulips. Interested, yes. In like would be fine. In love was not obligatory.

She certainly wasn't looking for love. Shanna blinked as the colors blurred before her eyes. She found it with Calder, but what she had felt didn't boomerang back.

When she met Calder, she thought she had found her Prince Charming. She had been ready to dive into a whirlwind affair complete with a happily-ever-after fit for a princess bride. Instead she discovered that she had fallen in love with a guy who was more cowboy than charming, who had little use for romance, and had no plans to treat her like a princess. It was no coincidence that there was a lack of cowboys in fairy tales.

Calder obviously thought she would "come to her senses," but that was three months ago. She thought it had been the right choice to stand up for what she wanted. Now she wasn't so sure.

No. She wouldn't second-guess herself again. Not this late in the game. Shanna blindly grabbed a bouquet of pink tulips. To hell with the cost. She was on a mission. This time she was looking for romance. She wanted to be wooed. Courted.

Was it so wrong that she wanted to be the center of a man's attention? She didn't think so. She wanted a man to do something goofy and stupid over her. That wasn't asking for much!

And she certainly wasn't asking for it to last forever, Shanna thought, as she paid for the flowers. She wasn't even asking for it to last a month. Just one day.

One *lousy* day.

Valentine's Day, to be exact.

Shanna turned at the sound of screeching tires next to the lobby's back doors. Her eyes narrowed at the sight of a familiar silver sports car.

February 14. The same day when even the most unworthy of women were treated like princesses. Women like her boss Angie.

Shanna took a prudent step behind the cart and watched Angie's husband—Ted, Ed, Fred, or something like that—bolted out of the car and hustled around the hood to help Angie out from the passenger side.

Shanna didn't get it. Ted-Ed-Fred was successful, sweet, and good-looking. How'd he wind up with a witch like Angie? Some sort of court-ordered community service?

And Angie sure didn't appreciate what she had, Shanna decided, her mouth twisted with disapproval. It wasn't enough to have the lapdog. Oh, no. Not nearly enough. Angie's secret lover, Tony, was always dropping by the office. He was extremely sexy, extremely attentive, and from the occasional grunting heard in Angie's office during lunchtime, extremely well hung.

So the witch had two men who made her the center of attention, and Shanna had no one. On paper, it didn't compute. She played by the rules. She was the good girl. How come she wasn't being rewarded?

Angie strode in, her obscenely expensive shoes clicking against the hard floor. She carried a platinum travel coffee mug in one overly manicured hand and gave a half-wave over her shoulder to her husband with the other. " 'Bye, Stan."

Stan. That was it. Heh. Close enough. She frowned as she noticed how Angie's new designer pantsuit hugged her toned body. Shanna's sigh reached to her toes. Why did the blonde have to have everything *and* a high metabolism? Why didn't the gods just make Angie a Charlie's Angel while they were at it?

"Shanna?" Angie's attention swiveled at the sound of the heavy sigh. "Why aren't you in the office yet?"

Why aren't you? Shanna bit her tongue before she said it aloud. "I'm early." Like stating the obvious was going to make a difference.

"There's no time to waste." She gestured for Shanna to hurry up, which she grudgingly obeyed. "We have to reach our project objective on Friday . . ."

Blah, blah, blah, blah, blah. Shanna stepped into the elevator with Angie, wishing she worked on the first level.

". . . So these are your assignments for the week . . ."

Like this couldn't wait for the department's morning meeting? Of course not. Angie had a captive audience, and everyone in the elevator was going to hear her wield her dubious authority.

All Shanna could do was nod and tune out. She stared at her bouquet as if her life depended on it. Her professional life, at any rate.

"I don't know why you spend money on bouquets," Angie veered off onto another topic. "Flowers are so boring. All they do is shrivel up and die."

Shanna wished there was a bumblebee in the bouquet. A big, fat one. It would then zip out and sting Angie on the mouth. That would shut her up. For maybe all of one minute.

"Of course, Stan's going to be out of town this week . . ."

"Oh?" Shanna perked up at this tidbit of information. "You're spending Valentine's apart?"

"No way!" Angie looked appalled at the very idea. "Stan wouldn't do that to me. He's going to take a cross-country flight back home so we'll be able to spend Valentine's night together."

It was a struggle to keep a blank expression, but Shanna managed. Barely. "That's so . . . sweet."

Okay. It was official. Valentine's Day was wasted on the wrong people. Or maybe V-Day was designed for the wrong people.

Hmm . . . Shanna returned her gaze to the bouquet. She might have something there. Maybe Valentine's was based on a Darwinian principle.

There were those who would always have spectacular V-Days. They would never spend February 14 alone. Angie was definitely one of them. It wasn't fair, it wasn't even logical, but it was the way the world turned.

Then there were those designed to endure. They were the ones whose Valentine's Days were less than spectacular. They would get potted plants instead of roses. Jewelry that turned skin green. Sugar-free chocolates.

And then there were those designed to envy. No gifts. No celebrations. No nothing. Shanna was stuck in that group. Figured.

Not this year, though. Shanna's jaw tightened. And if she had something to say about it, never again.

Because if it was about survival of the fittest, Shanna was going to win. She was going to have spectacular V-Days from this moment on. No matter what. Even if it meant sacrificing, adapting, eating her young . . .

She grimaced. Okay, maybe not that far. But Darwin had nothing on her. She wasn't going to let anything get in her way. If anyone tried, Shanna thought as she glanced in Angie's direction, they were going down.

It was revolution time.

Chapter Two

T minus 63 hours

"Have you seen the paper?" Heather asked as she pulled her backpack off the bus seat she had been saving.

Shanna sat down and brushed the rain from her coat. "Heather, you know if it's important, then I'll see it on the Web."

"You might find this important." She tossed the local newspaper at her.

Shanna grabbed it and reluctantly scanned the front page. She had other things to do on their commute. Reading the news was the last thing on her mind. "If you're upset about some comic strip character dying—whoa!" She felt like someone kicked her in the stomach. It hurt so much, she wanted to gag. In fact, she did.

"Told ya," Heather said softly.

She stared at the headlines until her eyes burned. She squeezed her eyes shut and forced them open. No good. The words remained in the same order. SWISH CLOSED DOWN BY AUTHORITIES.

Shanna slapped the newspaper on her lap and stared straight ahead. *I'm not going to cry,* she decided, as she pressed her trembling lips together. *I will not cry.*

She flopped back, her head hitting the hard plastic. "I can't believe this is happening," Shanna said in a daze. Her eyelashes fluttered as she tried to stop the first tear from falling.

"Yep." Heather took the paper back and clucked her tongue. "Who knew 'most romantic restaurant' was synonymous with 'a breeding ground for Hepatitis A'?"

Shanna leaned forward and thunked her head against the chair in front of her. Again. And again.

The skinny guy who always sat there turned around and scowled. "Do you mind?"

She drew back and slouched in her seat, waiting until the man turned around before sticking her tongue out at him. Couldn't anyone show some compassion? Just a speck? She was having a crisis here!

"Why? Why?" She tossed her hands up in the air and looked skyward. "Why this week? Couldn't the authorities have closed it next week? Saturday, even?"

"So unsuspecting customers like yourself could contract a liver disease?" her sister said as she turned the page of her newspaper.

"Come on, how dangerous is Hepatitis A?"

Heather flipped back the page and leveled her with a look. "Wouldn't you rather have good health over a good Valentine's Day?"

Shanna pursed her lips as she considered the question. Healthy liver or a happy Valentine's Day . . . Healthy liver, happy Valentine's Day . . .

"Shanna?" Heather sounded just like their mother when she did that.

"What does a liver do again? Ow!" She flinched as Heather elbowed her in the ribs. "Yeah, yeah," Shanna agreed as she rubbed the sore spot. "I want the healthy liver. I guess."

"I can't believe the way you're acting." Heather returned her attention to the newspaper.

"I can't believe this is happening." She combed her fingers through her hair. "What am I saying? Of course it's happening. Because this is my life we're talking about."

"Calm down. It's going to be fine."

"How can you say that?" She already felt the panic clawing its way up her throat. There was no way she could bounce back from this setback. Screw revolution.

Her sister shrugged. "You can go to another restaurant."

Shanna scoffed at the idea. If only it were that simple. "Right. Don't you think that all of the romantic restaurants are booked up at this time?"

"You don't know that for sure unless you call other places."

"I don't *want* another restaurant. I want Swish." She folded her arms and pouted. She planned on it, waited for almost a year, and now it was snatched from her days before she could enjoy it. Her luck blew.

Heather put down the paper. "Don't you think you're asking for too much out of this day?"

Shanna flinched at the absurd idea. "Too much?" she said in a low, fierce tone. "Hardly. Too much would be expecting a Valentine's Day *wedding* with Calder Smith."

Her sister's eyebrows shot up. "I should say so, since you barely speak to him."

Damn, she wished she hadn't said those words out loud. It hurt more having her dream out in the open. And, if the rules were right, it would never come true.

"Forget I said that," Shanna said from the corner of her mouth.

"Done." Heather looked out the window as if she hadn't heard a thing. "Forgotten. Purged from my memory."

Now if only she could purge it from hers. Shanna's shoulders sagged. "This was supposed to be a Valentine's that couldn't go wrong."

"Just because you went for the downgrade version?" Her sister shook her head. "Think again."

If she reached for the moon, she'd crash and burn. Asking for the minimum was already showing cracks in her plans. It was time to regroup and go straight into crisis management.

"Stop worrying." Heather lightly tapped her on the shoulder with the paper. "You'll come up with something. Better yet, have Dominic take care of it."

"Have a guy be in charge of my Valentine's Day?" Shanna snorted. "Puhleeze."

Shanna rushed into her department, wondering how to conduct a fast search for romantic restaurants. She needed to get a head start before the other Swish patrons nabbed all the alternative reservations. Damn, she hated the sense of urgency pulsing through her veins. It was enough to make her want to curl up into a fetal position.

She skidded to a stop the moment she saw her two coworkers. They were huddled next to her office space, and once again Shanna hated being in the middle cubicle. It was bad enough that she could hear everything between the thin walls, but it was worse when everyone gravitated to her "door." She knew it wasn't for her cheerful disposition or her stash of candy. More like geographic bad luck.

"Shanna!" Megan jerked her head up. "Hi!"

"Hi," she replied cautiously to what could only be described as the dishwater blonde. She never knew what that meant until she met Megan.

"Hey, Shanna," Kerry said, flipping her brunette hair away from her face before walking back to her cubicle. "How's it going?"

"Good." Okay, something was up. That was about as chatty as Kerry got in the morning. And what was with these two? They barely tolerated each other. Whenever Kerry wasn't in the office—which happened a lot—Megan would gossip and badmouth her to Shanna. And vice versa. It made Shanna wonder what they said about her when she wasn't around.

"Hi, Angie!" Megan said past Shanna's shoulder, her brightness level going up a notch, where it would remain until Angie left the room. "Oh, love your shoes."

Shanna tried to keep her expression blank as she took off her coat. Megan's brown-nosing was really annoying. Probably because it worked so well. Shanna didn't think she could stoop that low. And even if she did, she would still get caught for pulling stunts. Megan had the unique talent of getting away with anything.

"Thanks, Megan. I just bought them yesterday." Angie stopped and rotated her ankle so everyone could get a better look. She glanced up when Shanna stowed her purse away in the bottom desk drawer. "Shanna, are you just getting in?"

Are you? She bit the tip of her tongue. "I'm early." She didn't know why she kept telling Angie that.

"Doesn't matter."

Yep. Never works. Shanna kept her mouth shut and booted up her computer.

"We need to have all the bugs fixed by the end of Friday," Angie continued, gesturing with her travel coffee mug as she warmed up to her gloom-and-doom speech that she had given every day for the past two weeks.

"Oh, speaking of Friday," Kerry said. "I need to leave early."

"Hot date?" Megan asked. There was a sharp edge to the cheerfully curious question.

Kerry flashed a warning look at her coworker. "No, my grandmother is getting out of the hospital and they need me there before the visiting nurse shows up."

Good one. Shanna grabbed a tissue from her box and wiped the water circling the base of her vase. Kerry was getting more creative with her excuses. She had to; she was running out of the usual ones.

"I thought your grandmother died on New Year's Eve," Angie said, perplexed. "I remember something about you having to leave early for the funeral home."

Kerry paused. "Right—that was for my other grandmother."

Yeah, Grandma #7. Shanna pinched off a dead leaf and tossed it in her wastebasket. She was not going to get into this. It had nothing to do with her.

"Well," Angie shrugged, "I guess that can't be helped. Do as much as you can in the next few days." Angie walked off and stopped. "Hold on a second."

Shanna perked up. Did she finally add up all of Kerry's relatives and realize they didn't compute? Oh, please, please.

"Shanna?"

Shanna froze. She was wrong. She winced and closed her eyes. Kerry's lies were going to affect her. She could hear it in her boss's voice. She could feel it coming.

"Weren't you planning on leaving early?"

She forced her eyes open. "Yeah."

"Come on, you guys." Angie raised her voice. "We can't have two people out on the day of our deadline."

Shanna had a hard-won appointment at a chi-chi salon and was getting the works done. Had scrimped and saved for almost 365 days. Had figured out her schedule with the intensity of a general going into battle. But would Angie understand any of this? "I know, but—"

Angie's hand sliced through the air, her coffee mug reflecting against the fluorescent light. "If it's not an emergency, forget it."

Why was *she* getting the attitude? Shanna glanced at Kerry, who suddenly appeared to be very busy.

"You're going to have to stay until five," Angie decided, as she walked toward her office.

"But—" Shanna had requested that time off months ago. Earned it. Was truthful about it.

"Kerry has a family situation. And she has seniority," Angie pointed out and stepped into her office.

Shanna stared as Angie closed the door, the impotent

anger crashing through her. She wanted to scream. Stomp her feet. Quit on the spot. If only she could.

She dragged her gaze away from the door and saw Kerry looking at her. "Sorry," her coworker said with a small smile.

Shanna looked away. "Yeah." *And may all eight of your grandmothers come back and haunt you.*

"Dominic, I'm sorry . . ."

Calder paused upon entering the office suite, which at first glance appeared empty. His gaze snagged on Shanna's head peeking above her cubicle wall. The bright red hair looked tousled. Just the way he liked it.

"Yes, I know . . . I know . . ."

Regret suffused her voice. Was she canceling the date? Hope swelled inside his chest.

Striding over to where Shanna sat, Calder felt a pang of guilt for listening in on her conversation. He immediately squashed it. If she wasn't going on a date with Dominic, he wanted to be the first to know.

Shanna's back was turned. She combed her fingers through her hair and Calder let his gaze drift as the long, soft tresses cascaded down her blue sweatshirt. He leaned against the plastic-and-fabric wall, wondering when she started wearing bulky clothes and how he was going to get her out of them.

"I realize that you're busy," Shanna continued in a hushed voice, "but if we want dinner reservations on Friday, we need to act now. Surely you must know of at least one restaurant."

Calder now understood the reason for all the phone books blanketing her desk. If the creases, wrinkles, and impatient pen scrawls on the yellow pages was anything to go by, her search wasn't going well.

He glanced around the cubicle and noticed the gigantic crystal vase stuffed with pink tulips. A cheerful bowl set next to him, overflowing with candy hearts. Valentine decorations dotted the boring beige wall. It was a hodgepodge of flowers, lace, and ribbons.

Any of those items would make Calder break out into hives. The combination should be deadly to him, but he wasn't backing away, forming the sign of the cross with his fingers. It wasn't his taste, but he liked the design because it was pure Shanna.

"Okay . . . okay . . . you ask around and let me know. Okay . . . talk to you later. 'Bye!" She hung up the phone and muttered, "Ask around. Like that's going to happen."

"Problem?"

Shanna yelped and jumped. She swiveled her chair around, her eyes widening when she saw him. "Calder. I didn't see you."

Whatever happened to her ability of knowing the moment he stepped into the room? When she knew exactly where he was and what he was doing? He hadn't believed in all that lover mumbo jumbo while they were together. Now he missed the intuitive connection they once shared.

Once? Nah. They still had it. It was rusty, that's all. "What's up?"

"Nothing." She shook her head and immediately changed the subject. "If you're looking for Angie, she's still at lunch."

Nothing? Yeah, right. That was another thing he was surprised he missed. She used to be very open with him. Told him everything, whether he wanted to hear it or not.

"Your reservations fell through?" he asked.

"Something like that." Her eyelids drooped but Calder caught the disappointment she was trying to mask. Shanna twitched her mouth to one side. Like she was undecided about something. "You . . ." she paused, sinking the edge of her teeth into her bottom lip.

Calder felt the buzz as he stared at her mouth. Shanna did the sexiest things and never seemed aware of it. God help him when she was being seductive on purpose. "What?"

She drew back at his harsh tone. “Never mind. I’ll ask someone else if they can recommend a nice restaurant.”

Calder stood immobile. He didn’t think he heard correctly. Shanna wanted restaurant recommendations from him to go with *another man*?

The caveman impulses roared through him. He clenched his teeth until they threatened to shatter. “What do you mean by *nice?*” Did he just growl? He needed to pull back before all those weeks of patience were wasted.

“A place that offers a wine list instead of a kids’ menu,” she immediately responded as she closed the phone books and stacked one on top of another.

Okay, he didn’t expect that answer. Shanna always had definite standards about this kind of stuff. “Not even romantic?”

“No.” She cast a quick glance at him as if she heard something judgmental in his tone. “I hit all the romantic ones, but I can’t get in. I’m sure you know of at least one nice one.”

He did, but he wasn’t chivalrous enough to let on about them. “What would I know about restaurants? According to you I’m in the office 24/7.”

Shanna pressed her lips in a firm line, the only indication that she heard the latent argument. “You know of a few,” she pointed out, refusing to get into past history. “There were one or two neighborhood restaurants where they knew you by name.”

Uh, no way. No way was he going to let her go there. “Try them,” he suggested, ready to call them up and block her reservation. He didn’t want Shanna reenacting those moments with another guy.

“I did try,” she confessed, “but they can’t fit me in. At this point I’m willing to drop the *nice* requirement as long as I don’t wind up at a drive-thru.”

“Why don’t you cook dinner?” Hell, where did that come from? What was he doing?

She gave him a horrified look. “Cook?”

"Yeah." Why wasn't he shutting up? "That lasagna you made from scratch for my birthday was good." He placed his hand over his stomach as he remembered. It was better than good. And then what they did with the leftover sauce . . .

"You think I should cook?" Shanna's raised voice cut through his carnal thoughts. "On Valentine's Day?"

She said it like it was a bad thing. "Does that go against your beliefs?"

"A little," she said in a huff. "I'm not going to spend hours in a kitchen on a special day."

"Oh, yeah. What was I thinking?" The woman expected to be treated like a queen for a day, wanting all other moments to pale in comparison. She was getting hung up on all the shiny trappings and didn't see she was tossing away the good stuff.

Shanna shook her head. "Next you'll suggest I bake my own wedding cake."

"It's not unheard of," Calder said as her phone rang.

She held her hand up at him as if she were controlling traffic. "No more suggestions out of you. Cook. For Dominic. On Valentine's Day." She picked up the phone. "Hello, this is Shanna Murphy."

He suppressed a smile. Dominic didn't rate a home-cooked meal. Probably not even a pot of coffee. That would hold him . . . for now. Calder backed out of the office suite, feeling like he just dodged a bullet.

"Shanna? This is Tony."

Tony. Tony? Shanna frowned as she flipped through her mental Rolodex. She didn't know of any Tony. "Tony . . . ?"

"Angie's . . . friend."

"Oh, hi." *That* Tony. She twisted her lips before she mouthed off, but she just *loved* how everyone assumed she remembered everyone and their full personal history. As if she didn't have a life of her own. Which she didn't, but that was beside the point.

Her mind rewound to what Tony labeled himself. *Angie's friend.* Ha. What a joke. More like *lover. Inamorato. Bed-buddy.* For someone who gets it on with Angie during office hours, it was useless to practice discretion now.

"I don't know how you got transferred over to my line," Shanna told him as she reached for the buttons on her phone. "I'll connect you to Angie's voice mail."

"No, wait," Tony said in a rush. "It's you I want to talk to."

"Me?" Her stomach clenched. Why? She was surprised that he was aware of her existence. That he knew her name. Her work number.

What would someone like Tony want with her? The possibilities were bizarre. Tantalizing. Each one feeding her vengeful fantasies against Angie.

A wicked smile curled along her lips. Tony wants to dump Angie for someone nicer. No, someone beautiful and sexy. No, wait . . . a goddess. A *love* goddess.

Of course, she would turn him down flat, Shanna decided as she leaned back against her chair. But she could carry on, knowing that the boss's *friend* wanted her more than the goddess Angie. Her days would be spent finding ways to remind Angie of that. While dodging the unemployment line. Hmm . . . being lusted over by your boss's lover was a hazardous pastime, but oh, so worth it.

"Shanna?" Tony repeated with a trace of exasperation. "Can you hear me?"

"Hmm?" Shanna mentally prepared her thanks-for-the-offer-but-I-find-you-disgusting-and-no-STD-free-test-results-would-change-my-mind speech.

"I said, what does Angie have planned on Friday afternoon? I'm planning a surprise for her."

The revenge fantasies skidded and hit the wall of reality. Eh, no big. Actually, it was a relief.

But did he have to make her an accomplice in giving the witch a perfect Valentine's Day? Ugh. The indignity of it all! "Oh, that's so"—*unfair, unjustified and just plain wrong!*—"sweet."

"Yeah," Tony said bashfully. "But I need to know if she has any important meetings."

And he was asking her because . . . ? "I wouldn't know."

"Can you check her schedule?" he prompted, as if she was brainless. "It would be on her computer."

That's another thing she loved. Everyone assumed she was a lackey. "I don't have her password. Sorry."

"Oh, that's all right. I'll figure it out some other way. Just don't let Angie know about my plans."

"Not a . . . problem." She stumbled to a stop as Tony hung up. Before she could ask him if he knew of any romantic restaurants. Bummer.

As she returned the phone to its cradle, her gaze caught the familiar scrap of paper nestled underneath the yellow pages.

THE LIST

1. Receive a dozen long-stemmed red roses. At work. In front of everyone.
2. Dinner at ~~the~~ **a** ~~most~~ ~~romantic~~ **nice** restaurant in **the** ~~downtown~~ Seattle **area.** Champagne **or wine** optional, but would gain bonus points.
3. A date with someone who knows where my G-spot is without asking for directions. And knows what to do with it.

It doesn't look bad. That bad. As bad as it could be. She had to remember that it was all about adapting. Adjusting. Hanging on.

She wondered to which restaurant Tony was taking her boss. Probably something fabulous. Ultraromantic. Angie probably wouldn't appreciate it unless it was ultraexpensive.

Why did guys do this kind of stuff for someone like Angie? She was demanding, ungrateful, and thoughtless. Shanna couldn't imagine that would be an aphrodisiac to men. Everyone knew men have fragile egos.

The woman must make it up to them in bed. Shanna shuddered at the thought. It was unimaginable, but as Sherlock Holmes once said, if you eliminated all other factors, the one that remains must be the truth. Or something like that. But if someone as hard and unloving as Angie could lure guys into acting stupid and goofy in the name of love and sex, any woman could get romanced.

Shanna grabbed her to-do list and added the pharmacy to her errands. Hope surged through her for the first time since she'd read the paper in the morning. If the promise of incredible sex was all that it took, Dominic was going to romance her brains out.

Chapter Three

T minus 36 hours

Calder looked up from his computer screen. He thought he had seen a glimpse of flame-red Murphy hair next to his door. Anticipation buzzed through his veins until he saw the porcupine hairstyle.

He quashed the disappointment welling in his chest. "Heather," he greeted evenly.

"Cut the chitchat," Heather demanded as she strode into his office. "It's time to take a walk."

When it came to Shanna's twin sister, he always felt like he walked into a conversation midway. "Where?"

"To our friendly neighborhood drugstore. The one across the street." She clapped her hands. "Come on, let's hustle."

He propped his chin on his fist. "Not that I wouldn't *love* to spend time with you . . ."

"I'll explain it on the way." She gestured to the open door.

"I have work to do." He thought it was obvious. He couldn't see the surface of his desk. Hadn't seen it since the last time Shanna clucked her tongue and straightened it up for him.

"Dude," Heather glared at him. No tongue-clucking out of her. "I'll give it to you straight. You're blowing it with Shanna."

His chest clenched and he felt something shift. It was like the void yawned bigger. Calder remained still, but the restraint that had gotten him this far in life slipped. "How do you figure that?"

"You're giving her some slack before you reel her in." Heather acted like she was fly-fishing. "I know it. You know it. Shanna doesn't know it."

"That's my plan."

"Yeah, it was a brilliant plan. In November." She splayed her hands in the air. "But it's freaking February and she has just made a To Do Dominic list."

He flinched at the news. It ate at his gut like acid. He wanted to punch something. Rip apart everything in his path until the world matched the destruction that was going on inside him.

Shanna didn't want him anymore. He felt like he was falling into a black hole. He had nothing to hold onto.

Had Shanna ever made a To Do Calder list? Did she complete it and decided it was time to move on? What if there was something on the Dominic list he didn't have? His gut twisted. Better not be.

Calder noticed that Heather was watching him closely. He schooled his expression but felt his skin drawn tight against his face. "What does this have to do with me?" he asked. His voice was cold. Arctic. Too bad Heather wasn't one to get frostbitten.

"She doesn't want Dominic." Heather waved her hand as if the guy was a nonissue.

"It doesn't sound that way," he replied.

Heather's eyebrow rose from the lethal softness of his voice. "She isn't going to bed him because she's still hung up on you." Heather leaned her arm against his monitor. "Take my word on it."

"You're that sure?" He wanted to believe her, but Shanna never said she loved him. Yeah, he felt loved, but for someone who was into anything mushy and sappy, Calder had to wonder what kept her from saying those words.

"Shanna wants romance." Heather made a face and a retching noise. "Something Dominic will give without backing it up with any real feelings."

"More power to him." He returned his attention to the screen, but it was all a blur.

"Why you couldn't give it to her remains a mystery," she said, as she inspected her nails.

He swerved his attention back on Heather, surprised by the accusation. "You're asking me that? *You* are?"

Heather held up her hand. "I back up your sentiments one hundred percent, Calder. You know I do. But is it really that hard to give a dozen red roses when you know how important it is to Shanna?"

"I'm not going to pretend to be someone that I'm not." What he felt for her wasn't soft and fragile. It wasn't refined. Roses and lace didn't explain how he felt.

But it was more than that. He wasn't sophisticated. The stuff Shanna wanted might as well be from a foreign culture. He didn't understand it, didn't know how to get it for her. And if he tried, he would mess it up.

"Okay, Calder," Heather said, as she snapped her fingers in front of his face. "Now is not the time to think. It's the time to act."

He leaned back in his chair and sighed. He couldn't. He had responsibilities. Obligations. Deadlines. No one seemed to understand this. "I have work—"

"It'll be here when you get back. I promise, no one will steal it from you." She shifted impatiently. "Don't you want to see for yourself if Shanna is over you?"

Not really. He didn't know how he would cope if the interest was gone from her blue eyes. If the glimmer of attraction had dimmed. But he had to know.

"What, exactly, am I supposed to do?" Calder asked as he rose from his chair. "Storm into the pharmacy, throw her over my shoulder, and see if she calls security on me?"

"That's Plan B," Heather said, as she pushed him out the door. "Plan A is much more subtle."

Calder looked over his shoulder. "What do you know about subtle?"

"Trust me."

That was hard to do when the simple suggestion made his stomach cramp. "Do I have a choice?" he muttered under his breath.

"Not really," Heather admitted, coming around to his side. "Here's the plan. All you have to do is troll the condom rack . . ."

"Oh, hell." He turned around and headed back for the safety of his office.

Panic, hot and pure, nearly blinded Shanna. The need to unsheathe her claws was instinctive. But that wouldn't get her anywhere.

She knew better than to cause a scene. She would be sweet but insistent. Do whatever it took to overcome this obstacle.

And that meant she couldn't lunge over the counter and grab the pharmacist by the lapels of his crisp white coat. No matter how much she wanted to.

Shanna rested her wrists on the counter. She folded her hands together, ignoring the urge to ball her fingers into fists. "What do you mean," she said through a fixed smile, "that you won't give me my birth control?"

The older man looked at her from over his half-glasses. "Your prescription has expired," he replied in his typical, no-nonsense manner.

Shanna wanted to shrug and make a face. Instead she went for a wide-eyed-innocence look. If acting stupid could cajole men into changing their minds, she'd give it a whirl. "Not by much," she said.

"Enough," he replied, mimicking her tone.

Okay, Shanna decided, as her eyes narrowed. He wasn't going to fall for that. But after polite, sweet, and stupid, she was running out of tactics. What was next in her limited repertoire?

Tears. Ech. She absolutely hated when women did it, but it seemed to work. She had to give it a try.

"But you don't understand," she said, looking up, trying to get tears to form. She looked into the lights and blinked frantically. Nothing. Her eyes, if anything, felt bone-dry and itchy.

Apparently she couldn't cry on demand. Especially when a very unfriendly guy was waiting with impatience for her to leave. Wish she had known about that earlier. She should have practiced before trying it out in public. Now she had to fake it.

"It's going to be"—she sniffed and fluttered her hands next to her face—"Valentine's Day."

The pharmacist appeared unmoved. Shanna wondered if he was waiting to see tears stream down her face. It was going to be a long wait. She ran the tip of her finger under her eyelashes, pretending to wipe away the moisture.

"Facial tissues are in aisle three."

Shanna sighed and slouched. She never did like this pharmacist. He was old-fashioned, judgmental, and disapproving. Basically, he was like her dad, with an authoritarian white coat as a bonus. And access to her birth control. That would explain the awkwardness she always felt when getting a refill. Trust her to find a pharmacy that would give her a complex along with her medicine.

It was time to beg for mercy, no matter the consequences. The loss in dignity . . . The absolute humiliation . . .

Shanna threw herself facedown on the counter, her arms

stretched out wide. She winced as she bumped her nose. Hard. It stung. *Oh, sure, now the tears come.*

The sharp corner dug into her stomach. Her toes dangled a few inches from the floor. Shanna had no idea she was that short.

The pharmacist exhaled sharply. "What is it now?"

"Isn't it against some Hippocratic oath to prevent me from having my birth control on the most romantic day of the year?" Her voice sounded muffled. She was about to blow her hair out of her way when she felt herself slipping.

"No," the man replied firmly. "I suggest you call your doctor and schedule an appointment."

That wasn't going to help, Shanna thought, as she grappled for traction. It took months to get an appointment with that woman. Hmm . . . now that she thought about it, this medical insurance program she was in really wasn't working out for her.

What was she doing? She didn't have time to think about that, Shanna reminded herself, as her fingers squeaked down the smooth counter. She needed to focus. Get birth control in the next thirty-six hours.

Shanna raised her head. "Do you have anything that would tide me over?" She puffed some of the hair away from her face.

"Try the contraception aisle," he suggested in a cold tone and walked away without a backward glance.

The contraception aisle. Shanna's feet hit the floor with a thud. Great. Terrific. Didn't the guy realize she had a prescription so she wouldn't have to deal with the contraception aisle?

She turned away from the counter and read the signs hanging from the ceiling. The aisle in question was in between the feminine hygiene products and diapers. Shanna sensed there was a hidden message in the layout, but felt some things were better left alone.

Turning the corner into the aisle, Shanna stumbled to a

halt. People with more forethought than she had picked the row clean. Someone was going to have hot and heavy Valentine sex. Too bad it wasn't going to be her.

So why did she feel relief? No. That can't be it. She was looking forward to her date with Dominic. Wasn't she? He was reasonably attractive and somewhat attentive. More importantly, he wasn't married, gay, or hung up on his mother. And he was marginally employed. Other than the fact he wasn't Calder, what was the problem?

Calder. Stop thinking about him. No more thinking of C—He-Who-Shall-Not-Be-Named. Shanna determinedly studied her purchase options. Spermicides . . . caps . . . condoms . . . Which one would offer her a more romantic evening? She was thinking, none of the above.

Okay, which offered less interruption? Less mess? How about no assembly required?

Sheesh. Shanna dug her fingers into her hair. Why did she let her prescription expire? Okay, yeah, there was that ridiculous vow when she believed she was never going to be in another serious relationship again. Heather tried to stop her from doing something rash, impulsive, and incredibly stupid. But did she listen? Nooooo.

She hated when her twin sister was right. But at the time she knew she wasn't going to want anyone as much as she wanted Cal—her ex-boyfriend. Sad thing was, it was still true.

Shanna felt herself wallowing in self-pity. Nothing could be done about it now. She had to move on.

She reluctantly picked up a box of something called dental dams. She frowned, wondering why it was shelved in this section. Shouldn't it be with the toothbrushes and mouthwash?

Seeing someone step in the aisle, Shanna shoved the dams back on the rack. The box teetered and fell onto the floor.

She glanced at the person who just entered. And did a fast double take that made her neck pop. *Calder!*

He strode in, his scuffed boots echoing against the tiled floor. It was like watching raw nature sweeping in. Calder was untamed beauty from the quiet hunter stance to the scent of rain clinging to his tanned skin.

"Hey, Shanna." She felt her heart flip-flop as his slow smile completely captivated her.

"Hi," she greeted weakly. Taking a step back, the toe of her sneaker hit something. Shanna looked down and saw the box. She bent down to retrieve it, mentally cursing her awkward movements.

Calder was already there, crouched and watching. Shanna couldn't shake off the sense that he was ready to pounce. But that was ridiculous. Still, it made her hesitate before she accepted the box from him.

His fingers brushed against her skin. She closed her eyes as sensations erupted in her. Her instinct wasn't to yank back. She wanted his touch to linger. Thread her fingers through his and hold tight.

Shanna pulled away, desire roaring through her. "Thanks," she murmured.

"You're welcome." His voice was low and intimate.

She didn't look at him as she straightened to her full height, which didn't come close to his. It was more than his stature that was overwhelming. His broad shoulders were made for clinging. The smoke-colored Henley brushed against his sculpted chest. It looked soft and well-worn. The classic cut of his faded jeans emphasized his lean, muscular legs. She knew the back view would make her stomach flutter.

Everything about the man invaded her senses. He was pure male, elemental and sensual. She wanted to meld into him, whether he was in bed or in a crowded store.

Which reminded her . . . What the hell was he doing in the contraceptive aisle? Not that she could necessarily ask that. She had to be blasé. Nonchalant. "How's it going?"

"Good." He scanned the row of condoms. "You?"

"Good," she answered, striving for a casual tone. Her eyes widened as he reached for a box of ribbed and studded condoms.

Shanna froze as she felt everything fall away from her like tinkling glass. He was buying condoms. Condoms designed to stimulate a woman's nerve endings. A woman who wasn't her!

The jagged pain ripped her in half. She struggled to remain upright instead of doubled over. How was this possible? When did he find someone new? How much did he like this woman? Okay, cut to the chase. The real question was, how hard was it to replace her?

"Sorry," Calder looked down at her. "Did you say something?"

"Huh?" Her gaze collided with his. She saw the satisfaction flaring in his dark, slumberous eyes. For the night that lay ahead of him?

She hurriedly looked away and pressed her lips together. *Remain calm. Walk to the nearest exit. Do not run . . . This is not a drill . . .*

"Say something?" Shanna pulled a box off the shelf in front of her. "Me? No." She snatched a bag of something dangling at eye level. "But wow,"—she grabbed for a tube of this and a bottle of that—"my lunch hour is almost over. I better get going."

"Big night planned?"

She stilled as her hands clenched around a tube she pulled off the shelf. Shanna was surprised she didn't squeeze the cream out of it. "What?" She looked down at the boxes, bottles, and bags in her arms. "Yeah, well. Valentine's Day, you know."

"Uh-huh," he said. Something different edged his voice. Like he understood. But how could he? Unless . . .

"Valentine's plans?" She barely managed to choke out

the words. Shanna nodded at the box in his hand. *So help me, if you made V-Day plans with another woman, I will not be held accountable for my actions.*

"Me?" He frowned at the thought. "Hell, no."

No. She felt a moment of absolute relief. Pain followed up so fast she thought she was going to be sick. That meant that the box was for incredible weeknight lovemaking. The kind of hot sex that had them instinctively searching for each other throughout the night. The kind that made her fall asleep at work the next day.

Somehow she felt worse. She needed to remember how many of those nights he worked late, how often he wasn't around. Of the many nights she fell asleep alone. Only to have Calder gently wake her up, cradling her spine against his chest and sharing his heat, his hands gliding down her abdomen . . .

Shanna clenched her thighs. She had to get out of the store. Right now. She grabbed a pump bottle. "Gotta go."

"I'll see you later, Shanna," Calder said as he reached for another box.

She couldn't move. Another box? Extra large? Fiery jealousy whooshed through her, leaving nothing but cinders. Shanna couldn't take it. She dipped her head and rushed to the cashier, her actions on autopilot.

Move on. Adapt. Any of this ring a bell? The words bounced around her chaotic mind as she waited in line. It didn't matter whose nerve endings he pleasured on a Wednesday night. Not at all.

By the time she reached the cash register, her arms ached and her heart felt like it was going to shatter. It took all of her willpower not to stomp back, tape off the contraceptive aisle, and direct Calder away from the scene.

Shanna dumped her purchases on the counter and ignored the cashier giving furtive glances under her lashes. What was she going to do with all this stuff? Shanna wondered as she opened her purse. At least the money she had saved for the salon was being put to good use.

Good use. Yeah, right. Who was she kidding? She hadn't even kissed Dominic. What made her think she was ready for a sex marathon?

She had a feeling half of the lubes and condom stuff was like swimwear; it was nonreturnable once you stepped out of the store. But she had too much pride to go back and return the items while Calder was there. She might as well consider it an investment in her future dating life. Whoo. Hoo. Keep her feet from dancing.

"Do you know the price for these?"

Shanna stopped hunting through her purse and looked up. The cashier held up the dental dams. "Uh, no."

The woman picked up the intercom. "Price check for dental dams. Price check on dental dams."

Those dental dams were out to haunt her. What were they for, anyway? Shanna leaned over and read the box.

Use these latex barriers for safe oral and anal sex. Available in a variety of flavors. Now in cherry!

Shanna felt the blush creep through her face. Her skin felt hot. Scalding. When she got back to the office, she was definitely going to check her horoscope. She had a feeling it was going to mention something about the Fates laughing their asses off at her.

From where he stood, Calder could see Shanna getting flustered at the register. He wondered what could have possibly rattled her. As far as he knew, only he had that power over her poise. Was he losing that, too?

He gripped the box tightly in his hand, the hard edges digging into his palm. He looked down at the box and smiled. The possessiveness flashing in Shanna's eyes was all he needed to see.

Relief flooded through him. The way she was going after

the Valentine's Day date with that loser had him worried. He knew that she didn't *really* want Dominic, but rather a date for Valentine's.

He knew that, but still . . . How was he going to keep Shanna from going out on Valentine's Day? He could go the easy route and do exactly what was on Shanna's list, but that would make his feelings a lie.

And he wanted her to understand that. He thought she would have by now. But Heather was right; it was time to reel Shanna Murphy in.

Calder replaced the box on the shelves. He still had the ones he bought while dating. If all worked out, he would use those condoms for their original purpose before their expiration date.

Chapter Four

Valentine's Day

Shanna quietly sat down next to her sister on the morning express bus. Heather cast a cautious sideways glance. "How's it going?" her twin asked.

Shanna stared straight ahead, right at the skinny guy's bald spot. She decided that it was as good a view as any. "He didn't call back."

"Who didn't?"

She swallowed hard. "Dominic."

"Ah." Her sister closed the newspaper.

Shanna blinked when the bald spot started to rotate like a kaleidoscope. "I left messages all day yesterday and he didn't return any of them."

Heather stopped folding the paper. "How many messages? Enough to qualify as a stalker?"

Most likely. "His cell phone was out of range," she said by way of an explanation. Shanna turned to her sister and made a helpless gesture with her hands. "Where could he be?"

Heather hunched her shoulders. "I dunno."

"What could send him out of range unexpectedly?"

Her sister's shoulders reached ear level. "Dunno."

"Do you think he would have the decency to let me know?"

"One can only hope."

Shanna chewed on the corner of her bottom lip. "Maybe he's looking for the perfect Valentine's Day card."

Heather arched an eyebrow. "And the quest took him to Canada?"

"Yeah, I thought that might be stretching it, too." The theory sounded better at four in the morning. Shanna returned her attention to the skinny guy's head. "I guess it's official."

"What is?"

Shanna exhaled shakily. "I ran my Valentine's date out of the country."

"You don't know that for sure."

"Heather, if your date doesn't even try to contact you on Valentine's Eve—"

"Oh, *God*," Heather muttered.

"Then he's probably dumping you and trying to lay low in another country so you don't hunt him down."

Heather rolled her eyes. "Try not to take the dramatic option for once in your life. He could be sick. Or dealing with an emergency."

Shanna folded her arms across her chest. "He had better be in the hospital suffering from amnesia."

"Your concern for him is overwhelming."

"I ran off another guy," Shanna said, slouching in her seat. "And I was so close. Right up until Valentine's Eve."

"For. The. Last. Time. There. Is. No. Such. Thing."

"And now look at me. I'm all dressed up and nowhere to go." She had picked out the chunky red sweater, long, flowing black skirt with a heart design, and black ankle boots specifically for the holiday. Early this morning she had to upturn her jewelry box to hunt for her diamond heart earrings. It had been that long since she had a reason to dress for a romantic occasion.

"Cute outfit," Heather said. "Not like I would want to borrow it or anything."

"But it's all a waste. And do you know why? Because I have no date," Shanna said, as she started ticking her list off with her fingers. "No dinner at a restaurant, and I can safely assume no dozen roses."

"Okay, so what are you going to do?" Heather asked with a hint of exasperation. "Go home, put on your old sweats and sulk? Eat a quart of ice cream and watch *Casablanca* for the five-hundredth time?"

"Maybe." She thought she had good cause for it. "Why do these things always happen to me? Why can't the forces of nature go my way for once?"

Heather paused. "Have you ever thought that this might be of your own making?"

Shanna flinched. "Say *what*?"

"Let me ask you something," Heather turned and faced Shanna. "With all this planning you did for the perfect V-Day, what did you plan to do for Dominic?"

"I—" Shanna blinked rapidly. "Well, I—" Somehow he-gets-to-find-my-G-spot wasn't the right answer.

"Yep, that's what I thought."

"You don't understand. This day was supposed to be about *me*." She thumped her palm against her chest. "Focused solely on *me*. Make *me* the center of attention and have my fantasy come to life."

"Hmm."

"Don't *hmm* me. Yes, I know that it sounds selfish and grabby. That's because it is! It's the one holiday designed for women to feel loved and appreciated."

"No, it's not. Valentine's Day is an excuse to have sex. As long as the guy romanticizes it, he's guaranteed to get laid."

Shanna's jaw dropped as she stared at her sister. "I can't believe you said that. To my face."

"If you think about it, V-Day is a lot like prom night."

The skinny guy in front briefly turned around to stare at Heather with disbelief. Shanna ignored him. "I don't want to hear it."

"As long as he dresses up, gives you flowers, plies you with alcohol, and doesn't buckle under the high expectations . . ."

"Valentine's Day," Shanna said through clenched teeth, "is supposed to be about showing love and appreciation."

"Nuh-uh." Heather turned and gave her a sly look. "You just said it was about a woman having her romantic fantasies fulfilled."

Shanna growled. "Oh, shut up. What about all the other days when I show love and affection? When I give and give and nothing comes back? I wanted one day when it comes back to me, and I wanted to *wallow* in it."

Heather arched her eyebrow. "You wanted it from Dominic?"

"Sure, if he was the only guy who was going to give it to me." Shanna sighed and wearily closed her eyes. "I wanted to be the center of a guy's existence for once in my life. It didn't matter that it was fake. I just wanted to know what it felt like."

"Well, don't give up hope." Heather patted Shanna's arm. "It still might happen. Dominic hasn't officially bailed."

"Yet." Shanna added and opened her eyes. She knew the signs of a potential dump, and it was just a matter of time. Shanna stared at the skinny guy's bald spot, wishing it would pull her in. She didn't think she had the strength to face yet another sucky Valentine's Day.

Shanna breathed a sigh of relief when she walked into her department and noticed she was the first one there. She hurried to her cubicle and stumbled to a stop. Her desk was dripping wet.

Paper was plastered against the desk surface. Droplets of

water dripped from the edge of her desk. Shanna glanced up, but saw no brown spots or other telltale signs of a leaky ceiling.

She walked toward her desk with trepidation. What the hell happened? Sweeping the sodden papers to the side, she grabbed a handful of tissues and mopped up some of the water. Where did all this water come from? Shanna wondered, just as she lifted her vase that felt suspiciously light.

No. Her eyes widened as she stared at the vase. She noticed the crack that started from the scalloped edge to the flat base. *Noooo.* "Cheap piece of—"

She gritted her teeth. *Don't lose it. Do not lose it. Your coworkers are going to arrive any minute.*

That reminder was enough to force her into action. Shanna clenched her fingers around the vase and marched straight to the women's restroom.

This was *not* an omen, she reminded herself, barely noticing the other employees milling around the hallways. It was *not* a punishment for putting herself first.

Shanna swung open the door to the restroom. *All that effort . . .* She tossed the traitorous crystal vase into the trash. *All that money. And for what?* She glared at the seesawing trash lid. *Nothing.*

Shanna grabbed a handful of paper towels as the tears pricked the back of her eyes. *Don't cry. Not now. Wait until you get home. You can do it.*

When she marched back to her cubicle, she saw Megan and Kerry had just arrived. Shanna mumbled something that resembled a greeting and set to work at mopping her desk as the other two women compared their Valentine plans. Shanna tried to block out the discussion, but the phrases "spa getaway" and "birthstone tennis bracelet" kept filtering through.

And all she had asked for was dinner, roses, and Valentine sex. She couldn't even get that. It wasn't fair. Shanna glared accusingly at the Valentine's Day decorations strung along her cubicle, fighting the urge to tear them down and rip them into itty-bitty pieces.

"Cupcake?"

Shanna flinched and glanced up. Megan had reached over the wall adjoining their workspaces and offered a plastic tray of pink-frosted cupcakes with heart-shaped sprinkles.

Shanna really didn't want one, but she took a cupcake in the name of office diplomacy. Anyway, her stomach was grumbling. "Thanks."

"Morning, girls," Angie greeted as she strolled into the department, wearing a sophisticated ruby-red pantsuit. Up until that moment, Shanna thought her own outfit had looked pretty good. That was until Angie's attire practically screamed *Sexy!* while hers was more of a hoarse *Nice try!*

"Hi, Angie," Megan bubbled in the only way Megan could. She approached their boss and offered a cupcake naked of frosting. "Here, I made this especially for you."

Shanna held her breath as Angie frowned at the dessert. *Yessss!* Megan overplayed her hand. No way would refined-sugar-is-evil Angie accept it.

"It's low-fat, low-carb," Megan added. "Not to mention organic."

Ugh. Shanna wrinkled her nose and gave a suspicious look at her own treat, wondering if there was something nutritious lurking under the mound of pink icing.

"Why, thank you, Megan." Angie smiled big and accepted the cupcake. "That's thoughtful of you."

Shanna set her cupcake down with a thump and twirled around to face her computer. There really was no justice in the world.

Or maybe she wasn't doing it right. As much as Shanna was reluctant to admit it—and no way would she say it out loud—her sister had made a valid point. She hadn't thought of others on this holiday.

Not that she felt guilty about ignoring her coworkers. Wasn't it enough that they grazed from her candy dish? They didn't deserve baked goods. Yet, Megan was thinking of others on V-Day. Sure, for her own gain, but it worked.

She did, however, feel a pang of guilt about Dominic. Why hadn't she even considered doing something for him? Was she that out of practice? Come to think of it, when was the last romantic thing she did for someone else?

But that was different, Shanna decided, as she booted up her computer. Calder hadn't been into romance. She showed her love in other ways. And she did it every day. But she would have done them anyway.

Except for one. Shanna winced as the regret welled up in her chest and pressed against her ribs. She would have told Calder that she loved him.

Instead, she held out on him. She secretly tested him, waiting for a sign in the form of a romantic gesture. She had thought that would have been enough proof that he loved her. She had thought wrong.

Shanna sighed, wondering if she did anything right when it came to Calder Smith. And was there any way she could make things right? Probably not, considering he was buying condoms in bulk to use with someone else.

She swallowed back the bile-green jealousy and clicked onto her e-mail. Scanning through the multitude of spam, Shanna's attention zoomed in on one sender: Dominic.

Her stomach pinched. Her hand hovered over the mouse. Dread, thick and hot, spread through her as she clicked open the e-mail.

Can't make it tonight. Some other time.

That was *it*? Shanna shook her head sharply and read it again. That's all he had to say when he sends it at—she glanced up at the time of the e-mail—1:30 this morning? He didn't even *sign* it.

Her fingers itched to type a reply that would place a curse on a certain part of his anatomy. No, she decided, and swiftly deleted the e-mail. She'd wasted enough time on the louse. *There's a reserved spot for you in hell, Dominic.*

But that didn't explain the sense of relief washing over her. She couldn't possibly be happy about getting dumped on Valentine's Day.

Okay, okay. Shanna rolled her eyes. So maybe she wasn't so happy about going out with Dominic. She really didn't want him. He was, after all, a slut.

She wanted Calder. She still did, with or without the romantic wrappings. She wanted him more than anything, now that she knew what it was to be without him.

But she'd blown it, and had wasted too much time not fixing it. No, instead she'd busied herself on the perfect V-Day project that was destined to fail.

She needed to make up for her mistakes. She had to do it now. Do it before she talked herself out of it.

Shanna pushed away from the computer and stood up. Her Valentine's Day wasn't going as planned, but if she was lucky, it would be better than expected. Who would have thought Dominic's chickenshit cowardice would have been a good thing?

Calder stood at the whiteboard hanging in his office designing an algorithm, when he felt Shanna's presence. He tensed as his mind went blank. Today was not a good day to see her. He didn't want to see men with ulterior motives giving her gifts.

Why you couldn't give her a dozen roses remains a mystery. Heather's comment managed to dig under his skin and he couldn't shake it free. Yeah, he'd been wondering about that, too.

"Calder?"

Her soft, clear voice washed over him. He glanced up, bracing himself for the impact of seeing Shanna. His chest tightened as he took it all in: her long, red hair that always felt soft under his fingers, blue eyes that had the power to turn his mind into mush, and the sweater and skirt hiding her beautiful and surprisingly flexible body that haunted him in his sleep.

She looked so damn good. *For another man*. He scowled at the reminder. "Yeah?"

"You're busy," she said, and took a step out of his office. "I can come back another time."

She looked like she was about to make a run for it. "No, what's up?" Calder dropped his marker and grabbed her before she escaped.

The minute he touched her he knew his restraint was not up for the test. Images collided and crowded his mind. Of him caging her in his arms and not letting her go. Of slamming the door closed and pressing her against it. Of kissing her senseless until her lips were reddened with his mark. He wanted to burrow his fingers under her sweater and palm her breasts, teasing her nipples until she called out his name . . .

"Do you have any plans for tonight?"

. . . wrap her legs around his hips, shove her skirt up and—what? "Uh, no," he answered dazedly. "Why?"

She nervously hooked her hair behind her ear. A diamond heart earring winked back at him. "I was wondering if you'd like to come over to my place after work."

Calder frowned, shaking the image of her, wild and willing, against his door. He couldn't follow what she was saying. "Your place." Sounded crowded.

"For dinner," she clarified. She looked up at him from beneath her lashes and smiled.

His body grew heavy and his cock stirred. That was the same look she always gave right before she blew his mind with staggering pleasure. The kind of pleasure that hurt so good and left him gasping for air.

His gaze drifted down Shanna's face, his heartbeat skittering. Calder wanted to brush his mouth against each freckle before tasting her lips and dipping his tongue inside her wet heat. He craved her so much that he almost couldn't stand it. But she was worth the agony.

"I'll make your favorite," she promised.

He was really confused. Tempted and bedazzled, but confused. Calder dragged his gaze away and glanced at his calendar. Yeah, it was February 14, unfortunately. "You don't cook on Valentine's Day."

"Eh, so what?" Shanna waved off his concern. "I'll break tradition."

Calder swallowed roughly. He wanted to grab the surprise gift with both hands, but he didn't want to share, either. "What about Dominic?" he asked, reluctant to mention the guy's name.

She pulled away from him. "Oh, yeah. Dominic." She rolled her eyes and made a face. "We're not going out tonight. Or ever, for that matter."

"Why not?" He liked the annoyance burring her words. Dominic somehow screwed up—or else Shanna came to her senses.

"He canceled." She shrugged. "It's no big deal."

Pain slammed deep in his chest. Calder was surprised he didn't stagger back from the force. Shanna's plans fell through and she was going to fall back on Calder. Not because she wanted to go out with him, but because she wanted to go out.

"So? How about it?" The soft promise in her voice had the same effect on his defense as a battering ram. "You, me, and a home-cooked dinner?"

She was even going to forgo her cardinal rule to make something out of what's left of the day. Damn, this was going to hurt. But he had to do it. When they got back together—and they would—it would be for the right reasons. Not because no one else was available. "No," he answered gruffly.

"Does seven—I'm sorry?" She frowned. "What?"

"I said, no." He turned away and walked to his desk before he ruined it by falling to his knees at her feet. "I don't want to be the alternate date," he continued in a hard, flat tone. "You want to be with someone for Valentine's and since I don't have any plans, I'll do."

Shanna looked stunned. "That's not the reason at all."

"Right." Calder sat down, grabbing a pen between tense, whitened fingers. He needed distance. He needed to be at least a room's length away with as much furniture between them as possible.

He wanted to grab for the one thing he had been wishing for, and he barely had the strength to deny himself. Calder's hand shook slightly and hoped Shanna didn't notice. He now understood how she felt when she refused to accept the terms of their relationship.

And she managed it for three months. He didn't think he was going to last three more minutes. The woman had more strength than he gave her credit for.

Shanna glared at him. "You know what? Never mind. Forget I said anything," she ordered, her voice rising. "Forget I was here."

Now *that* he couldn't accomplish, even if he wanted to.

He said no.

Shanna exited the elevator like a sleepwalker. She felt dazed and couldn't shake out of it. She couldn't believe it. *Calder had said no.*

Well, what did she expect? She broke up with him months ago, had just accepted a date with another man, acted like she was ready to sleep with that other man, and thought Calder would be panting at the possibility of getting back together.

She was an idiot. She threw away the possibility of a really good thing for a fantasy that was never going to happen.

Shanna walked into the department and froze.

The florist deliveries had already arrived.

That is, florist deliveries for *other* people.

Megan's large, beautiful bouquet peeked over her cubicle wall. The flowers were bright. Cheerful. Nauseating.

Shanna slowly walked to her desk, glancing at Kerry's. The woman had received a darkly exotic floral arrangement. She hadn't even realized Kerry had someone special enough to send flowers.

Shanna quietly sat at her computer, hoping no one would notice the lack of greenery on her desk. She tried desperately to focus on the line of code, never feeling so empty in her life.

"Shanna?"

You can do this. Your breakdown will resume at 6:00 P.M. Shanna fought for a polite expression and turned. Her breath caught in her throat as she saw Angie standing at the cubicle doorway holding the most enormous bouquet of red roses.

The gray Seattle clouds parted and a stream of sun hit the blood-red petals. Shanna felt the constricting binds of misery breaking free from her ribs. Tears of joy burned the back of her eyes and she realized that Dominic had planned to send her flowers. She could have sworn the angels were singing the "Hallelujah Chorus" in the background.

"Well?" Angie's strident voice halted the music to a screeching stop. "Are you going to take them or do I throw them in the trash?"

"*What?*" Her boss had gone too far. *Harm one petal, harm even one leaf, and you're a dead woman.*

"You weren't listening, were you?" Angie sighed, her nostrils flaring. "Both Stan and Tony sent me flowers. I can't have this bouquet," she shook the vase slightly "from Tony in my office when Stan picks me up tonight."

"Oh. Right." *Angie—2, Shanna—0.*

"I was going to throw them out when I realized you don't have a bouquet."

Shanna felt the blush crawling up her neck as her coworkers glanced in her direction. *Go ahead. Turn a spotlight onto my flower-free cubicle.*

"Do you want them?" Angie asked impatiently.

No. She didn't. Why would anyone think she wanted hand-me-down flowers! Who cared if they were her dream floral arrangement right down to the baby's breath, fern fronds, and bright red satin bow?

But what excuse could she possibly give, since she had flowers on her desk for the past six weeks? "Thanks," Shanna said, as she accepted the heavy arrangement.

"No problem," Angie replied, and walked away without a backward glance.

Shanna stared at thc bouquet. Why wasn't there a patron saint for women who were dumped on Valentine's Day? She could use some divine intervention right about now.

Chapter Five

Shanna tried to work steadily for the rest of the morning, but her gaze kept darting to her clock.

She blocked out the oohs and aahs her coworkers made about the teddy bear Angie received a half an hour later.

She ignored Kerry's covert whispering on a phone call with her "grandma," who apparently goes by the name of "Snake."

And when Angie found it necessary to unwrap a present in front of everyone, even though it had a designer lingerie emblem on the box, Shanna didn't gag once at the sight of the crotchless underwear in her boss's hand.

Shanna thought she was doing well under the circumstances, amazing even herself when Angie's husband sent a huge box from a local chocolatier. As her boss passed the treats around, Shanna went so far as to blindly grab the closest chocolate and politely say thanks.

A lot of good *that* did her. It turned out to be a raspberry cordial. Figured. If there was one way to ruin a good piece of chocolate, add sticky-sweet fruit syrup that dripped everywhere.

She glanced again at the flowers on her desk. At least she got one thing on her list. A dozen red roses. Sent by a man. And she received them in front of everybody.

Shanna determinedly looked away. Next time she'd be more specific on her list.

No. Wait. There would be no next time. She did everything possible to ensure a proper V-Day and it didn't work. Nothing worked. She was giving up, rolling over, and playing dead.

" 'Bye, girls."

The ebullient voice jarred Shanna out of her thoughts. She glanced up and saw her boss waltzing out of her office, heading for the exit.

" 'Bye, Angie," Megan piped up.

"When I get back," Angie said, and took another sip from her coffee mug, "I expect to see major progress."

Hot anger boiled inside Shanna, crackling through her composure. She wanted to take that coffee mug and ram it down Angie's throat.

"When can we expect you back?" Megan asked.

"I don't know for sure," Angie said with a coy smile. "I'm having a long lunch."

Shanna rolled her eyes. "Oh, give me a break!"

After a tense silence, Angie said sharply, "Excuse me?"

Damn! Shanna winced. She hadn't meant to say it out loud. *Don't say anything else. Keep quiet!*

"Did you say something, Shanna?"

She heard Angie by her cubicle doorway. Shanna slowly opened her eyes. *Think Nancy Reagan! Just say no!*

But she couldn't. It was as if her body were rejecting everything obedient. "You shouldn't be taking a long lunch," Shanna said softly through clenched teeth.

Angie drew to her full height. "*I* shouldn't?"

"If this deadline is so important," Shanna reluctantly continued, knowing she was digging herself a deeper grave yet unable to stop herself from disaster, "everyone should work until it's finished."

"That's for me to decide," Angie said coldly. Her eyes were like shards of ice. It made her look scarier than usual.

"I had to give up my half-day because of a deadline." Shanna swiped her tongue against dry lips, her heart pounding furiously against her breastbone. "But you're going to take several hours off?"

"I'm the boss. What I say goes." She leaned forward, and Shanna saw a glimpse of the pure ruthlessness that she knew had always lain under the surface of the beautiful face. "Got it?" Angie said with lethal softness.

And that was the problem. Angie *was* the boss, and Angie always won. Unemployment was looking better all the time. "Got it."

"Good." Angie turned on her heel and marched out of the office.

Shanna glared at Angie's back until the woman was out of the door and turned the corner. Her courage burst to the forefront once she was out of earshot. "I hope you get hit by a bus!"

"Shanna!" Megan said with a gasp.

"An express bus going a hundred miles an hour," Shanna continued, her voice rising as she warmed up to the idea.

"Uh . . ."

Shanna launched from her chair and leaned against the cubicle wall. "A bus stuffed with sumo wrestlers!"

"Shanna?"

"With a driver suffering from PMS!" She clenched the edge with tight hands.

"Yo, Shanna!"

"And when the bus driver hits you . . ." Her fingers dug into the fabric on the wall.

"Are you—"

"I hope she slams on the brakes. Hard!"

"—okay?"

"And goes in reverse!" Shanna suddenly decided.

"I guess not."

"Leaving tire tracks permanently tattooed on your face!"

"God, Shanna," Kerry said, as she turned off her computer. "Grow up."

So says the woman who gets her half-day. The same woman who approaches every workday with the plan to slack off, leave early, and slough the workload onto her coworkers. Shanna gave Kerry a warning glance.

Kerry rose from her seat and hooked her purse over her shoulder. "I'm out of here. See you guys Monday."

"Say hello to Grandma Snake for me," Shanna said. She didn't feel a spurt of victory at Kerry's guilty flinch.

Shanna returned to her chair and stared at the computer screen. She was still meditating on the same line of code when Megan cautiously left for a lunch with her fiancé.

"And then there was one," Shanna muttered to herself. Once again, she found herself alone making sure the work got done. Having the least seniority meant the last for lunch because "someone had to be in the office," the last to leave work, the last to pick vacation time. Dead last in everything.

When it was nearly 2:00 P.M., Shanna found herself staring at the screen, waffling over the plan to change a few variables in the program to mess with everyone's mind. But that would only cause more work for her in the long run.

It really was hell being the lowest on the totem pole, Shanna decided, rubbing her stomach as it growled. Especially when there was no opportunity to move up. And now she had made it nearly impossible when she mouthed off.

Shanna shook her head, mourning the years of good behavior dashed by one fit of temper. She knew she was going to suffer for her outburst. She didn't know when or for how long, but she was going to pay. Through the nose.

"Uh, hello?"

Shanna whirled around and saw the cute but exhausted delivery guy at her cubicle.

"Yeah?" Shanna asked, eyeing the flat, pale blue box

from a well-known jeweler. *Please tell me you are my fairy godmother—er, godfather—and whatever you have in the box will bibbidi-bobbidi-boo me outta here.*

"I'm looking for Angie . . ." he squinted at the last name.

Shanna sighed. "She's not in."

"I need you to sign for this." He thrust the clipboard in her face.

Could Valentine's Day get any worse? Shanna wordlessly signed the sheet and grabbed the box. She watched the delivery guy leave and decided this was the suckiest of days.

Rising from her seat, she headed toward her boss's office. She glowered at the box, reading the sappy love note Angie's husband had attached, and her feet faltered to a stop. Should she take a peek? Just a small one?

Shanna looked right and left before she unlatched the box and opened the lid. Her gasp rang out as she stared at the diamond necklace.

Shanna snapped the lid closed.

You know what? Valentine's Day is a stupid holiday. It was designed *all* wrong. There was something seriously faulty about a holiday where a woman was too busy boinking her lover to accept diamonds from her husband.

She stomped into Angie's office and tossed the box onto her boss's desk. When it went down with a thud, Shanna cringed. If that turned out to be broken and she signed for it—it would be the suitable ending for a crummy day.

She retrieved the box and flipped the lid open. Shanna sighed as the diamonds sparkled back at her. She lovingly traced the snowflake design with the tip of her finger. What would it be like to receive something so beautiful? To wear something this gorgeous?

A naughty thought invaded her mind. She *could* try on the necklace. Right here and now. Her eyes shifted right and left again. No one would know.

Shanna nibbled her lip as she studied the diamond-encrusted necklace.

No. Shanna closed the lid and latched it. No. No. No. Considering how her day had been going, the hook would get stuck and she wouldn't be able to get it off.

Anyway, Shanna thought as she placed the velvety box in the center of Angie's desk, she didn't want diamonds. Well, actually, she did. But she wanted the *meaning* behind the diamonds even more.

She just had to stop holding her breath for that fairy tale to happen, Shanna thought with a slump of her shoulders. Her head dipped and she frowned when she looked inside the wastebasket.

What the . . . ? It was the cupcake Megan made especially for Angie. Nearly untouched. Hmm . . . not everyone was getting their way. Good to know she wasn't the only one.

Calder stood by Shanna's cubicle and dragged his gaze away from the amazing bouquet of roses. Who was giving her flowers? Dominic? His competition was smarter than he thought.

He wished he had given her those roses. He wished he had put the smile on Shanna Murphy's face. He bet her expression would have taken his breath away.

He didn't begrudge her flowers, Calder thought, flicking his gaze back at the offending petals. He knew she should be surrounded by them. Every day.

Acid ate away at his stomach. Or maybe it was regret. Possibly—though he wouldn't admit to it even under torture—fear.

All that I-refuse-to-take-part-in-all-things-romantic was crap. He had been blowing smoke. He hated to admit it—God, he hated to admit it—but he was scared. Scared of messing up. Scared of making a fool of himself when deep down he wanted to be her Prince Charming.

He didn't have what it took to be a prince, but he wasn't going to let that hold him back anymore. He was going to pursue Shanna again. He might get it wrong. He probably would leave out something important, but he'd take the risk.

He saw Shanna stepping out of Angie's office. She hesitated before walking over to him. "What's up, Calder?"

"Is your date with Dominic back on?"

"No," Shanna replied.

The knot that had formed in his chest loosened. He gestured at the flowers. "Then who?"

Shanna looked away and down at her feet. "Angie received two bouquets, and since I was the only one without flowers . . ."

Calder winced. His pursuit wasn't going to be easy. He had a lot of mistakes to correct.

"So," Shanna folded her arms across her chest, "why are you here?" She suddenly glanced at the door.

Calder followed her gaze and saw Angie breezing in. The tousled hair, the secret smile, the creased red suit told him just what Angie had for lunch.

"Shanna?" Angie's voice rose with irritation. "Are you just getting back?"

Calder silently observed the muscle twitching in Shanna's cheek. "I haven't gone to lunch," she answered carefully. "I'm not allowed to leave the office unattended. Remember?"

"Where is everyone else?" Angie gestured at the empty cubicles.

"Kerry left early to take care of her"—she paused—"*grandmother*, and I don't know why Megan hasn't shown up yet."

"It's too late for you to go to lunch. You need to get back to work," Angie said as she waltzed into her office and closed the door.

Shanna turned and faced Calder. "I really do hate her," she said matter-of-factly.

"I heard." As much as he wanted to whisk Shanna away from the woman's claws, any interference would only make it worse. He was already failing as Prince Charming, but that guy was too impetuous, anyway. "Runaway bus? Sumo wrestlers?"

"How'd you hear about that?" she asked in a whisper, darting a guilty look at Angie's door.

Was she kidding? Everyone from the CEO to the cleaners gossiped. "You were shouting it and someone overheard."

She made a face. "Terrific."

"You shouldn't have done it," Calder was compelled to say. He couldn't take her away, but he might be able to guide her. Although she probably wouldn't appreciate it. "Angie is going to give you hell."

"Yeah, I know." She rubbed her forehead tiredly. "So, what were you going to talk to me about?"

Yep. Didn't appreciate it. "I changed my mind about tonight."

Her eyebrows shot up. "You have? Even though you think you're an alternate date?"

"I don't think that. I—I . . ." Okay, he might be doing his best to transform into Mr. Romance, but he had no idea what he was doing. "I want to take you somewhere tonight."

"Really?" He heard her catch her breath. "You don't have to."

Calder looked intently in Shanna's eyes. "As a Valentine's date," he clarified.

Shanna froze. "No way," she said, her mouth barely moving.

Calder waved his hand in front of her eyes, snapping her out of the daze. "How about I pick you up at five?"

She frowned, looking more confused by the minute. "That's early for you."

"Yeah, I know."

"O . . . kay."

Angie burst from her office, the door banging against the wall. She hurried over to them. "This is terrible," she announced, flattening her hands against her chest. "Megan left a message on my voice mail. She's been in a car accident and she's in the emergency room being treated for whiplash and a concussion."

"Impressive," Shanna murmured. "Can't prove it. Can't disprove it."

"She can't make it back to work!" Angie announced. "Doctor's orders!"

"I want to see it in writing," Shanna said under her breath.

"We have to meet our project objective by midnight." Calder watched Angie's wire-hanger-thin shoulders rise and fall, the diamond necklace twinkling under the harsh lights with every move. "Shanna, you're going to work until they're done."

"What?" Shanna exclaimed in a squawk. "I haven't—"

"You'll stay all night if need be." Angie pointed a bony finger, and Calder noticed the lethal length of her manicured nails.

Shanna didn't respond.

"I have to update my boss on the project." Angie shoved her hands in her hair. "Fuck!" She pivoted on one spindly heel and stormed out.

Calder stared after Angie as the room suddenly plunged into silence. What the hell was that? Interference or not, he had to get Shanna away from that woman.

"Can we have a rain check on the dinner?" Shanna asked in a tight voice. She was doing her best not to look at him. "Like tomorrow night?"

"It won't be Valentine's night," he reluctantly reminded her.

"I know." She nodded her head briskly. "It's okay."

But this time, it wasn't okay for him.

"I better get to work." She turned and looked at her desk, and Calder saw the glitter of tears.

"I'll wait for you."

She blinked and her mouth parted open in surprise. Calder almost felt offended by her reaction.

"You don't have to," she said with shy uncertainty. "I might be here all night."

More reason for him to stay. "And I'll be in my office until you need me."

Calder liked the way she was staring at him. It made him feel powerful.

Who was he kidding? He was getting a buzz from it. She usually had that awed and dazed expression when he took her to his bed. That look was even more potent outside the bedroom.

He brushed his mouth against her cheek, inhaling her scent and enjoying the softness and heat of her skin. He paused, savagely reining in his impulses. He quickly strode out the door before he did something uncivilized and wound up with rug burn on his knees.

He might get the hang of this Prince Charming thing. Either that, or it'd kill him.

"Are you crying?" Heather asked, her suspicion loud and clear through the telephone.

Shanna wiped the moisture lying right under her eyelashes. "No."

"Uh-*huh*. So . . . Psycho Boss expects you to stay late and you told her to take this job and—"

"No," Shanna interrupted, squeezing the tissue against her nose.

"But—but—but—" Heather spluttered. "Calder asked you out! On Valentine's Day! This is monumental!"

"I'll go out with him tomorrow," Shanna said as she tossed the tissue into the wastebasket. A night with Calder was the most important thing. The date was no longer crucial, although she'd prefer something sooner than later.

"It's not the same," Heather said.

Shanna drew the phone away, and stared at it before placing it back on her ear. "I can't believe you just said that."

"Neither can I. But you know what I mean."

She did, just as she knew she couldn't alter the chain of events. Shanna sighed in defeat. "I better hang up before Angie finds me on the phone. Just don't expect to see me on the bus."

"What I don't understand," Heather quickly added, "is why you aren't fighting for it. You could tell the bitch that you aren't going to make the deadline and there's no way you're going to work late."

"And after I do that and get fired—which would be the perfect ending to this holiday—do I get to move into your place, and have you financially support me?"

"Forget that," Heather replied. "You move in with Calder."

Shanna felt her stomach do a funny little jump. "Don't get your hopes up. It's a mercy date."

"Oh . . ." Heather said. "So *that's* why you're not fighting for Valentine's night."

Shanna glanced at the door as she heard fast, angry footsteps thudding down the hallway. "I hear Angie coming," she whispered, leaning down toward the phone.

"Okay, okay. But all I have to say is that Megan had better be black and blue Monday morning or I'll do the honors for you."

"Sounds good." She hurriedly hung up the phone and placed her fingers on the keyboard as Angie rushed in. Shanna glanced out of the corner of her eye, but Angie made a beeline to her office. When her boss slammed the door behind her, Shanna slowly exhaled.

She absently wondered if there were any countries that didn't observe Valentine's Day. Shanna grabbed her computer mouse and started searching online. She might just go ahead and find out how much international flights cost. While she couldn't do anything about it now, there was no way she would suffer through another Valentine's night.

Shanna stretched her arms overhead and groaned. It was 9:00 P.M., her fingers were stiff, her back was sore, but she was buzzing with energy, wondering if she could salvage any part of Valentine's night.

Don't get your hopes up. She needed to approach the night with no expectations. Especially since it was probably a mercy date. But could she get some mercy sex with that? No, she shouldn't think of that. It was too presumptuous. Wasn't it?

Shanna rang Calder's office, glancing at the wrinkled wrapper and bread crust from her deli sandwich that he'd dropped off hours ago. "Hey, I'm done," she said breathlessly when he answered.

"I'll be right down."

Was she imagining the dark promise lurking underneath his words? And was mercy sex worse than no sex? And would it help if she managed to get him stripped naked in her bed by midnight? Because then it would still be Valentine sex.

She pondered the question as she took the last sip of her hazelnut latte. A smile slowly formed on her lips as she remembered Calder surprising her with the large cup made just the way she liked it. Shanna sighed and closed her eyes as she felt the caffeine hit. She hadn't had a latte for six weeks. It beat a box of chocolates any day.

Logging off her computer, Shanna paused while grabbing her purse and glared at Angie's closed door. She hadn't heard a thing from the woman since she stormed in there hours before. And that's the way Shanna preferred it.

She would have liked to continue the silent treatment by leaving without saying good-bye to her boss, but what was the point in that? She wanted Angie to know just how long she'd stayed.

Shanna strode to the door and knocked loudly, but there was no reply. Yep, the silent treatment continued. She listened at the door, but she didn't hear any noise.

She knocked harder. "Angie?" Jeez. Her boss could be such a big baby sometimes. Shanna creaked the door open, hoping she wasn't going to interrupt another X-rated videoconference. "Hey, Angie?"

Angie was sitting at her chair, her head resting against her desk, turned toward the computer. The screen was blank, indicating the screen saver had turned off hours ago.

This is *so* unfair. Rage bloomed and stung against her ribs. She had been doing the work of three people, and her boss was in here taking a *nap*?

"Yo, Angie!" she said loudly, stomping around the desk to face her lazy boss. "I'm going now. Okay?"

She faced Angie and drew back. Alarm tingled in the back of Shanna's neck as the fine hairs on her arm stood to attention. Something was wrong.

Angie didn't wake up, but her eyes were wide open. Her lips were parted. Her skin didn't look right.

Shanna cocked her head to the side. That was weird. It almost looked like Angie was . . . dead.

Chapter Six

Calder was in the hallway strategizing how the evening was going to end—preferably with Shanna in his bed, underneath him, over him, and all the prepositions and positions that were humanly possible—when he heard her cry out.

The scream was primal and blood-chilling. Calder bolted into a full run. "Shanna?" he called, careening into her department.

Fear, icy and tight, gripped his heart as he ran to her desk. She wasn't there. A quick look at the other cubicles showed that they were empty.

So where was she?

"Shanna!" He ran by Angie's office and stopped at the doorway. The first thing he saw was Shanna standing at the desk. Her arms were wrapped tightly against her midriff, but she was visibly shaking.

He glanced at where she was staring with wild eyes. Angie's head rested on the desk, pitched forward as if she had fallen asleep. Dread filled his chest as he slowly walked over to where Shanna stood and looked at Angie.

The woman's eyes were open and stared blankly at him. Her lips and skin were blue. Oh, yeah. That woman was dead.

"Don't touch anything," Calder told Shanna, unable to stop staring at the stiff, almost rigid body.

"I wasn't planning on it," Shanna whispered.

He studied Angie's desk. It was cluttered with flowers, files, chocolates, reams of paper, gift boxes, a travel coffee mug, and a teddy bear. But no blood. "I'm going to call Security."

"Okay." She didn't move.

He made himself look at Angie, but Calder didn't see anything that would give him a hint of what happened. As far as he could tell, there was no sense of panic in Angie's last moments. No outstretched hand or contorted expression. Not a hair was out of place.

He slowly surveyed the room. The bookcases were crammed with awards and plaques. The computer equipment hummed quietly. The desk and chairs were in the same spot as always. Nothing looked out of the ordinary. There was no sign of struggle. "Was anyone here this evening?" he asked.

Shanna shook her head dazedly. "No."

He cast a sharp look at her. "Are you sure?"

She pulled her attention away from her boss and met his eyes. "I can see and hear everything that goes on in this department."

"Then what happened here?"

"I don't know."

"Did you have anything to do with this?" He ran through the list of possibilities. Accident, self-defense . . .

Her mouth slowly dropped open as realization hit. "What?" She nearly hissed the word. "No!"

He held his hands up. "Just asking."

Shanna took a step back, her eyes widening. "How could you even suggest such a thing?"

Calder motioned at Angie. "I find you standing over the body of a woman you hate." Obviously the question wouldn't help his new romantic image, but he couldn't ignore the possibility.

She put her hands on her hips. "Do you think I have it in me to kill someone?"

He never said the K-word, but now wasn't the time to point that out. "I'm trying to find out how much I need to protect you."

Shanna's eyes grew impossibly bigger. In fact, she was looking at him as if he were insane. So much for being her knight in shining armor.

"Are you okay?" Calder asked.

"No." She hunched her shoulders and closed her eyes. "I think I'm going to be sick all over the floor."

"The cops won't appreciate you contaminating the crime scene." Calder placed his hand on her back.

Shanna flinched, and he silently prayed it wasn't because of his touch.

"What makes you think a crime occurred?" she asked, finally moving toward the door. "For all we know, she could have keeled over from a heart attack."

It was possible, but his instincts were screaming *foul play*. "Do heart attack victims turn that blue?"

She looked over her shoulder at Angie. "And she *still* looks good. Damn it."

Whew, Calder thought as he gently guided her out of the door. He was worried for a minute there, but Shanna was back to normal.

After spending most of the evening in silence, the crime scene was almost deafening. Plainclothed and uniformed officers crowded her department. The atmosphere buzzed with urgency, interspersed with jolts of heightened activity.

Since Shanna wasn't allowed in her cubicle, she took the opportunity to station herself at Kerry's desk and look through the drawers. She learned more about her coworker than she ever wanted to know.

Shanna grabbed a women's magazine off Kerry's desk and flipped through it. She stopped at a romantic quiz. "If you were a famous lover in royal history, who would you be?" she read aloud softly. "a), Cleopatra, b) Wallis Simpson, or c) Grace Kelly."

Well, that was a no-brainer, Shanna decided with the wiggle of her eyebrows. It was "c" all the way.

"If you chose Grace Kelly," Calder said over the cubicle wall, "you got the answer wrong."

She glared at him. "There's no right or wrong answer," she answered primly.

"Yep." He rested against the wall. "You picked 'c'."

"Lucky guess." She slapped the magazine closed and paused. "How did you know?"

"Because she was the closest one to a fairy-tale princess."

She felt her jaw tighten. "That's not why I chose her." At least, it wasn't the *only* reason.

"Suuuure."

She tossed the magazine back onto the desk. "Who did *you* pick for me?"

His slow grin turned her inside out. "I'm not telling."

Shanna scowled at him, wishing her heart didn't kick up a beat at the sight of one of his rare smiles. "You think you know me and how my mind works, but you don't. Now go back to your corner." She motioned for him to leave. "You're not supposed to talk to me while they investigate."

"Why are you mad at me?"

Was he serious? "You think I"—she dropped her voice a level—"did it!"

"No." He splayed his hands over the wall. "I *asked* if you did."

Didn't he get it? A guy who was head over heels in love with her would never ask. Come to think of it, neither would a guy deep in infatuation. Or attraction. "This day truly sucks," she decided. "It's an omen."

"Not that the world revolves around you or anything," Calder muttered dryly.

"Okay. I get it." She crossed her arms and twirled the office chair around. "I get that I'm selfish and self-absorbed."

"I didn't say that. You are one of the most giving—"

"And I feel like I'm being punished for asking something in return," she said, twirling back to face him. "I wanted some romance and you acted like I was requiring you to risk your life for me."

His face tightened. "I *would* risk my life for you," he said in a dark, low voice.

"Yeah, I know." Which was a romantic thought, in a disturbing way, but she wanted action! "Not to worry—I'll probably die of extreme old age. Don't get me wrong—I appreciate the offer."

"Uh-huh."

"Sorry. Nothing seems to come out right." Shanna sighed. She shoved her hands in her hair. "What a day. My perfect Valentine's Day went down the toilet, and the love of my life thinks I have homicidal tendencies."

His head jerked up. "Love of your life."

Jeez. He didn't have to act all poleaxed about it. "As if you didn't know." Did he think she was this attentive and loving to every guy she dated? She didn't cook, dress up, or swallow for just anyone!

Calder's eyes glittered with a possessiveness that took her breath away. "You never said—"

"Shanna Murphy?"

"Yes?" She turned and saw a handsome man in a dark suit standing in front of her.

"Sergeant Donovan Anteros," he said by way of greeting and shook her hand. "I'm the investigating officer. So what happened here?"

"I have no idea." Which is what she'd told about a dozen other officers.

"When was the last time you saw her alive?"

"Four . . ." she shrugged, "four-thirty."

"What was she doing?" he asked, scribbling down notes on his pad of paper.

"She returned from a meeting." She pointed at the pathway Angie made hours ago. "She went straight to her office and slammed the door."

The sergeant's brow wrinkled. "Did she do or say anything unusual?"

"No, she was bitchy as usual."

A pause hovered between them. The officer looked directly in her eyes. His eyebrow quirked up.

"Sorry, did I say that out loud? God!" She thwacked her palm against her forehead. "I've been doing that all day."

"You didn't get along with the victim?" he asked.

Shanna made a face. "No one did."

"Why not?"

Calder jumped in. "Uh—"

Sergeant Anteros pointed the tip of his pen at Calder. "I'll get to you in a minute, sir."

"Before you continue," Shanna said, "let's get something straight. I don't know what happened and I had nothing to do with Angie's death." She glared pointedly at Calder.

"Sergeant!" one of the officers called out from Shanna's cubicle. "Can you come here for a minute?"

"I'll be right back," Anteros promised.

Shanna leaned back into the chair. "Can't wait."

Calder watched the police officers crowd into Shanna's cubicle. Something close to panic pressed against Calder's ribs as he watched them point out something on Shanna's computer. The way they whispered and put their heads together said it all. Shanna was in trouble.

She might not have had anything to do with the death, but circumstantial evidence was building up against her. He had to do something about it. But what? He looked around the department, praying for a sign, for inspiration, but came up with nothing. If it was any other day, he *might* find a clue, but Valentine's Day screwed everything up.

"If you think about it," Calder said, as an idea slowly formed, "Valentine's Day is a good setup for a homicide."

Shanna flashed him a cold look. "That is blasphemous."

Calder felt his mouth tug up into a grin. "I thought you were off V-Day."

"Not *that* much."

"Come on, Shanna. On February 14 everything is off-schedule. You do things you wouldn't normally do."

"And isn't that sad? Shouldn't every day be like Valentine's?"

He shuddered. He then noted another officer had joined the others in Shanna's cubicle. "So," Calder said as casually as possible, "who do you think killed Angie?"

"I don't think you should be so hasty. Right now it's considered a suspicious death."

"A woman who was rabid about her health and fitness level suddenly dies. There's an overwhelming possibility someone killed her."

"Then that would mean I might be working next to a murderer. Thanks, Calder. Like I didn't have enough trouble psyching myself up to go to work."

He didn't want to hear that. "My bet is Tony. He was the last one around her. Other than you," he added under his breath.

"Not true. She went to a meeting after she got back from her nooner. As far as I know, her boss has no motive."

She was right. Calder rubbed his forehead as an ache bloomed against his temples. "Damn."

"Now that I think about it, it couldn't be anyone I work with. Kerry and Megan left early. And honestly, I think they had better things to do on Valentine's Day than come back to the office to bump off their boss."

"That doesn't leave us with a lot of choices," Calder muttered.

"We don't need to come up with the culprit," Shanna said. "Let the police do their job."

"Shanna, don't you see? You're the prime suspect."

She froze. "*What?*"

"And if we don't come up with some reasonable doubt—like, say, another suspect—in the next five minutes, the rest of your Valentine's Days are going to be spent in prison."

She was the prime suspect? *She* was?

Shanna stared at Calder, feeling dizzy and nauseous. Her mouth was suddenly dry. Her tongue felt thick and swollen.

She didn't do a damn thing wrong. She stayed in her cubicle, did what was asked of her, and kept her hands to herself. Everything was going to be fine.

Riiiight.

Don't freak, she told herself silently. Calder was here. He wouldn't let them take her away. Calder, the guy who just vowed to risk his life for her. The same guy who also just suggested that she'd bumped off her boss.

Shanna hunched her shoulders. She was so going to fry. To a crisp.

"Poisoned?" she heard Calder ask. Shanna froze, tuning back in to the conversation.

"There are many poisons that can cause cyanosis. You know, the skin turning blue," Anteros explained. "Anything from a plant, spider bite, or a chemical."

"That's strange," Shanna murmured.

The officer picked up on that right away. "Why?"

"I can imagine a stabbing, or a shooting," Shanna said. "Even pushing her in front of a bus."

"Shanna," Calder said with warning, "now is not the time to critique a murderer."

"But poisoning?" She clucked her tongue. "It doesn't fit Angie. It's not aggressive enough."

"Murder is always aggressive," Sergeant Anteros said.

"Well, fine." She rolled her eyes. "If you look at it that way."

"You'll have to excuse her," Calder told the investigating officer. "She's in shock."

"Ms. Murphy, did you bring her coffee at any time during the day?"

Shanna huffed and looked at Calder. "Why does everyone think I'm the lackey?"

Calder shrugged.

"So," Anteros tapped his pen against his notepad, "that's a . . ."

"It's a no." She returned her attention to the sergeant. "A big, fat one."

"You sure? Not even a cup?"

"No one touched Angie's coffee mug," Shanna explained. "She never let it go. I bet she never washed it." She wrinkled her nose at the thought.

"Do you know what she had to eat or drink?"

"No. I only saw her drink from the coffee mug."

"There's more than one way to poison someone," Calder said. "Sergeant, you might want to look at those flowers on Shanna's desk."

"Hey!" Shanna jumped up from her seat. "Those are mine."

Calder ignored her. "They were given to Angie. Who knows what's in them. Inhale and you're dead."

Anteros gave a nod at one of the officers listening in. "Bag 'em."

"Well, thanks a lot, Calder. My one and only bouquet of roses, and you're going to have them dissected."

"Did she give away anything else she received today?" Anteros asked.

"She passed out the chocolates. Oh, man." Shanna sat down with a thump. "I knew this Valentine's Day was going to be the death of me."

"Are you okay?" Calder asked.

"I'm feeling a bit weird." She looked up at him. "Tell me the truth. Am I turning blue?"

"Uh, no."

"Oh, good. Wait, there was also the cupcake." She paused and waved the concern away. "But it should be okay. Megan made one especially for Angie."

The sergeant perked up. "Especially?"

"But I doubt she ate it. Everyone knew that . . ." she drifted off. No one would put poison in the food. They would put it in a gift Angie couldn't refuse.

"Knew what?"

"You know," Shanna said, standing up and staring at the open doorway of Angie's office. "Maybe we're looking at the murder scene the wrong way."

"How so?" Calder asked.

"You need to see it from a girl's point of view."

"You're saying the murderer was a woman?" Anteros asked.

"No, but the victim is. And a princessy girl, at that," she added in a confidential voice. "Rather than thinking how the murderer would administer the poison, let's look at how the victim would accept it."

"Shanna, I don't know if this is a good—"

"Take the flowers, for example."

"What about them?" Anteros looked at the flowers in Angie's office and the ones on Shanna's desk. "Which ones?"

"Both are beautiful. No woman could resist. But Angie could. Why? She was never into flowers, and she easily got rid of the second bouquet because she didn't want her husband to see them."

"Okay, so they might not be in the flowers," Anteros admitted. "But we need to check them anyway."

"And the cupcake," Shanna continued. "I'm betting Angie didn't even take a bite. Not even out of courtesy."

"We can check on that."

"And the teddy bear?" Calder asked.

Shanna chuckled at the idea. "No way was Angie going to cuddle that thing."

Calder nodded in agreement. "Got it."

"Putting poison in a chocolate box is too risky," Anteros decided. "You wouldn't know how long it would take for her to get to the one filled with poison."

"And the murderer wouldn't know that Angie was going to be generous about it," Calder added.

"It's more than that," Shanna said. "The murderer knew Angie well enough to know she probably wouldn't eat the chocolates."

Calder squinted as he tried to understand. "So why would anyone send her chocolate?"

"Oh, Calder," Shanna said with a sigh. "You have so much to learn."

"Where was the poison?" Calder asked.

"The necklace." Shanna said.

"Necklace." Sergeant Anteros repeated.

"The necklace!" Realization dawned on Calder. "I noticed she was wearing a diamond necklace when she told you about Megan."

"Yep, it was on her desk when she came back from lunch." Shanna leaned her hip against Kerry's desk. "This all makes sense to me. A woman can resist chocolate if she's determined to stick to her diet, but no woman—especially a princessy one—can resist trying on expensive jewelry. It doesn't even matter who it's from."

The guys stared at her funny.

"Doesn't everyone know that?" she asked.

The guys looked at each other and shrugged.

"Apparently not."

"How can someone poison another with a necklace?" Calder asked.

"How should I know?" She shrugged. "That's not my expertise."

Calder shook his head. "I don't buy that theory."

"Hey," she flattened her hand against her chest, "I couldn't resist the necklace."

"You tried on the necklace?" Calder's face paled.

"No—I mean, I almost put it on. But considering how my luck has been going, I knew I would get caught." Wow, who knew her bad luck would actually turn good? Shanna's knees got a little shaky just thinking about it.

"The necklace was in your possession?" Sergeant Anteros interrupted.

"Yeah," she glanced at him, "I signed for it."

"I'll get you your own damn diamonds," Calder said in a soft growl.

Shanna smiled. "That's very sweet of you, but—"

"I can't believe that you are so hung up on Valentine's Day that you almost wore a poisonous necklace."

"I didn't know it was poisonous," Shanna said, her patience wearing thin.

"Enough!" the investigating officer raised his voice. "We don't know if the necklace is poisonous, or if we are purposely being led in the wrong direction."

Shanna glared at Anteros. "Hey!"

"Ms. Murphy, is there any reason why you would want to kill the victim?"

"Sergeant, I just solved the mystery for you and this is the kind of gratitude I get?"

"You had the necklace in your possession, you were the last person to see her alive," Anteros said, beginning to list the evidence.

She raised her palm at him. "Don't even go there."

"Witnesses say you had an argument with the victim."

Shanna crossed her arms. "She started it."

Anteros pointed at her computer. "And this afternoon you were looking online for plane tickets to Calcutta."

"*Calcutta*?"

Shanna looked at Calder. “Did you know that there’s a strong movement against Valentine’s Day in parts of India?”

“Ms. Murphy!” Once again, the investigating officer raised his voice. “Is it true that you were angry with the victim because she made you work late on Valentine’s night?”

“Let me put it to you straight. My Valentine’s Day already sucked. Why would I purposely make it worse by spending it at a crime scene?”

“She does have a point,” Calder inserted.

“If I was going to do it, I would have done it yesterday so I would have today off from work.”

“Ms. Murphy,” Anteros said over Calder’s groan, “please retrace your activities on Valentine’s Eve.”

Shanna’s eyes lit up. “Valentine’s Eve?”

“I mean, yesterday.” A blush crept up the officer’s neck and spread in his face. “February 13.”

“Sergeant Anteros,” Shanna asked, tilting her head to one side as she studied him, “are you married?”

The investigating officer had the deer-caught-in-the-headlights look. “Um, no.”

Shanna smiled. “You should really meet my sister.”

Chapter Seven

"Only you would try to hook up your sister with the investigating officer at a crime scene," Calder said as he drove his sports car down the rain-soaked Seattle streets.

"Donovan Anteros is a romantic," Shanna decided as she curled into the warm leather seat, enjoying the simple pleasure of sitting next to Calder. "He would be good for Heather."

Calder glanced over at her. "You didn't even like him until he said the words 'Valentine's Eve.' "

She arched her eyebrows. "I was gradually warming up to him. Anyway, that doesn't matter. I'm still waiting to hear it." She made a give-it-to-me motion with her hand.

He sighed. "You were right. The back of the necklace was coated with poison."

"I know!" She slapped her hand against her leg. "I still can't believe it. I hope they catch Ted-Ed-Fred—"

"Stan," he corrected.

"And put him away for life!"

"Wow. You're taking this to heart." Calder said as he took a turn.

"Any guy who turns a beautiful and romantic Valentine's gift into the means of murder," Shanna said, raising her finger to make a point, "is obviously twisted and should not be a member of society."

"Obviously."

"I should have guessed it when Angie's husband hadn't dropped by the office to pick her up. Someone who catered to her every whim would not make Angie wait that long. How much do you want to bet that he's already out of the country? Probably left Monday morning."

"Stan is the prime suspect," Calder reminded her as he slowed the car down. "He hasn't been charged with anything."

Shanna sat up straight. "You know, this is wrong."

"It's called the legal system."

"No, not that." She noticed they were in front of Calder's town house community. "You were supposed to take me home."

"I changed my mind," he said as the entrance gates slowly opened. "You're staying with me tonight."

Her breath caught in her throat as excitement trickled through her veins. "Oh, I am?" she asked, her voice huskier than she intended.

"Yeah." He turned and looked at her, doing nothing to hide the possessive gleam in his eyes. "You are."

So he wasn't going to woo and court her into it. He wanted to claim her, and he wasn't going to wrap up the primal feelings with civilized words or traditions. Honestly, was she going to quibble about it? No.

But she wasn't about to fall into bed with her ex-boyfriend at the first opportunity. She had standards. She'd wait until he begged. "Don't you think it's too soon?"

He parked his car in his garage and closed the door with the push of a button before he answered. "Do you?"

She could lie and say she needed time. But all he would have to do was touch her and she'd start mewling and clawing his back like a cat. "I guess my question is, why am I staying with you tonight?"

"'Cause I need you with me."

He said "need." She'd count that as begging. "Well, if

you put it that way . . ." Shanna said, unsnapping her seat belt. She leaned over and kissed him.

The first touch instantly blew her away. Her lips tingled, her veins fizzed with excitement. She felt the kick, the insistent throb deep in her belly, the buzz skittering up her spine.

She gasped with surprise when Calder lifted her from her seat. Shanna stared at him wide-eyed as he carried her across to his side. She straddled him, her skirt bunching up around her bare legs.

She saw the desire and the need stamped across his face. Shanna inhaled the faint scent of his cologne as she curled her hands behind his head and kissed him.

The taste of him was addictive. She had no idea how she managed to go so long without him. All thought fled from her mind as his hands glided along her bare thighs.

She needed to press her skin against his. Share her heat with him. Shanna pulled Calder's shirt free from his trousers as her kisses grew rough and frantic.

Their ragged breathing echoed in the silent car. The insistent throb between her legs was suddenly too much. Shanna bucked and flexed against Calder. She rubbed against his hard cock and closed her eyes, craving him. She was ready to take him right there and then in the front seat. Sooo ready.

Calder shifted forward and turned. She opened her eyes and realized the interior lights were on. Then she noticed the dinging bell. He nudged the door open with his elbow.

"Where—"

"Bed." His hands shook slightly as he grabbed the keys from the ignition. "My bed."

She liked hearing those words coming out of his lips, reddened from her kisses. But that's not the point! "We're doing just fine—" she squealed as he dipped her back, her hair cascading behind her and out of the car.

She clawed the tight muscles of his shoulders as he guided her out of the car. Falling on her head would put a damper on her plans. Shanna wrapped her legs tightly around his waist as he stood up. She noticed he didn't grimace or buckle under her weight. She liked that in a man. *Her man.*

Her kisses grew wet, slick, and slid along his strong chin. Where was he going to claim her? she wondered as he walked, carrying her with him. The wall? The trunk of the car? Anywhere was fine as long as it happened *right now.*

Calder managed to open the door and step inside. He slapped the light switch on the second try and she saw the long flight of steps all the way to the first floor.

Shanna unwrapped her arms from his neck. "Put me down," she said, her lips against his jaw.

Calder seemed reluctant to let her go. "Not yet."

Didn't he get it? Shanna wondered as she wiggled against him, her heart pounding fiercely. If they didn't race to his bedroom on the second floor—*right this very second*—she was going to take him on this very hard, very cold tile floor. Especially if he didn't stop touching her like that.

She had to hurry them, or their reunion wasn't going to turn out as she had planned. Shanna grabbed the hem of her sweater and shucked it off. She shivered as the air brushed against her heated skin. She froze when she captured Calder's hot, dark gaze.

Need slammed against her, knocking the breath out of her lungs. Desire rippled across her skin. Something powerful hummed inside her, like she was ready to burst into someone bold, beautiful, and free.

Shanna met his eyes as she brazenly reached for the back of her bra. Her chest rose and fell as she unhooked the strap and peeled it from her body.

Calder leaned down to taste the slope of her breast and she felt herself being lowered. Her fingers bit into his arms as he laid her on the steps. The carpeted edges bit against her shoulder blades and the small of her back. Strangely, she didn't care.

Her fingers fumbled against the front buttons of her skirt. She couldn't get them unfastened quickly enough. She managed to undo a few by the time Calder shucked off her ankle boots and tossed them down the stairs. Shanna yanked off her skirt and panties, kicking them to the side.

She lay sprawled before Calder, naked and willing, her long hair fanned across the step above her head. She parted her legs and opened her arms, urging him closer.

Calder hovered above her, bracing his arms by her head. He dove for a ferocious kiss, darting his tongue deep into her mouth. She greedily suckled his offering when his hands skimmed down her curves before cupping her sex.

Shanna arched against Calder's hands as his finger stroked against her slit. A moan caught in the back of her throat as he rubbed small, teasing circles against her clit. She tossed her head from side to side as pleasure pulsed from her center until every inch of her skin tingled.

She murmured incoherently as Calder dipped his fingers into her wet core. With a knowing curve of his fingertips, he pressed against that secret spot.

Shanna was pretty sure she screamed. Her voice was definitely echoing in her head. But once he replaced his hand with his mouth to suckle her clit while stroking that special spot, she was cocooned in a white silence.

Dark spots danced before her eyes as she slowly recognized the slanted ceiling above her. The carpet underneath her back pricked against her skin. She was limp, still shuddering, when she heard the rustle of Calder's clothes. She blinked as she heard the clatter of keys and the thud of his wallet hit the tile floor.

She felt the tip of his cock against her as his face burrowed into the dip of her neck. Calder surged inside her, the powerful move sending her sliding up the steps. Shanna grappled for the banisters, her knuckles bumping against the wall as she reached for something to hold onto. She held on tight to the banisters, the wood biting into her sweat-slick palms.

Calder grasped her hips and lifted her off the steps. His hands supported the small of her back, and suddenly she was suspended in the air, taking flight with each thrust . . . soaring . . . until she burst free and unfurled into a rainbow of colors.

"Can you believe that all this time I was envious of Angie?" Shanna said aloud much later in the darkened bedroom.

The pillows shifted as Calder raised his head. "You were?" he asked as he gathered her hair and brushed it out of his way.

"Okay, that's not true. It wasn't envy. I was pea-green with jealousy," she admitted. "Choking on it, actually."

"Why?"

Was he kidding? "She was gorgeous," Shanna said reluctantly, "successful, powerful, and could make guys do anything for her without asking."

"Are we talking about the same Angie?"

"And her husband was the epitome of devotion," Shanna continued. "Or, so I thought. It was all an illusion."

And it seemed so genuine. So perfect. It was her romantic fantasies come to life. That was what probably freaked her out more than anything. Well, maybe not as much as seeing Angie blue and dead.

Shanna didn't like what she was seeing now. Hindsight was a bitch. While she had been tallying up all the unromantic things that were happening to her, she had almost missed the fact that she had found a guy who she truly loved, trusted, and respected. Someone whom she wanted to spend forever with. Someone who would be there for her no matter what.

All this time she'd felt she had nothing, but instead she'd had everything she'd been envying. Huh. She should have seen that one coming.

"At least I don't have to worry about you," Shanna said as she snuggled against him. She smiled as she felt hard, warm muscle against her back. "If you ever send me a diamond necklace, I'll know something's up."

"I meant what I said." He spanned his hand against her stomach and pulled her closer against him. "I'm getting you diamonds."

"I don't want them."

He caught the tip of her earlobe with his teeth, and wild sensations raced down her spine when he bit down and pulled. "Yes, you do," he said against her ear.

Okay, he got her there. "I want the meaning behind them," she conceded.

"You already have it." He paused, the taut silence building before he whispered, "I love you, Shanna."

Her heart stopped and her eyes widened. "You do?"

"And, I'm going to marry you."

Her pulse began to gallop. She couldn't believe that someone who was allergic to all things romantic just mentioned the words "love" and "marriage" within a minute of each other. He was making up for lost time!

Of course, there is that rule of never believing what a man says while in bed. Especially declarations of love and proposals of marriage. Although, Calder wasn't really asking, was he? "Oh," she croaked out, "you are?"

He pressed his mouth against the tender spot on her neck and she shivered. "How does a Valentine's Day wedding sound to you?"

She tensed. "Horrible," she blurted out.

He raised his head. "It does?"

She turned to face him. "I'm not waiting a *year* to get married to you."

Calder frowned. "Don't you want the—"

"I want you," she said. She tilted up her chin and pressed her lips against his.

This was all that mattered. They were the center of their universe. Everything they did would reflect that. It might not be roses, but it would be something straight from the heart. She got that now.

"I'm not really good at the whole romance stuff," Calder

muttered against the corner of her lips as his fingers skimmed her rib cage. "But I'm going to work on it."

"You're doing just fine," she said, her eyelids fluttering closed as his hands cupped her breasts. In fact, his instincts were almost on target. *Just a little to the left* . . .

"Starting with the wedding," he promised, brushing the pad of his thumb against her nipple. "We are going to get married as soon as possible."

"O . . . kay." *Harder* . . .

"I have some vacation time coming up," he said softly as he captured her other nipple between his fingers. "And my project deadline is in about six weeks."

Now squeeze . . . "Perfect." Her skin felt hot and flushed. And why was it that every time Calder touched her breasts, the sensations were magnified between her legs?

"Good," Calder said, his voice thick and low. "April 1. Save the date."

April 1? Why does that sound familiar? Shanna opened her eyes. "Wait. April *Fool's* Day?"

"Problem?"

She knew Calder was very new to this romance stuff, but some things were self-explanatory! "That's not the most romantic holiday," she began.

"Didn't you say that we should treat every day as Valentine's Day?" he asked with a teasing glint in his eyes before he lowered his mouth against the peak of her breast.

"Yes-s-s," she said, trying to think straight when he did that amazing thing with his tongue. "But—but—but, there are exceptions. Like April Fool's Day. First of all, you don't—" her breath snagged in her throat as she arched off the bed.

"I promise," Calder said, barely lifting his head. Jagged tremors forked through her body as his warm breath wafted over her wet skin. "We'll make it the most romantic day of the year."

Here's a sneak peek at Sylvia Day's
"Stolen Pleasures"
from her new anthology,
BAD BOYS AHOY.
A February 2006 release from BRAVA.

British West Indies
February 1813

He'd stolen a bride.

Sebastian Blake gripped his knife with white-knuckled force and kept his face impassive. If the beauty in front of him was to be believed, he'd stolen *his own* bride.

He watched as her chin lifted with defiance and her dark eyes met his without fear. She was tall and slender with blond curls tumbling down from a once stylish arrangement. Her lovely watered-silk dress was torn at the shoulder, revealing a tempting display of creamy breast. There was a sooty handprint marring her flesh, and unable to help himself, Sebastian reached out and rubbed the offending mark away with gentle strokes of his thumb. She stiffened and lifted her bound hands to knock his away. He met her gaze and held it.

"Tell me your name again," he murmured, his hand tingling just from that simple contact with her satin skin.

She licked her bottom lip and his blood heated further. "My name is Olivia Blake, Countess of Merrick. My husband is Sebastian Blake, Earl of Merrick and future Marquis of Dunsmore."

He lifted her hands and stared at her ring finger, noting his crest etched in the simple gold band she wore.

He scrubbed a hand over his face and turned away, striding to the nearest open window for a deep breath of salt-tinged air. Staring out at the water, he spied the debris from her ship bobbing in the waves. "Where is your husband, Lady Merrick?" he asked, keeping his back to her.

Hope tinged her voice. "He awaits me in London."

"I see." But he didn't, not at all. "How long have you been married, my lady?"

"I fail to see—"

"How long?" he barked.

"Nearly two weeks."

His chest expanded with a deep breath. "I remind you that we are in the West Indies, Lady Merrick. It is impossible that you were married only a fortnight ago. Your husband would not be able to await you in England if that were true."

She was silent behind him and finally, he turned to face her again. It was a mistake to have done so. Her beauty hit him with the force of a fist in his gut.

"Would you care to explain?" he prodded, relieved he sounded so unaffected.

For the first time her bravado left her, her cheeks flushing with embarrassment. "We were married by proxy," she confessed. "But I assure you, he will pay whatever ransom you desire despite the unusual circumstances of our marriage."

Sebastian moved toward her. His calloused fingers caressed the elegant curve of her cheekbone and entwined in her hair. Her breath caught, and her lips parted in response to his gentle touch. "I'm certain he would pay a king's ransom for beauty such as yours."

Through the smoky smell that clung to her, he could detect the arousing scent of soft woman, warm and luxurious. He reached for the blade strapped to his thigh and withdrew it.

She flinched.

"Easy," he soothed. Sebastian held out his hand and waited patiently for her to step forward again. When she did, he sliced through the rope that tied her hands together and sheathed his knife. He rubbed the marks on her delicate wrists.

"You are a pirate," she murmured.

"Yes."

"You have taken my father's ship and all of its cargo."

"I have."

Her head tilted backward on the slender neck and she gazed up at him with melting chocolate eyes. "Why then are you being so kind to me, if you intended to rape me?"

He caught her fingers and placed them on his signet ring. "Most would say a man cannot rape his own wife."

She glanced down and gasped at the heavy crest that mirrored her own band. Her eyes flew up to his. "Where did you get this? You can't possibly . . ."

He smiled. "According to you, I am."

Olivia stared up into the intense blue eyes and felt certain her heart would burst from her chest. Her mind faltered, stumbling over the shocking revelation that the notorious Captain Phoenix was claiming to be her husband.

She backed away from him in a rush and he reached to steady her when she would have fallen. A whimper escaped as his touch burned her skin. The day's events had shaken her, but it was the gorgeous face of the infamous pirate that made her weak-kneed.

Tall and broad shouldered, his presence sucked all of the air from the tight confines of the cabin. His black hair was unfashionably long and the darkness of his skin betrayed how much time he spent outdoors. He was wild, untamed—a man of the elements.

She'd watched, fascinated, as he'd swept onto her ship and taken command of it within moments. Phoenix had executed the attack with brilliant precision—not one man was seriously injured and no one had been killed. Having spent most of her childhood on her father's ships, Olivia recognized singular skill when she saw it.

The way he'd used his sword and barked commands, the way loose tendrils of his hair had blown across his face, the way his breeches delineated every stretch of his muscular thighs . . . she'd never experienced anything so thrilling. So exciting.

Until he'd touched her.

Then she'd discovered what excitement truly was.

Shouldering her way through the people at the bar running the length of the room, Alex waved at the bartender. The girl turned bright blue eyes on her and flicked one of her black braids over her shoulder.

"What can I get you?"

"Nothing . . . yet," Alex shouted over the noise of two guys arguing about the Mets. "I'm actually looking for someone I'm supposed to meet here. I know it's crowded but . . ."

The girl grinned as she swiped the bar with a damp rag, shouting back, "A guy? Tall, dark hair, leather coat? Kind of slick?"

Oh, good. She swallowed. "That should be the one."

The bartender jerked her head toward the tables in the back corner, on the other side of the room. "Make him pay for the first round," she said with another grin. Her tongue was pierced with a tiny silver barbell.

Alex nodded as she walked away, nudging past a girl doing a Jello-O shot of something the color of Windex. It was hard to see very far beyond the shifting crowd of bodies, but as she got closer to the back of the room, she spotted her date, sitting alone at one of the corner tables, just like the bartender said.

Wow. Sydney wasn't wrong.

He was gorgeous. Well, maybe not gorgeous in the traditional sense, but definitely her type. In fact, the secret type she hadn't even known she had until she laid eyes on him and found his close-cropped dark hair and strong jaw shadowed with stubble the sexiest thing she'd ever seen. He was leaning back in his chair, the fingers of one hand carelessly circling the lip of his empty glass, his dark eyes shifting back and forth over the crowd, watching, waiting.

He didn't look like a real estate broker. Unless he only sold homes to the mob, or in the kind of neighborhoods other agents were afraid to drive through. And his leather jacket wasn't exactly what she'd pictured, either. She'd been thinking tailored, metrosexual, buffed to a buttery sheen; his looked as if it had been tied to the bumper of a speeding car and dragged across an uneven pavement. Scuffed, worn, lived-in but, she had to admit, as natural on him as a second skin.

He looked . . . dangerous. Which was certainly different, for her, at least. She'd never known dangerous could look so tempting.

With a deep breath for courage, she edged past a couple who were taking turns sipping from the same drink and walked up to his table. *Now or never. Nothing to lose.*

"Hi," she said. "Alex Ramsay. I'm sorry I'm late, but . . . well, there's never a good excuse for that, is there? I hope you haven't been waiting long."

His mouth curved into a smile and he shook his head slowly. "Not long at all. Just long enough, I guess."

She pulled out the chair opposite his and sat down, nestling her bag on her lap. Now what? He was looking at her so strangely, as if he wasn't exactly sure what she was doing there, but definitely not unhappy that she'd shown up. Except for the way he kept glancing past her toward the short hallway that led to the bathrooms, if the stick figures of a man and a woman posted above the archway meant what she thought they did.

She wanted him to look at her again, she realized suddenly. Maybe it was the heated, sexually charged atmosphere, or the simple fact that she'd taken the plunge and come on this date, but she wanted to make the most of it. Getting out of a rut seemed a whole lot more appealing if she was going to be doing it with someone who looked like him.

"Have you been here before?" she asked him, wishing she had a drink in front of her. It would have given her something to do with her hands, at least.

"A couple of times," he said, that same slightly confused smile playing around his mouth. "Usually on business."

What kind of business could he do here? She couldn't imagine discussing escrow and variable rate mortgages in a place like this.

"You?" he asked, leaning forward, his elbows on the table. Beneath the sweaty, faintly electrical haze of too many bodies, the sharply spicy scent of perfume, and too many speakers blaring at once, she could suddenly smell him—dark and warm, like a crisp night in front of a fire.

Delicious, she caught herself thinking as she looked up and into his eyes. Oh yeah, they weren't bad either. A rich dark brown, intent and curious and intelligent, the kind of eyes that saw everything.

"No," she answered finally. "I work a lot of nights."

His gaze sharpened, and she found herself explaining before he asked. "Teaching. Adults usually need evening classes, and after a few hours of the tango and the foxtrot I'm usually too beat to do anything but collapse in front of the TV."

"The tango, huh?" His head tilted sideways as his mouth quirked into another grin. "I didn't know anyone did that anymore."

"Oh, lots of people still want to learn." She crossed her

legs under the table and her foot brushed against the solid weight of his calf. "Sorry. I'm usually more graceful than that."

His grin changed into a sultry smile. "I believe it."

She fought a blush. What were they talking about? Was this flirting? Because it felt pretty good—a little vague, certainly, and a little dangerous, but exciting. As if the conversation could twist into something new at any moment.

Maybe she should slow things down a little. She cleared her throat. "So, how long have you been in real estate?"

Now his grin was a frown. "What makes you think I'm in real estate?"

"Uh . . ." *What?* She was trying to think of how to respond to that when someone tapped her on the shoulder. She turned her head to find the bartender she'd talked to earlier leaning down to speak to her, blue eyes wide.

"The guy who told me he was waiting for someone," she whispered fiercely. "That's not him."